SH

y
ll
is
g
o
s:
l,

Richmond upon Thames Libraries

Renew online at www.richmond.gov.uk/libraries

9071

D0268593

Also by David Owen

Panther

The Fallen Children

All the Lonely People

DAVID OWEN

GRIEF ANGELS

ATOM

First published in Great Britain in 2020 by Atom

1 3 5 7 9 10 8 6 4 2

A CIP catalogue record for this book is
available from the British Library.

ISBN: 978-0-349-00342-9

Printed and bound in Great Britain by Clays Ltd, Elcograf S.p.A.

Papers used by Atom are from well-managed forests
and other responsible sources.

MIX
Paper from
responsible sources
FSC® C104740

Atom
An imprint of
Little, Brown Book Group
Carmelite House
50 Victoria Embankment
London EC4Y 0DZ

An Hachette UK Company
www.hachette.co.uk

www.atombooks.co.uk

For Nigel, Miggy and Junaid.
Twenty-one years and counting.

The Persistent Dream

The dream is fractured by the crackle of frost in his throat. Goosebumps pucker pale skin as the boy lifts his head to cough glassy shards of ice into his palm. Propping himself on his elbows, he sees he has once again strayed from his bedroom. A wide, round window cups his body like a shallow basin, his lingering warmth melting his profile into the thin, chill layer of frost that rimes its surface.

'I'm still asleep,' the boy tells himself, every word a wintry puff of breath. 'This isn't real.'

The view beyond is boundless vertigo, giddiness lurching through him. A legion of winking stars are blunted by the curve of the Earth. The planet – *his* planet – glows as if lit from within. He expects to shudder awake again, break the surface of the dream, sit up in bed with sweat on his forehead and panicked breath in his lungs.

The dream persists.

'Not here,' says the boy, trying to scrabble away from the window, the polished ice slipping under his hands to leave him stranded. 'Not again.'

This is the third night he has been brought here, and he braces for what must come next –

Pain, fierce and familiar, a physical entity expanding and contracting inside his stomach. A stowaway strong enough to curl him into a ball. The boy grits his teeth and clenches his eyes shut. It will pass. It always does, retreating to a hidden corner to convalesce.

The window is set into compact metal walls thick with ropes of bundled wires, bulbs blinking red and green. The cold clings to him like a second skin.

'I can't stand it here,' whispers the boy.

You asked for solitude. The answering voice slinks, teasing, from the darkness. There's nowhere more solitary than here, hundreds of miles from any other soul.

The satellite – for what else could it be? – is lightly whirling. The planet below, its homespun tattoos of continents, drifts out of view. In moments, there is nothing to be seen but stars and void.

'I've changed my mind,' says the boy. 'I thought this was what I needed, but—'

I'm on your side. The voice belongs to a boy. It's strikingly similar to his own, but is somehow . . . primeval. A voice to whisper arcane sins in your ear while you sleep. I'll take you wherever you need to go.

'I need to find the right way out of this,' says the

boy, straining to peer through the darkness. 'That's all I need.'

A moment brittle with promise passes before the voice speaks again. How do you know there is any such thing?

The vacuum of space beyond the window tugs at him, exerting a hypnotic pull he can hardly resist. It will claim him, he knows, and the boy will let it.

'There has to be,' he says.

The satellite turns, turns.

I might know a place. A long way from here. Look out for me.

The bulbs sputter and fail. Underneath him, a biting *crack* is chased by the insistent hiss of escaping air. A fracture spider-webs across the glass, corrosive veins of ice splitting it into jagged plates.

There is nowhere to run. The boy reaches out for something, anything, to hold on to. Silent, the void inhales.

The glass is sucked out.

He is expelled, the satellite a cocoon breached too early to have given him wings. The incalculable emptiness catches him, turns him over, snatches him ever further from home. An impossible distance.

And then the black, soft as a feather, caresses his face. Wraps his body up tight in its embrace. Takes him—

Now the boy wakes with a start. The dream recedes. He stands shivering in the sitting room, still unfamiliar, one hand resting on the cool grey stone of the mantelpiece. The photograph and the box are inches from his fingers.

It was a dream. Only a dream.

A tickle against his bare toes. The boy leans down, fingers hesitant as if reaching for an apparition, to brush the single black feather that lies across his feet.

Chapter One

Duncan

My phone vibrates in my pocket at the same moment the football clips my toe and spins up to hit me in the face. I ignore the notification in favour of rubbing my nose to keep my eyes from watering. Nothing is more important than my friends not thinking I'm crying.

'Lovely bit of skill, Spunk,' says Lorenzo, flicking the stray ball into the air to catch it deftly on the back of his neck, before propelling it upwards to knock a header across our ragged circle.

The genesis of my undesirable nickname is too lacking in imagination to bother telling in full. At two syllables, 'Duncan' was of course considered by my peers to be too long to ever be uttered in its entirety. Rapidly, it was shortened to 'Dunc', which upon the arrival of puberty was promptly discovered to rhyme with the newly identified fluid brimming inside our teenage bodies like untapped oil wells.

I like to think the nickname became established as a sign of affection.

Narrator: It wasn't.

My brain is always quick to correct any such favourable delusions.

The ball comes at me again and I jerk a knee up in time to keep it from hitting the ground. It floats across for Saeed to control with his chest.

'You're getting better at this,' says Matt through a cloud of breath.

'That's what your mum said,' Saeed shoots back as he loops the ball into the air.

Matt considers this for a moment. 'Solid five out of ten.' I don't know when they started scoring their *your mum* jokes but they have come to enforce the criteria with unflinching rigidity.

Lorenzo flicks the ball high and manages to wriggle it across his wide shoulders before using an elbow to push it up on to his head. Any compliment not aimed at him is clearly a challenge not to be ignored. He tries to hold the ball on the tip of his nose but loses his balance. It hits the ground and rolls away towards the maths block.

'Good one, mate,' says Matt, taking the opportunity to cram half his sandwich into his frighteningly large mouth.

Lorenzo shrugs. 'At least I tried to give it a bit of finesse.'

'Twenty-three kicks,' says Saeed, nodding approvingly. 'Not far off the record.'

The record – twenty-nine touches without the ball hitting the ground – was set on a day I was off sick, a fact

I am never allowed to forget every time we've failed to beat it since. I take out my phone to note down the day's effort, but open a waiting message instead. There's an image, the wheel spinning for a moment as it downloads.

'Hey, new boy, send it back!' shouts Lorenzo. The ball has rolled under the sheltered walkway of the maths block, and the new boy is there alone, leaning against the railing. The football is practically at his feet, but he doesn't seem to have noticed. Instead he's sticking his head out from the shelter to peer at the sky, eyes wide behind his glasses, like a mouse being circled by an owl.

'Forget it,' says Lorenzo, shoving his hands into his pockets.

'You think he's a bit . . . simple?' asks Saeed.

Lorenzo sighs. 'He wouldn't be here if he was.'

'They let *you* in, didn't they?'

Lorenzo aims a kick at his shin that Saeed dodges. 'What d'you think, Spunk?'

There are a lot of rumours circulating about the new boy. It's only his second week, and I've already heard that he's here variously because he was caught having sex with a male teacher at his old school, because he sexually assaulted a year seven with his ponytail, or because he murdered his dad.

Obviously, it's none of the above. But it is weird for somebody to move schools in February, in the final term of GCSEs, after which at least half the school will be leaving for pastures new.

We haven't really talked about what will happen after we finish school. Matt's going to the same college as his girlfriend Becky, while Saeed is half-heartedly applying for apprenticeships instead ('Engineers make bare money!') while secretly waiting to see what Lorenzo, who still can't make up his mind, will do.

It's going to be the biggest change of our so far largely uneventful lives. Except . . .

The change has already started. In the last year Lorenzo has become obsessed with the gym, so now he looks like he could crush a double-decker bus into a cube using his bare hands. Despite his undying devotion, that's one hobby Saeed hasn't managed to copy, instead opting to become so obsessed with pornography I'm surprised he can still walk. Matt spends most of his time outside of school and his part-time job at Asda doing the real thing with Becky, which in turn has made him as much Lorenzo's rival in performative masculinity as his friend.

All they seem to care about now is girls, clothes, getting served in pubs, eating clean to get better erections. Or whatever.

And then there's me. I'm not really interested in any of that stuff. At least, I don't find any of it remotely as urgent as they do. I just miss hanging out and playing *Mario Kart*, when the most important thing was who had the best lap-time on DK Mountain. I haven't changed at all, which I guess means there must be something wrong with me? They're leaving me behind. It's only a matter of time before they realise it.

Unless I can cling on by my fingertips to hide it and act like I'm one of them, like a spy, or a camera disguised like a penguin for a nature documentary.

We watch the new boy. After a minute he snaps his head away from the sky, like he's spotted something in the empty space beside him. He starts talking, even though there's clearly nobody there.

The new boy is really not doing himself any favours.

'We should probably just leave him alone,' I say.

Lorenzo deliberately steps on the toe of my shoe, smearing it with mud. 'Yeah, because I was planning on asking him out on a date.'

'Speaking of which,' says Matt through a mouthful of sandwich, 'how's it going with that girl from the gym?'

Lorenzo watches him for a second, like it might be a loaded question, and then smiles slowly like he's harbouring an elicit secret. The group he hangs out with at the gym are all older than him, but they don't know it. I tune them out as they begin discussing what his next move should be. It's absolutely not because I'm jealous about his new mates.

This is the strangest thing about how our friendship has changed: it's almost as if I'm *unimportant* to them now. Surplus to requirements. Like I'm a spectator rather than part of the group. If I disappeared from the face of the Earth – *poof!* – I'm not sure they'd miss me. They might even be glad I wasn't cramping their style any more.

When I look back at my phone, the image has finally downloaded. For half a second I'm not sure what I'm seeing. It's a picture of a girl, naked but for a red ribbon wrapped artfully around her to cover anything too private.

'Why did you send—' I say, thinking it must be one of the guys messing with me, before I clock the name at the top of the screen.

'Hello, who's that?' says Saeed, porno-sense tingling as he grabs at my phone. I try and pull it away but he's too quick. He practically presses his greasy nose against the screen. 'Bloody hell.'

The others crowd around. I consider making a run for it and leaving my phone behind, but there isn't a chance before the penny drops.

'What the fuck?' says Matt, grabbing the phone and glaring at the picture.

The message is from Becky.

Matt and Becky have been going out for around six months. It's fair to say it came as a bit of surprise – Matt's belly and distinctly potato-shaped head always put him at the bottom of our unspoken internal hotness rankings. His unforeseen sexual triumph upset the natural order more than we could ever have expected.

Firstly, we had always thought that whoever of us got a girlfriend first (and everything that came with it) would be worshipped like a god by the rest of the group. Instead it just made things *weird*. We could no longer talk endlessly about sex – how it worked, the things we'd like to do, what we were doing to ourselves in the meantime – because one of us was actually *doing* it. The rest of us just seemed pathetic in comparison.

Secondly, it practically gave Lorenzo an aneurysm. He had always been the de facto leader and king-in-waiting to the throne of masculinity we were all scrabbling to claim. He should be able to have any girl (and probably a lot of the boys) at school that he wanted, but for some reason he always ignores their attention. Still, Matt's behaviour was practically mutinous.

I hold my hands up, an innocent man, but it does nothing to keep Matt from charging me. He grips my throat with both hands and propels me back until I hit a wall. Air rushes out of me in a cloud.

'I swear, I don't—'

'Shut up!' His breath is hot on my face.

I can see in his eyes that he wants to hit me, but I'm not sure Matt has ever actually hit anybody in anger before. He's a gentle giant, really – his gargantuan hands are usually reserved for holding kebabs.

If he punches me – if he *actually* punches me – our friendship will unravel for good. Not just mine and Matt's; all four of us. He lifts his fist. It trembles, either with rage or reluctance. I clench my whole face in anticipation of the blow.

'Hold up,' says Saeed.

He's retrieved my phone from where Matt dropped it. As much as I'm sure he's savoured the image (and mentally tucked it away for later), he's also scrolled up to earlier messages between Becky and me. There are precisely two of them.

'Look,' he says, holding the phone in front of Matt's face.

Matt is strong enough to open his fist and take the phone, while still using the other hand to pin me against the wall.

'"Does Matt like *Attack on Titan?*"' he reads.

'It was your birthday,' I say. 'She didn't know what to get you.'

'I hate *Attack on Titan*.'

I nod at the phone. 'That's what I told her.'

11

The second message corroborates my story. Matt thinks about it for a moment, and then lets me go. I take a breath, trying to ignore the ache in my throat.

'Then why's she sending you this?' Matt says.

'It was blatantly an accident,' says Lorenzo, who's been quiet until now. 'It must have been meant for you.'

Matt frowns. 'She's never sent a sext before.'

'Then I guess it's your lucky day, bruv.'

I hear Lorenzo's phone chime in his pocket, but he ignores it. He watches jealously as Matt deletes the picture from my phone before handing it back to me.

'Sorry about . . .' Matt says, not looking me in the eye.

'Don't worry,' I say, shoving the phone inside my school blazer before it can do any more damage.

Taking out his own phone, Matt begins making a call and stomps off across the playground. I guess our friendship is going to survive another day. I just have to hope its days aren't already numbered.

Narrator: They blatantly were.

Thanks, Brain.

That pessimistic voice is my depression talking. In fact, *that's* the biggest sign that our friendship has changed: I still haven't told them about my depression diagnosis. It's been around a year, but every time I'm about to do it, I realise I don't know how they'll respond. I can't risk it.

'Christ,' says Saeed, grinning wide enough to reveal his vampire teeth. 'I'll never look at Becky the same way again.'

'Leave it out,' says Lorenzo, checking his phone and quickly tapping out a response.

Without these guys, I wouldn't have any friends.

12

They've been a part of my life for so long. No matter what has changed, I have to cling on to them for as long as I can. I don't know what I would do – who I would be – without them.

A bell rings all around the school, signalling the end of lunch break. Everybody on the playground immediately begins sloping inside.

'The new boy's coming to my house tonight.'

Lorenzo pockets his phone. 'You what?'

'Owen Marlow. That's his name. His mum's joined the same church as my parents.' I huff a cloud of air. 'They want to welcome her to the community.'

'New recruit for the God squad,' says Saeed. 'I wonder if she's hot?'

As the playground empties, I look back towards the maths block. The new boy – Owen – is the only person who hasn't moved. The bell rings off, and his eyes seem to follow something invisible up into the sky.

'Go on, head boy. I'll see you in English,' says Lorenzo, slapping me hard on the back. 'Get the football while you're at it.'

My parents insisted that being head boy would look good when applying to colleges and, eventually, universities. Unluckily for me literally nobody else rivalled me for the job. One of my so-called responsibilities is to make sure everybody gets inside quickly after break.

So I shoulder my bag, and make my way over.

Owen

There's hardly any shelter on the playground. The canteen was too hot, too busy, condensation fogging the windows. At least it's quiet under the maths block entrance. Just a few guys kicking a football around nearby. It's enough that I don't feel completely exposed.

I lean out as far as I dare and look up at the sky. The birds are circling lower than before. Close enough that I can see the dull winter light through the gaps between feathers. They look like herons, but three times as big. Oily black, legs, wings and necks stretched out of proportion. If I close my eyes and listen, I'm sure I can hear the wind whistling through their feathers, like a storm passing through a cave.

A shout across the playground snaps me out of my trance. I pull back under the roof. It's been four months since the birds appeared. A few days after Dad died. At first, I tried pointing them out to other people. They laughed, thought it was a joke. When I insisted, they looked at me like I was more broken than they'd thought. Nobody else could see them.

After that, I kept the birds to myself.

I googled if it's normal to hallucinate manifestations of your grief. Unsurprisingly, it is not. That didn't stop me from coming to think of the birds as Angels – not guardians, but heralds. Of what, I wish I knew.

I yawn and rub my eyes. Last night's dream still clings to my mind. The darkness, the solitude, the peace of the vacuum. After waking, I stayed downstairs until morning. Looking at the photograph on the mantelpiece. Trying to resolve it with the way I remember things.

A new house. A new start. Just like that, everything I knew is gone.

I rub my fingers against the feather in my pocket.

When I lean out from cover again, I'm sure the Angels are lower than a moment before. There are five or six of them. It's hard to tell as they cross paths, lazily change direction, like cells merging and dividing.

They're not angels, you know.

I rear back under cover. The boy is beside me. Somehow I didn't hear his approach. He looks roughly my age, dark hair cut into a too-straight fringe. There's something familiar about him, like he's somebody I knew in a past life. He smiles at me without warmth, lopsided dimples puncturing his cheeks. Tugs on the lapels of his school blazer like wearing it is a novelty. It leaves dusty black stains on his pale fingertips.

'You can see them?' I say.

It can make you think you're going crazy, can't it? he says, gazing up. Now I recognise his voice – last night it existed only in the darkness of a dream. When I look into his eyes they're as black as the void.

I back away from him so quickly that I almost fall, the wall of the maths block catching me. 'What can?'

The boy's lip twitches. Grief, of course.

A football rolls up behind him and knocks against his ankles. He doesn't seem to notice. The pain in my stomach is roused, threatens to double me over.

'Leave me alone.'

The boy grins. You told me you wanted somebody to help you through this.

'What if nobody can? I keep being told I have to grieve *properly*. That I should be sad, or angry, or accepting,' I say, the urge to retaliate driving me forwards. 'But I still don't know how I feel.'

The boy steps closer. Who are you grieving for?

We're close enough now that I can lift a hand and reach for him. My fingers hover inches from his skin. The boy doesn't flinch. I want to know that he's real. But then I imagine my hand pushing through his body, closing on empty space. A breath shakes itself from my lungs and I drop my arm.

'You already know.'

I think I do, says the boy. But I can't say the same for you.

A shout and a scuffle somewhere across the playground. A fight kicking off. I don't take my eyes from the boy.

I told you I knew a place, he says. I've found somebody to guide you there.

The pain begs for attention. I grit my teeth and wrap my arms around myself, my blazer stretching at the shoulders. 'It was only a dream.'

I jump as the bell rings all around us. Everybody on the playground moves in slow motion. Delaying the inevitable as long as they can.

The boy wags a sooty finger at me. You can cling to dreams as long as you want. It won't get us anywhere.

A shift in the air. One of the Angels drops out of the sky with its wings wide and talons outstretched. I stagger back under shelter as it swoops. In a single moment I see how its dull eyes are set deep in its head, catch the smell of rain on its feathers. My ears pop as it beats its wings to stall its descent. It hasn't come for me – not yet. Instead its talons sink into the boy's shoulders, the school blazer disintegrating into dust as he is plucked from the ground.

I'll come for you again soon, the boy calls down as the bird steals him for the sky. That's a promise.

The loose circle of birds tightens and hides the boy from view. When they open out again to resume their patrol, he's gone.

I'm still staring after him when I realise another boy in a school blazer has stopped a few paces away from me. I know he's real because he looks at me like I might collapse or explode at the faintest touch. I'm used to that – I have been for four months now.

'Are you all right?' he says.

I wish I never had to hear that stupid question again.

Duncan

It's almost always a stupid question, and this occasion is clearly no exception. He's drenched in sweat and holding his belly like an alien is about to burst out of it. I know his name, but for some reason it seems too familiar – too presumptuous – to use it.

He takes a deep breath and fixes his eyes on the ground, never once looking at me directly. When the younger kids drag their feet after break I usually threaten them with a visit to the head teacher, Mr Spencer. The playground is almost empty now, and I don't want him getting into any trouble.

'Lunch is over,' I say, relying on the age-old practice of shamelessly stating the obvious. 'Do you know where you need to be?'

He looks at his watch, and then finally at me. 'Yes,' he says.

I begin to follow as he steps past me, but instead of heading inside he makes straight for the front gate.

'You can't just . . .'

The real problem with being head boy – apart from everybody saying I suck off Mr Spencer under his desk – is that I have no actual authority. If Owen hears me, he doesn't show it. He must already know that the main gate is kept locked during the day, because he heads for the staff car-park entrance and on to the road. He glances up at the sky, and then puts his head down, feet pounding away from the school without looking back.

Chapter Two

Duncan

I invoke Emergency Girl Protocol #3 to tidy my bedroom quickly enough: dirty clothes kicked under the bed, antidepressants hidden in the bedside table, dirty plates piled outside the door where Dad will spend five minutes loudly refusing to pick them up before doing it anyway, then spray enough air freshener to drown a canary and delete every last cookie of my internet search history.

The entire process is designed to take less than two minutes so that if a girl was about to arrive on short notice she would never see how I really live. Owen isn't a girl, obviously, but despite the extraordinarily low probability of such an occurrence it's only sensible to run a drill now and again.

I hear Dad come to an outraged halt outside my bedroom door. 'I'm not picking up these plates!' he sing-songs.

While I wait for the air to become breathable again I set

19

an episode of *Battlestar Galactica* playing on my laptop. It's the one where the exiled fleet meets another ship full of survivors and everybody realises they're not the only humans left in the entire universe. The new ship has a hard-ass lady captain who awakened in me an interest in tightly fitted military gear I never knew I possessed.

I check the clock. There isn't time, and it definitely wouldn't help with the smell.

It's strange when you introduce somebody to your room for the first time. I don't bother cleaning up for Lorenzo or the other guys because they've known me long enough that they won't judge. It's not like they bother coming over much now anyway. When it's a *new* somebody it feels sort of intimate, like you're showing them a little piece of your soul. Except, for somebody new, you always clean up and hide your terrible secrets so what they see isn't quite real at all.

Whatever Owen was feeling on the playground earlier was *definitely* real. I hardly recognised whatever emotion that look on his face was betraying: an over-priced smoothie of fear, sadness, dread and anger. Intense enough to make him run away from school in the middle of the day.

My phone vibrates. A message from Lorenzo: *Ready for your big date?*

He's being a knob, obviously, but I'm jittery enough that it could be a date. Not that I'd know what going on a date feels like. My assumption is *TERROR* with multiple exclamation points.

Before going downstairs I do one final sweep of my bedroom and wonder what it says about me to a stranger

20

– the *Battlestar Galactica* poster on the wall (signed by precisely one-fifth of the main cast), the bank of shelves containing sci-fi Blu-rays, books and graphic novels, the games consoles piled in a tangle of wires around my tiny TV, and the threadbare armchair shoved into a corner because I refused to let it be thrown away. Lorenzo has started referring to the room not-so-affectionately as my *sad nerd cave*.

Lorenzo's room is now poster-free in what I assume is an attempt to seem more grown up. The only concession to his personality is the assortment of free weights leaving dents in the carpet.

I'm pretty sure I know which room I like better.

The plates are gone from outside my door. By the time I head down to the kitchen, full hospitality protocol is in effect. The thickest tablecloth we own covers the table, which is now laden with plates of quiche, halloumi skewers, prosciutto on crackers, and other fancy stuff I don't even recognise. Mum has applied to be on *Come Dine With Me* so many times they must have blacklisted her by now.

'Did you get my instant noodles?' I ask.

Mum sighs theatrically and throws me a packet of Asda-brand chicken-flavoured noodles. 'Some mothers might take offence that you prefer those over my best spread.'

I'm so happy Saeed isn't there to hear my mum say 'best spread'.

'It just means Dad can eat double in my place,' I say, snapping on the kettle.

Dad flicks soapy water at me from the washing-up

bowl. 'I'll blame you when *I'm* the one who has a heart attack.'

Mum gives him a non-jovial frown and he turns away sheepishly. There isn't time to find out why before the front door bangs open, sending a gust of cold air through the house. It's raining outside, and when Emily storms into the kitchen her wheelchair leaves faint wet trails across the hard floor.

'They quit,' my young sister snarls, throwing off her raincoat.

Mum hurries to retrieve it. 'Who quit?'

'Steph and Renata!'

'They're not doing the talent show?' says Dad, snapping off his yellow rubber gloves.

Emily growls in frustration, as if we should telepathically know exactly what's happened. 'Cowards! Abandoners!'

Every year our school holds a talent show that generally serves only to demonstrate the profound dearth of talent among the populace. Emily and her friends had entered with some kind of dance routine we haven't been allowed to see yet.

'Why have they quit?' I ask.

Emily scowls. 'I'm not telling.'

That's one thing I like about my sister: she never lies, she just stubbornly refuses to tell the truth.

'I'm sorry, darling,' says Mum, just as the doorbell rings. 'Can we commiserate about it later?'

'There's no need to commiserate!' Emily proclaims, as Mum hurries off to answer the door. 'Those deserters won't stop me from performing!'

I grimace. 'You're going to dance by yourself?'

She fixes me with a steely glare. 'If I have to.'

By the time I reach the front door our guests are already shuffling inside, carrying the smell of rain with them. Mrs Marlow stamps her feet on the mat, shaking raindrops from her red anorak. She's tall and skinny, bony fingers wrapped around the neck of a bottle of wine that she thrusts at Dad to parry his enthusiastic attempt at cheek kissing. Her small eyes flick rapidly around the hallway, like she's scanning for threats. Mum takes the anorak and hangs it dripping on a peg.

'It's blowing a gale out there,' says Mrs Marlow, pulling an opener straight from the awkward-conversation handbook.

'Oh, it's terrible,' says Dad, meeting the play head-on. 'Come on through and dry off.'

Owen is still half hidden by the door, cleaning rain from his glasses. His long, dark hair hangs in limp strands across his face. There are heavy bags under his eyes, like he might not have slept for days.

'Do we need to take our shoes off?' he asks.

'If you wouldn't mind,' Mum says sweetly, like she wouldn't amputate his legs at the knee if he dared take another step.

I nod at Owen, and he nods back, apparently remembering me from earlier. It's official – we are on embarrassed masculine nodding terms.

Emily pivots her chair to lead us all through to the kitchen.

'Have you eaten?' Mum asks.

'Sorry, yes,' says Mrs Marlow, goggling at the

abundance of food. 'I hope you didn't go to too much trouble.'

Mum deflates a little. She'd already been cooking for hours by the time I got home from school.

'It's all right, I'll eat your share,' says Emily, reaching for a plate.

Dad crams a handful of peanuts into his mouth, which rather undermines the clipped posh tone he always assumes in company. 'Duncan, I believe you already know Owen from school?'

'Yeah, sort of,' I say.

Owen nods, eyes on the food. It's as if he's been told he can only eat one thing, and he wants to make sure he chooses wisely.

'I'm making some noodles if you want some?' I tear open the packet of flavour, pour the bright yellow powder over the block of dry noodles, and add the boiling water before shoving the whole thing into the microwave.

Mum throws up her hands in despair, but Owen nods. 'All right.'

We all share a painfully extended silence as the microwave hums and Dad crunches another mouthful of peanuts.

'We're really grateful for the invite,' insists Mrs Marlow.

The microwave finishes with a *ding!* I grab a tea towel and retrieve the steaming noodles, now dyed a luminescent yellow.

'Duncan, why don't you show Owen your room?'

'I would be delighted,' I say with a mock bow. 'Care to follow me?'

Mum lightly slaps the side of my head and I flash her a grin. Emily glares at me – apparently there'll be no such easy escape for her. I swaddle my hands in tea towels to carry the steaming bowl. Owen grabs a couple of forks and follows me out of the kitchen.

For some reason I'm relieved to find my room still tidy, like it might have thrown a tantrum of disarray in my absence.

'Sorry if you had better plans for tonight,' I say, shutting the door behind us.

Now he looks at me, cheeks flushing red. 'These are the first plans I've had since we moved here.'

'No pressure, then.' I wave him to the bed and hand over the bowl of noodles. Rain drums against the window behind him. 'I don't know what you want to do – I've got movies, or we could play something?'

Owen digs a fork into the noodles and slurps up a mouthful. He chews once, twice, and then pulls a face like I've fed him boiled tapeworms. 'These are terrible.'

I blink at him, unsure what to say. 'I love instant noodles.'

'I do too.' He sets the bowl aside and wipes the back of his hand across his lips. 'But you need proper noodles. I'll get you some next time.'

'Oookay. Thanks?'

Owen glances back at the window and shoots to his feet, as if he's seen a monster lurking behind the glass. He recovers by crossing to my shelves to run a finger along the spines of my Blu-rays and games. 'Alphabetical order,' he says.

'Yeah, I know,' I say, waiting for him to find fault with the system or me for employing it. Lorenzo used to mix a few around whenever I went to the toilet, just to see how long it would take me to notice.

'And no Transformers movies,' he adds, nodding appreciatively.

I don't tell him that I torrented them because I knew they'd be rubbish but kind of wanted to see them anyway. I always buy the Blu-ray of something I really like. My shelf has plenty of choice, even though I mostly just re-watch *Battlestar Galactica*.

'You seen this?' I say, pointing to where the episode is still paused on my laptop.

'I don't watch much TV. What is it?'

I already regret mentioning it. '*Battlestar Galactica*, probably the greatest TV show of all time.'

He leans down to study the screen more closely, like he might have missed some important detail. 'What do you like about it?'

At first I think it's a dig, a little more subtle than his noodle criticism. Then he raises his eyes to mine and I realise he's genuinely interested. 'I don't know . . .' I say. But of course I *do* know, I think about it constantly, and all at once I'm too excited to *not* tell him.

'It's got all the cool sci-fi stuff – dog fights in space, alien planets, cool tech – with special effects decent for TV. But it's also, like, really human? It's got politics, and love, and it's funny. It's all about people trying to find where they belong after everything they knew is destroyed, trying to carry on like everything can be normal again, when it never really can be.'

Owen seems to think about this for a moment, his face unreadable until a smile creeps on to his lips. 'Wow. I thought it was just about killer robots.'

'It has those too.' I quietly kick myself for showing too much enthusiasm. 'Lorenzo refused to keep watching because he said the "hot robots" weren't naked enough of the time.'

'Lorenzo's your friend?'

'Yeah. My best friend.' It's weird that I can only say it with uncertainty.

Owen returns to the bed. Before he sits down he glances out of the window, and then pulls the curtains closed. I'm beginning to consider the possibility that he's going to murder me.

Narrator: He probably wouldn't murder him.

I pick up a fork just in case.

'I saw you all on the playground,' he says. 'So, which rumours have you heard?'

I've never seen a single person at school talk to him, so I have no idea how he could have heard the stories. He's caught me off guard, and he knows it.

'You're variously a murderer, a rapist, a torturer *and* rapist of animals, and a brainwashed Scientologist on the run from Tom Cruise,' I say, counting them off on my fingers.

Owen laughs loudly, the sound ringing around the room. It's matched by a muffled burst of laughter from the kitchen. 'Funny, isn't it, how I can be so many different things when everybody has stayed as far away from me as possible.'

Hello, uncomfortable silence, old friend.

I glance at my laptop. A Cylon disguised as a super-model is paused on screen, walking among humans and hoping nobody will discover the truth about her. My bedroom door nudges open, and our cat toddles inside, making straight to rub himself against Owen's legs.

'This is Cuthbert,' I say. 'You're not allergic, are you?'

He leans down to scratch Bert's squashy cheeks. 'Cuthbert is the most middle-class name for a cat I've ever heard.'

'For the record, I wanted to call him Starbuck.'

'Is that a . . . ?'

'*Battlestar Galactica* reference, yeah.'

'Approximately how much of your day-to-day conversation is about *Battlestar Galactica*?'

'At least 33 per cent.'

'Is that another . . .?'

'Yep.'

I have no idea if he hates me or not. He squeezes his eyes tightly shut and then smiles at me, almost like he's relieved the exchange hasn't offended me. For some reason I feel like I have to press the advantage.

'Were you okay today?' I ask. 'When you ran off after lunch I thought—'

'Do you want to know the truth?' Owen says, straightening up and tucking a strand of hair behind his ear. 'You'll hear it eventually anyway.'

Why does it feel like I'm being tested? 'Only if you want to tell me.'

He squeezes his jaw tight, and then winces as he reaches a decision. 'We moved here because my dad died.'

The room is so quiet that I just *have* to respond as quickly as possible. 'Oh, man. I'm sorry.' A sentiment that never sounds genuine, no matter how much you mean it.

He nods, crossing his arms over his chest. 'Four months ago he had a heart attack on a train. Nobody noticed for over three hours, until the guard tried to wake him up at the final stop. He was a teacher at my school, and going back afterwards didn't work out. Mum wanted a fresh start, so . . .'

His lip trembles, and he digs a finger inside his glasses to wipe his eyes. *Oh god.* He's crying. The weird new kid Owen Marlow is *crying* in my bedroom.

I remember – vividly – the last time I cried in front of anybody. It was year seven, only a few months after we had started secondary school. A year-ten boy punted a football directly into my stomach, knocking all the wind out of my body. As I gasped to suck down a breath, the tears just leaked out of my face. Lorenzo cussed the boy out, got him out of my face, and then laughed at me louder than anybody else. He still brings it up from time to time.

Owen hooks off his glasses and peers up at me with red-rimmed eyes. This is the test, and I'm pretty sure I'm failing. I should comfort him, or escape to the toilet to give him privacy. I should do *something*. Instead I'm frozen. It's like a terrible accident unfolding in slow motion right in front of me.

'Sorry,' he sniffs, lifting himself up and wiping clumsily at his eyes.

'No, it's—'

Before I can find the right words – or even *any* words – he crawls across the bed, throws the curtains back, and pushes open the window. Cold air and spots of rain gust into the room. Owen puts one foot up on the sill.

'Wait a while before you tell my mum I've gone, okay?' he says, climbing up and dropping out on to the driveway. It's a good thing we're on the ground floor.

I nod, flummoxed, and then he's hurrying on to the pavement and out of sight. I just stand there, half-expecting him to come back and tell me it was all a joke.

Narrator: It wasn't.

Owen

The rain soaks into my socks. I'd forgotten I took my shoes off. I keep my eyes firmly on the glistening pavement. Away from the sky. Move quickly between the waypoints of glowing streetlights.

The pain is back, gnawing at my stomach. I try to ignore it. It'll only slow me down.

How could I let it get the better of me back there? Because I've run out of energy to hide the truth. When we moved here I was determined I wouldn't tell anybody about Dad. It would be simple enough to be vague about why he's out of the picture.

Maybe it's easier to be honest. I can't hold myself together all the time.

Clearly.

At least if people know what happened, they'll under-stand – or pretend to – when something like this happens. You're allowed to be fucked up and melodramatic when your dad dies, right?

Now he's gone, it's so much harder to contain the parts of myself I had to keep hidden before.

I don't look up. The Angels will be circling somewhere overhead. Seeing them now would only amplify the pain. I focus instead on the cold dripping from my hair and creeping down my back. My toes turning numb. The rhythm of my feet splashing on the pavement. For the briefest moment I thought I saw something familiar in Duncan. A sadness – no, a *lostness* about him that might mean we'd understand each other. It disappeared as soon as I started to cry. He froze up, just like they all do. Acted like I'm doing something wrong. Flouting the rules of decency by daring to show how I really feel.

It's not his fault. I know that. I just wish somebody would understand.

A wrenching in my gut forces me to stop. I lean against a lamppost for support. The orange light is warm enough that it might absorb me, phase me out of existence. I take a deep breath. Force myself to lift my head, push my sodden hair off my face.

I don't know the way home. I've been walking for at least fifteen minutes, and all I know is that I've never seen this street before.

The first bird misjudges its dive, swooping overhead and missing me by inches. It casts no shadow in the pool of streetlight as it lifts away to rejoin the formation overhead, hidden in the darkness.

The Angels are falling to Earth.

I run, feet slapping against the road. The street is deserted, the neat lines of parked cars like ancient relics.

31

The air shifts above me. I hear the rain drumming against outstretched wings.

Talons sink into my shoulders. Pain shoots across my back. I'm lifted from the road like a mouse from a field.

'Help!' I shout.

I'm already too high to be heard. Above the houses, rivers of rain rushing through their gutters. I see how the streets are sketched out in grids of light. The Angel lifts me higher to join its flock. They close around me in a protective ball, damp feathers slick against my face. We reach the clouds, and then there is nothing but cloying darkness.

The Devil on the Water

Campfire warmth teases Owen awake. His eyes focus sharply, the orange light forcing him to squint. He sits in a small clearing of dense forest. A sickly fire trembles at its centre, barely steady enough to expel shadows to cower between the close-pressed trees. There is no sign of the Angels, yet for a moment Owen expects to find himself ensconced in their nest, the heat of the fire nourishing him until he is ready to hatch.

This must be the new depths of a dream. Somehow he blacked out on the road and his ailing mind has conjured the warmth and comfort his body craves. Only . . .

His hoodie is still wet. The moisture grows hot from the fire and peels away as mist. His shoes are still missing.

A woman steps in front of him and offers a calloused hand. Bright orange hair trails in braids over the shoulders and down past the waist of a tattered raincoat. Owen realises he is not slumped on the ground, jetsam discarded by the sky; he is sitting with his knees pulled tight to his chest, as if he stumbled across the fire and stopped to rest awhile.

He takes her hand and she pulls him upright in one easy, practised motion.

'Where am I?' he says.

Finally, his eyes adjust. He sees the ring of mismatched stones around the fire; the wooden spit over the flames, blackened and greasy with fat; the shape of faces sketched by crude fingers in the dirt. This isn't just a fire – it's a camp.

'You're exactly where you're supposed to be, though it took you long enough,' says the woman, voice croaking as if it has been a long time since she last used it. 'My name is Luana. I've been waiting for you.'

A mottled grey animal pelt is visible beneath the braids, slung around her shoulders and fiercely at odds with the raincoat and the ragged trousers underneath.

Owen remembers what the boy told him on the school playground. I've found somebody to guide you.

It doesn't feel like dreaming. Somehow he has passed beyond sleep to a realm on the other side.

'It's time to go,' says Luana, kicking dirt to smother the fire. The night rushes eagerly into the clearing. The darkness is crushing, until faintly lambent shapes ignite inside the framework of the trees. The lights brighten, intensify, and then begin to skitter through the branches like embers in an updraught. Insects, thousands of them, fighting back against the tyranny of night.

'They absorb the light of the fire,' says Luana. She shoulders a pack and sets off into the blazing trees.

'Wait!' Owen calls after her. For a moment he is rooted, scanning the circle of starless sky overhead for any sign of the Angels coming to collect him. The only movement is a pinprick of light gliding across the clearing. Not a star – a satellite.

If he stands there long enough, the dream will end and he will return safely home. He clenches his eyes tightly shut, but the darkness there is harder to bear than this strange new place.

Owen hurries after Luana, stumbling on the uneven ground while she seems to flow through the forest, hardly disturbing the grasping branches and the flaming insects. He is breathing raggedly by the time he catches up, and wonders if he is insane to follow so easily, while knowing he is too frightened to let himself be left behind.

'Please,' he says. 'Tell me what's going on.'

'You're in the Forest,' she replies.

That much he had figured out for himself. 'But where – *what* is it?'

'Death.'

Owen stops as his legs wobble underneath him. Luana turns to him with a smile playing on her lips. 'Don't worry, it's not quite how it sounds.'

The insects fade to cinders as they walk farther from camp, but the forest stirs to life in other ways. Fallen leaves crackle in the spaces between trees and nearby branches sway with the passage of unseen travellers.

'This used to be a kingdom,' Luana says, still pressing ahead so forcefully that Owen struggles to keep up. 'It sits on the edge of the Sunday Water, an ocean vast enough that nobody has ever seen the other side and come back to tell of it. When somebody dies, their spirit must cross the ocean to reach . . . well, nobody knows.'

She stops for a moment to listen to the night, as if it might whisper the answer.

'The people here prepared the dead for their final journey. Most accepted their fate and went peacefully. A few tried to fight, or refused to believe it was their time. They needed guidance and understanding. Time. The kingdom could give them that.'

Luana sets off again to press forward through the trees.

'I know it sounds like a fairytale. The kingdom even had a beloved King and Queen, would you believe? And they a son who would inherit it all. It prospered, and the passage of the dead went unhindered.'

Owen trips on a tree root and staggers into her back. 'Until?'

'I have been told the story countless times, but nobody could tell me exactly what went wrong,' says Luana. 'The Prince went out into the world and never returned. The King and Queen passed across the Water when it was their time. The throne stood empty. The kingdom was neglected and fell into disrepair. After that, every time somebody died here a tree grew up in their place.'

Owen flinches away from the nearest tree. The Forest is too thick to see more than a few feet ahead, to possibly take a census. Luana glances back and catches his wide-eyed expression.

'Eventually the trees were abundant enough to snag spirits as they made their way to the coast. They became trapped here, lost in the Forest.'

'Is that what I am?' says Owen quietly. 'A lost spirit?'

'No. You and I are something else.'

She stops again to listen, and this time Owen hears it too. A sound like gentle applause easing through the fissures of the Forest. Luana sets off in pursuit, and soon enough the trees begin to thin. They emerge together on the bank of a river that has cut a wide, meandering path through the Forest. Their feet swish through long grass as they walk to the water's edge. Luana looks to the empty sky and frowns.

'We have to wait for the moon,' she says, and promptly drops to sit cross-legged in the grass.

'Are there still people living in the Forest?' asks Owen, watching the water ripple by. 'From before, I mean?'

Luana nods. 'You can't always tell them apart from spirits. Sometimes, even they don't know which they are.'

'Your story didn't explain why I'm here.'

She looks up at him and cocks her head. 'Are you a monster-slayer, boy?'

His throat is suddenly dry. He bends to the water and scoops a handful, bowing his head to drink. Before it can reach his lips, Luana appears at his shoulder and knocks his hand. The captured water spills back into the river.

'Make the sign of the cross before you drink.' She pinches her thumb, index and middle fingers together, before moving them between forehead and stomach, right shoulder to left shoulder. 'There are spirits in the water. You wouldn't want to swallow one.'

Owen decides he is no longer thirsty.

'We're looking for a monster?'

'The Fisher of Souls,' she says. 'It lives on the Sunday Water and catches crossing spirits before they reach the other side. We're supposed to find it, and kill it.'

'But why me?' Owen thinks of what the boy promised him. Somebody to guide him through everything that's happened in the last four months, to help him figure out why he can't grieve the way he should. An idea sinks talons into his flesh. 'Has it captured my father's spirit? Do I need to set him free?'

Luana takes his hands inside hers, callouses rough against his fingers. 'Now that you're here, we have to reach the Fisher soon. If we can't find our way, if we can't kill it, you'll be trapped here in the Forest for ever. Like I was, a long time ago.'

'Who brought you here?' asks Owen.

'The birds, same as you.'

The Angels only appeared to him after his dad died. 'You lost somebody too.'

'It doesn't matter.' Luana drops his hands and points to the sky. 'The moon is rising.'

The trees on the far side of the river are beginning to glow a ghostly white. Owen watches the pallid face of the full moon hoist itself above the tree line.

'You are going to be tested,' she tells him, urgently now. 'The Forest will do everything it can to keep you here. It's my job – my last chance at redemption – to help you through to the other side. I'll need more power before we can begin our journey.'

The moon rises quickly until it hangs large over the

river. Its light reveals the silhouette of a figure standing on the water's surface. It lifts a hand, palm upturned, beckoning one of them to join it.

'When the moon rises, the devil will call to me, and I will go to him.' Luana recites the words, as if she learned them long ago. 'Death rules this Forest. To reach its end, we either wield its power, or we die too.' She almost sounds relieved as she kicks off her boots and moves towards the water.

'You'll freeze,' says Owen.

Whoever waits on the water fills him with dread. He has to fight the urge to drag her back.

Luana steps off the bank. Instead of plunging into the water, her foot settles on its surface without even a ripple. It is as solid as ice, even though Owen can see that it continues to flow. Luana takes another step, confidence growing. Then she walks quickly to meet the expectant shadow.

Under the fragile illumination of the moon Owen's eyes cannot identify the figure. When Luana takes its outstretched hand, it offers her a courtly bow of its head. It is shorter than her. The pair seems frozen in time for a long moment, the air singing in anticipation, before the figure slips its free arm around her waist and they lift their joined hands high.

The dance begins slowly. Tentative steps, like anything bolder would break the spell, dare the river to buckle under their weight. When it holds, their footwork quickens, certainty flourishing, their bodies pressing closer together.

Owen's fear is blown away by the whirl of Luana's raincoat as the shadow spins her away and draws her back, the dip and lift of their arms, their feet skipping in perfect time across the surface of the water. The river is a conflagration of moonlight, shimmering around the dancers, fracturing and reforming under their tread.

It is the most beautiful dream he has ever had.

There is a moment, as the entwined figures bound and spiral, that Owen is sure he sees the face of the shadow: it belongs to the boy who brought him here, who claimed he knew a way to help.

Seconds or hours pass before the dance begins to slow. The shadow pulls Luana close one last time, dipping her low in the crook of its arm so that her braids trail in the water. As she rises, the shadow bows to her, kisses her hand, and then turns to look across the water at where Owen stands. He shrinks away, hoping the night will protect him. The shadow lifts an arm to wave, and then sinks into the water, the current swallowing it whole.

Luana sways with exhaustion when she returns to the riverbank. A dreamy smile is only just fading from her lips, but her skin is pale. Fresh streaks of grey cut through her orange hair. Owen offers her a steadying hand, but before she can take it the shade of a wing passes across the moon.

'No,' gasps Owen. 'Not yet.'

The Angels form up above his head, their ragged circle skimming the treetops.

'What was that?' he asks quickly as a bird breaks away from the flock. 'What happened out there?'

'I went out on to the water a woman,' says Luana. 'I return a witch.'

Talons sink into his shoulders. He is plucked easily from the riverbank. Luana lifts a hand to shield her face from the turbulence of its wings.

'Our journey is only beginning!' she calls as he is lifted away. 'We must follow the river to its end.'

Within moments he is high enough that the river is a shining ribbon, the Forest an endless stretch of silvered darkness. The moon looks near enough to catch in his arms, and Owen reaches for it as the dusty wings of the Angels close around him.

Chapter Three

Owen

Rain trickles down my forehead, glasses too steamed to see through. My head feels thick, like a loaf of bread is baking inside my skull. I sway tiredly on the spot.

'Are you even listening to me?'

I take off my glasses. Somehow, I'm standing in my bedroom. Steadily dripping on to the carpet, sodden hoodie zipped up to my throat. Mum stands in the doorway. The vein throbbing in her neck suggests she's been shouting at me for a while.

'You didn't even take your shoes!' she says, holding up my battered trainers.

My toes are numb, squeaking against the inside of my wet socks. Sheepishly, I take my trainers. We seem to be halfway through an argument, but I've only just arrived to deliver my lines. I shake my head, trying to dislodge the residue of the dream. Or nervous breakdown. Or hypothermic hallucination.

'What was I supposed to tell them?' says Mum.

'Who?'

'Mr and Mrs Cyman! I could hardly pretend you had slipped out of the door.'

My body yearns for the warmth of the campfire dream. It's cruel that my mind would conjure so effortlessly comforting a place.

'And Duncan, that poor boy,' Mum continues. 'Sitting in his room like he was covering up a murder.'

'He didn't come and tell you?'

At the time I hardly thought about it, but the look on his face when I began to cry suggested he would put in an immediate call to have me sectioned. Climbing out of the window in the rain without shoes is definitely aberrant behaviour to be reported.

'To be honest, Mum, I don't give a fuck what you had to tell them.'

Her face contorts, anger boiling over into rage. Before she can really let me have it, my whole body shudders, the cold biting through to my bones.

'Oh, darling,' she breathes, softening instantly. 'I'll get you a towel.'

As soon as she's gone I lean across the bed to peer through the window. The sky glow is too strong to see if the Angels are circling in the rain.

Most of my clothes are still bundled inside the boxes stacked against the wall, so I squelch downstairs in my wet outfit.

Not much has been unpacked yet. The back room, always chilly because of a crack in the sliding glass door, has a couple of pieces of furniture still wearing

43

dust-cover jackets. Dirty footprints from the movers are still tracked across the carpet. On the mantelpiece rests a single framed photograph and the white cardboard box. The first items that were taken out to christen the new house.

I pick up the photograph. It shows the three of us, the way we never really were – Mum, Dad and me, standing on a beach in our swimming gear, arms wrapped around each other. I don't remember it being taken. I barely recognise the happy faces.

Next, I pick up the cardboard box. Open the top. Inside is a thicker cardboard tube that holds a clear plastic bag filled with salt-and-pepper ashes.

My mind goes back to the Forest. The woman – Luana – told me we were going to take a journey together. Perhaps I already started it, four months ago. She might be able to lead me to its end.

I laugh bitterly. If only she was real.

'Have you thought any more about where to scatter them?'

Mum stands in the doorway behind me, a fresh towel clutched to her chest.

I reseal the box and return it to the mantelpiece. Then I take the towel and press it to my damp hair. 'I'm still not ready,' I say.

She nods, but it doesn't mask her impatience. The ashes tether us to the man of the past, while Mum is already reshaping him into the man she will live with for the rest of her life.

It's not as simple as my not being ready to let him go. Dad is already *gone*, in a way so much more profound than death. Mum just hasn't realised it yet. She probably never will.

'I'm worried you're not coping,' she says. 'I want to help you grieve in the right way.'

The right way. If I had a quid for every time somebody told me that. 'I know.'

I will grieve. I *am* grieving. And whenever I've cried or tried to talk to somebody about how it feels, they seize up and change the subject as quickly as they can. Like I'm doing it wrong by dumping it on them. They want to be there, but they don't want to have to care.

Exactly like Duncan. At least he didn't offer up some internet platitude about the ephemeral beauty of death.

It's not his fault. I just wish . . .

The way I'm *supposed* to grieve doesn't feel true.

There has to be a way I can stop getting it so wrong.

What would Dad say if he came back to haunt me? *Honestly, you can't even mourn me properly!*

'We came here to give you the best chance to move on,' Mum says.

I clutch the soggy towel to my chest. Keep my eyes firmly on the family photograph. 'Have you started to forget him yet?'

'Of course not.' She smiles uncertainly, like I might be making a joke. 'I never stop thinking about him.'

'That isn't what I asked.'

She turns and leaves the room quickly, which means she is probably going to cry. It would have been worse, if she had truly understood my question.

The towel snags in the zip of my hoodie. I reach inside to dislodge it, jerking the zipper open. I try to shrug off the wet hoodie, but it catches on something behind me. I turn on the spot but can't get it free, so I reach up inside my T-shirt.

Feathers. Soft and oily against my fingers.

I rush upstairs to the bathroom, lock the door. Peel away my clothes. Naked, something still tickles against my back. Slowly, I peer behind me into the mirror.

Two long, black feathers protrude from my shoulder blades, running almost the full length of my back.

I grasp one in my hand, tug at it, but it is rooted under my skin.

I squeeze my eyes shut and breathe, breathe, waiting for the feathers to disintegrate between my fingers. When I open my eyes, they are still there, folded tight against my body.

It wasn't a dream. The Forest. The woman who greeted me there. They were real. Another long breath holds me on the brink of freaking out. I wasn't scared, in that place. I shouldn't let myself be scared now.

Carefully, I wrap the towel closely around myself and hurry back to my room.

Chapter Four

Duncan

If there's a bright side to my sister falling out with her friends – by which I mean a bright side for *me* – it's that she needs somebody to hang out with at lunchtime the next day, so I have an excuse to avoid the guys.

'Are you going to eat that?' says Emily, already lifting from my plastic tray the remaining half of the burger I was very much planning to finish eating.

The downside to hanging out with my sister is that I will inevitably go hungry.

There are two main reasons I'm reluctant to see the guys today:

1. Despite what he says, Matt will definitely still be suspicious about the sext.

2. They're going to ask me what happened with Owen last night, and I have no idea what to tell them.

Lorenzo would have asked me this morning if I hadn't made sure I was late, and then again during double maths if an unannounced test hadn't taken away any chance to talk. It was the first time I'd ever been happy to see surprise equations.

The problem is that it would be *so easy* to tell them exactly what happened: the instant noodles, the crying, the unexpected jumping-out-of-the-window-without-shoes. It's kind of comedy gold. Currency I'd be a total dick to spend.

'Have you taken your happy pill today?' Emily asks.

She calls it that ironically, and I know she's genuinely asking, because when I was first prescribed antidepressants I was forever forgetting to actually take them.

'I took it at breakfast.'

Emily nods, satisfied. 'Nobody else will dance with me.' She snaps a picture of her lunch on her phone. She likes to post #foodie parody pictures of school dinners to Instagram. 'And I'll look like a complete loser if I do it by myself.'

'You could try making up with your friends.'

Steph and Renata are sitting in their usual cafeteria spot a few tables over, picking at their food and studiously ignoring us.

'Not going to happen.'

I wait a moment, hoping she might decide to tell me what happened between them. Pushing her to give it up will just make her less likely to ever tell me. She avoids my eyes and keeps photographing her meal.

'You could just not do the talent show,' I say.

'I have to do it. I'm proving a point.'

'And what point is that?'

'I'm not exactly sure yet.'

We're almost finished with lunch when Lorenzo slaps a tray down on the table beside me and hops into the seat opposite Emily. His plate contains only the limp remnants of a salad. His diet is slowly being taken over by protein shakes and power bars and alligator testosterone yoghurt or whatever.

'You should eat more,' says Emily around a mouthful of burger.

Lorenzo grins. 'I have to stay in shape for you, baby.'

'Maybe I want more of you to love.'

'There's plenty of me to keep you satisfied,' he says, flexing a bicep that threatens to tear straight through his shirt sleeve.

They've known each other almost as long as we've been friends, but the *flirty banter* is pretty new. I'm 99 per cent sure it's a joke. The idea that it might be real makes me want to slip them both veterinary-strength chemical castration tablets.

'I will pay you actual money to stop,' I say.

Emily grins. 'It can go towards our wedding fund.'

'You've already got me wrapped around your finger.' Lorenzo collects her empty tray and buses it. 'Mind if I borrow my future brother-in-law for a bit?'

He practically lifts me out of my seat and steers me towards the playground. Ten minutes of break left. I was *this* close.

Matt and Saeed are waiting in our usual spot by the bench around the side of the maths block. We're not supposed to eat outside, but Matt is halfway through a baguette that must have been as long as his arm. At least it keeps his hands full enough that he can't throw a punch.

'Dump or a wank?' grins Saeed. 'Maybe he's still got that selfie of Becky on his phone, eh?'

Matt chokes on a mouthful of sandwich and glares at me like *I* made the joke.

'Usually I just think about your mum,' I blurt to deflect attention.

Saeed considers the effort. 'Three out of ten.'

'I asked her about it. Becky, I mean, not your mum,' says Matt, frowning. He frowns a lot these days. 'It was meant for me. I'm sorry about . . .' He waves his free hand to roughly encompass all of yesterday's unpleasantness. 'Just forget you saw it, all right?'

'I'm sorry, but that image is *never* leaving my mind,' says Saeed.

'Just remember who gets it for real, yeah?'

Matt doesn't play his sexual trump card often, which makes it all the more devastating when he does. Me and Saeed can take it as a joke (or we're at least good at hiding the profound pubescent pain it causes us), but for Lorenzo it's like a rival lion rocking up to his den and stealing his kill. Matt watches him closely, like he might have gone a step too far but isn't sure if he cares.

'Whatever,' says Lorenzo, jaw flexing as he turns to me. 'You gonna tell us about last night or not?'

Matt redoubles his efforts to finish the baguette before lunch is over, and Saeed looks at me expectantly, leaving me no choice but to talk.

'It was all right.'

'Just all right?'

Matt burps. 'Still alive, isn't he?'

'Owen isn't a murderer or any of that stuff,' I say. 'He's just . . .'

For some reason I want to defend him. It would be so easy to tell them how he cried in front of me. They would actually be interested in one of my stories for once. Oh, how we'd laugh! At the expense of somebody other than myself. But I can't do that to Owen.

'Was his mum hot?' asks Saeed.

'Forget that,' says Lorenzo. 'He's probably grooming you, Spunk. You're gonna be his next victim.'

'He's not like that!'

They all watch me expectantly. In the space of a breath, I decide to tell them why Owen moved here, because it's the only way to get them off my back.

Narrator: That was not the only reason.

'His dad died.' I whisper it to add a touch of drama.

Their eyebrows lift like synchronised swimmers. 'Serious?'

'Had a heart attack on a train. They moved here to get away from it all,' I say, beginning to regret telling them anything, knowing it's too late to stop. 'You can't tell anyone.'

'Maybe his mum needs a bit of comfort,' leers Saeed.

'Shut up, man,' says Lorenzo, punching his shoulder. 'That has to mess you up.'

Lorenzo's mum died before he was old enough to really remember her. He doesn't talk about it much any more, but when we were kids he was obsessed with my mum, like he was trying to make up for lost time.

It makes the endless *your mum* jokes from Matt and

51

Saeed even more tiresome. Lorenzo pretends not to mind, even joins in sometimes, but it can't be easy.

As if my loose lips have summoned him, Owen steps out of the main building doors and dodges through the crowds to reach his spot under the awning of the maths block. Today he keeps his eyes firmly on the ground, glancing towards us. I lift a hand to wave, but his gaze has already dropped away. Matt and Saeed laugh and make pitying noises in their throats, before Lorenzo distracts them with a story about his new gym mates and their adventures in being testosterone-addled beefcakes.

Spilling Owen's secret earned me their attention for a grand total of ten seconds.

I can't help but watch him. After last night, I should want to stay away. I thought his mum was going to throw *me* out the window when I told her what had happened.

Lorenzo catches me looking and elbows me in the ribs, which is a bit like being hit by a medieval battering ram. 'Reminiscing about your date?'

I smile, trying to pretend I'm not bothered.

'Honestly, I'm out after the girls in my gym and you're getting all dreamy-eyed over the new boy.'

If Instagram and Snapchat are anything to go by, Lorenzo spends most nights surrounded by dudes taking selfies of themselves in tank tops. Half the people at school would drop their pants for him at the slightest invitation. If I didn't know better, I'd think he was frightened of them.

The bell rings for the end of lunch. I'm ready to use my head-boy duties as an excuse to speak to Owen again, but he sets straight off for the front gates like the bell was a starter's pistol. Before he can make his escape, Mr Spencer cuts him off and marches him inside.

Owen

The office smells like cigarettes and Blu-tack. Mr Spencer points me to a hard plastic chair, before rounding his desk and sighing into his plush office chair. Everything on the desk is arranged at right angles: laptop lined up with the edge, pens, phone, stacks of paper all straight. I wonder if he thinks it demonstrates authority. He's probably the kind of person that claims to be 'a bit OCD' because he likes things neat.

The feathers on my back press against the hard chair. They *itch*. That's how I know they're real. I can feel them rooted down deep inside my body.

'Where were you off to just now?' he asks.

I glance at my watch. If this doesn't take too long, I can still make it in time. The best strategy available to me is to tell him exactly what he wants to hear.

'Sorry, sir, I know I'm not supposed to leave school premises.'

'Then why did I just catch you trying to do exactly that? And why didn't I see you at school yesterday afternoon?' He leans back in his chair, clearly pleased with his strategy of having only asked questions to which he already knows the answers.

'I wasn't feeling well, sir.'

'And you didn't think you needed permission to leave?'

I let the silence stretch so I have time to work out

exactly what he wants from me. If it's remorse, I can fake it. I just need to do it quickly.

'Look.' Mr Spencer's chair squeaks as he leans forward on his elbows. 'I know things have been hard for you lately, Owen.'

Oh, it's going to be one of *those* chats. Pretence of empathy. The magnanimous act, like they're doing you a massive favour by treating you differently. I'd rather catch a bollocking, like anybody else would get if they left school in the middle of the day.

'I can't imagine how difficult it's been for you . . .' Mr Spencer is saying.

Dad used to treat me differently to everybody else at school too. If he caught me doing the slightest thing – talking, doodling, arriving a minute late after lunch – he'd tear into me in front of the whole class. Far worse than anybody else would ever get. At first I thought it was because he had higher standards for me, and as ever I wasn't meeting them. Eventually, I realised that he thought if everybody saw him treating his son that way, they wouldn't dare risk finding out what it would be like for them. The whole class saw through it, and whenever they tested him he would let it slide, saving his anger for me instead.

'You should give me detention,' I say.

Mr Spencer stops in the middle of his current platitude. 'Do you think that's necessary?'

'For leaving school at lunchtime without telling any-body?' I lean forwards, challenging him. 'It should be worse than detention. But I'll settle for that.'

He snorts, like I've told a joke. 'When did this become

a negotiation? I'm letting you off, but you won't be so lucky next time.'

It has nothing to do with luck. It's pity, and I don't want any of it.

'Back to class, please.' He dismisses me with a wave of his hand.

'Yes, sir,' I say, already checking my watch as I cross to the door.

Duncan

Ten minutes into English I spot movement on the playground. I look out of the window just in time to see Owen hurry across the playground, not even trying to keep a low profile. He goes straight for the staff exit, but it's locked after lunch. The teachers have electronic fobs.

He tugs at the gate, and then turns his gaze to the sky. I can't see his face from here, but I remember his fright last night when he opened my curtains to peer out at the night. In one swift movement he scrambles over the gate and drops on to the pavement.

'New boy's in a hurry,' says Lorenzo, leaning across me.

I turn back to my book, pretending not to care, while a single question runs rings around my brain.

Where does he go that's so important?

Chapter Five

Duncan

It took around a year of dedicated research to establish exactly which fried chicken shop is the worst in Westleigh. The working hypothesis was that it had to be the place named after the most obscure US state: Wyoming Fried Chicken. Chicken Temple proved bland rather than offensive, while Doctor Cluck gave Matt such severe food poisoning he had to seek actual medical attention. Cluckers is a chain so it doesn't count.

Yet every one of them is a Michelin-starred, influencer-catnip hotspot compared to Cockerel's, the grotty chicken shop hidden away (ironically) behind Whole Foods. The flavour is so bad we considered calling the police. The only possible explanation is that the proprietor squeegees the grease from his own forehead and injects it directly into the wings.

So, of course, a weekly visit to Cockerel's has become a ritual of sorts, a local badge of pride; we frequent it and survive, against all odds.

'I swear it's getting worse,' says Lorenzo, eyeing his shrivelled breast.

'I love their unique blend of one herb and one spice,' adds Saeed. Sometimes he tries to play the Halal card to get out of a meal, like we'll somehow forget he doesn't practise that.

After getting the chicken, we position ourselves half-way up the high street, perched on a low road gate for Asda deliveries. It's been dark about an hour. Most of the shops are closing up. A few schoolchildren are still hanging around town, and the charity muggers have given up, huddling together in a cloud of cigarette smoke.

Grease has soaked through the chicken box before I've even taken a bite. 'I'd dearly love to talk to Mr Cockerel about the quality of his meat,' I say.

Lorenzo kicks at the gate. 'Don't start.'

'I just think such an illustrious gentleman would be mortified to discover that an establishment bearing his good name is serving such sub-standard poultry.' I hold up a dripping wing to illustrate the point.

'Your mum never questions the quality of my meat,' says Saeed.

Matt groans and wipes greasy fingers on his Asda uniform. 'Late and crude, two out of ten.'

Lorenzo points a drumstick at me. 'The shop is *not* named after somebody called Cockerel.'

'That's *Mr* Cockerel to you.'

'They messed up the apostrophe! It's supposed to be cockerels, plural, because of all the cocks they're feeding you.'

We all look to Saeed expectantly. He waves us away. 'Too easy.'

'I can't eat this crap any more,' says Lorenzo, closing up his box and shoving it at Matt. 'I wanna try this clean-eating thing the guys at the gym told me about.'

I almost choke on a bone. Cockerel's is our tradition. It used to be *him* that kicked up a fuss if one of us refused the punishment.

'I don't want your scraps,' says Matt, though his eyes on the chicken say otherwise.

'Whatever.' Lorenzo crumples the box and drops it at my feet. He knows how much I hate littering, and the way he looks at me is a challenge to say something. A challenge I don't accept. His next move is to take out his e-cigarette, like that's *clean*, and blow a cloud of sickly strawberry vape smoke into my face. I don't rise to that either, and within seconds he's looking past me. 'Check it out.'

I follow his gaze. A trio of girls is trailing down the high street from the train station, wrapped up in their coats, moving closer to our side of the street so they can avoid the regrouping charity people.

'Dare you to go over,' says Lorenzo.

The chicken in my belly threatens to reappear. 'Me?'

'Yeah, Spunk.' He lifts his e-cig again. 'It's time to live up to your name.'

That makes no sense whatsoever. The girls pass us by, looking perfectly content with not being bothered by pubescent idiots. I've never been able to go up and talk to girls. My suspicion is that they prefer it this way. My allotted role in life is to stand at the back of any given group and look awkward, and it's a role I take seriously.

I'm formulating an escape plan when I recognise the girl in the middle of the three. It's Michaela, from my parents' church.

'All right then,' I say.

'Yeah, as if.'

Except I'm already hurrying after them. 'Michaela!' I call, quietly enough that the guys behind won't hear me using her name.

She and her friends all turn as one. I fight the urge to turn tail and run. It takes her a moment to recognise me, and I'm relieved that she smiles when she does. It reminds me that she has the most amazing dimples I've ever seen. Strands of dark hair have escaped her massive woolly hat, and when she brushes them out of her eyes I can't help but marvel at her flawlessly painted nails. Not that I always had a big crush on her or anything.

Narrator: He did.

'Duncan,' she says, as I hover close, trying to decide if a handshake is too formal a greeting. 'I haven't seen you in ages.'

A few months ago I stopped going to church with my parents. They were largely okay with the decision after I explained I am completely and irrevocably atheist and was only still going to keep them happy.

'My mum talks about you sometimes,' I say, almost wincing at how pathetic I sound.

'Aw, she's so lovely.'

I glance at her friends, expecting them to sneer at me, but they just look bored and cold.

Footsteps behind me. The guys are coming over. I have to abort before they manage to speak to her.

'I'll let you get on,' I say quickly.

'It was nice to see you. Say hi to your sister for me,' she says.

They're turning away when Lorenzo arrives at the head of the group, lips twisted into his smuggest smile and trailing vape fumes.

'Aren't you going to introduce me?' he says.

Lorenzo talks a lot about chatting up girls, and okay, maybe I'm not the best judge but . . . he always seems bad at it? Like, excruciatingly so. He'll also only ever do it when we're together as a group. It's more of a performance than something he actually wants to do.

'We're just going,' says Michaela with a tight smile, dimples disappearing.

'What's the rush?' Lorenzo and Saeed follow them closely, while I hang back with Matt, who has prioritised finishing off his chicken.

'Where you hurrying off to?'

'Stop and talk to us for a while.'

'No, thank you,' Michaela says firmly. She flashes me a look that's a livestream of her opinion of me plummeting.

I put a hand on Lorenzo's brawny shoulder. 'Maybe just leave it, yeah?'

He ignores me and pushes between Michaela and her friends, giving her no space to shrink away as Saeed pins them on the other side. I turn to Matt for help, but he just licks his fingers clean and shrugs.

Behind us, I notice somebody else has stopped to watch. Owen stands outside the Chinese supermarket, hands shoved deep into his pockets. His presence gives me a masochistic kind of courage.

'Lorenzo!' I say, grabbing him harder this time.

'What?' he shouts, spinning around to throw me off. The others stop too, giving the girls a chance to flee.

'They weren't interested,' I say, trying to sound nonchalant, like I've just done him a favour.

'What do you know about it?' He steps closer. 'You wouldn't know what to do with a girl if she was begging you for it.'

I can't remember when I first realised I was afraid of my best friend, but I'm afraid of him now. Usually I don't bother standing up to him, because all it means is that he has to put me back in my place.

'It's just –' I glance behind me in time to see Owen disappear into a passageway between shops.

'Just what?'

Matt and Saeed are quiet, waiting to see what happens next. My usual move at a time like this is to back down, apologise, and try to get things back to normal between us as quickly as possible. Before he has the chance to realise that maybe if they *didn't* go back to normal he wouldn't care too much.

My mouth opens. Before I can speak, I step past him and hurry away up the high street, swallowing down the words I wanted to say.

That this wasn't even the first time I've felt ashamed of my friends.

Owen

I hear somebody running after me before I reach the end of the passage. A voice calls out.

'Owen!'

By the time he reaches me, Duncan is out of breath. He needs a few seconds to catch it before he can speak again.

'I saw you on the high street,' he says.

'Yeah, I know.'

We're outside a small office building, the lights in the windows snapping off as somebody inside the foyer sets an alarm with a series of bleeps.

'It probably looked bad, but they were only messing around,' he says.

'Messing around. Sure.'

Duncan actually flinches. Like I've punched him. His eyes are wide and desperate, as if nothing in the world is more important right now than explaining himself. I force myself to soften.

'You don't have to make excuses to me,' I say.

He doesn't look so sure. 'Where do you keep going at lunchtime?'

That takes me by surprise. I knew he must have seen – I've hardly tried to keep it secret – but I'm surprised he cares enough to be curious.

'I'm not going to tell you that,' I say, and move towards the road ahead. Towards the new house. I've stayed still for too long. The Angels are circling overhead.

The office block is emptying out, people saying their goodbyes and heading their separate ways home.

'I'm sorry about last night,' Duncan calls after me. 'I didn't know what to do. But . . .'

I stop. A young guy wearing a tie bumps into me and swears under his breath. Duncan struggles to find the words he wants. There's no need for him to apologise

– he reacted how everybody else does. Yet I let him flounder, oddly curious what he has to say.

'I wish I'd done better,' he finishes.

He's practically a stranger, but I can tell he means it.

'Come over again,' he says. 'Tonight.'

I glance at the sky. The ragged shapes of the Angels cut a tireless circle out of the darkness. If they're going to come for me again, it could happen at any moment. Before they were merely ominous, a delusion to outlast. Now they are a threat.

In the corner of my eye, I see Duncan follow my gaze. I look down quickly. Even though he won't see anything up there. 'Sure. I'll head over after dinner.'

'We can watch *Battlestar Galactica*.' His smile is genuine. When he takes out his phone I realise I'm expected to do the same. We exchange numbers.

'Drop me a message when you set off,' he says.

I nod, and we go our separate ways.

Duncan

'I'm glad you've hit it off,' says Mum when I tell her we'll have a guest after dinner.

Hit it off might be a bit strong. I chased him down and demanded he come over to my house. I'm not even sure why I did it. Maybe to make up for last night. Probably to get back at Lorenzo. Why should I need a reason? The main thing is that I don't regret doing it.

'Did he tell you why they moved here?' says Mum.

I nod, shovelling peas into my mouth.

'It's important to have friends at a time like this.' She looks at me with pride I almost certainly don't deserve.

'Friends that don't quit your dance group at the last minute,' mutters Emily.

It turns out nobody has told her the situation, so Mum begins to fill her in.

Everybody needs friends. I've been waiting for a message from Lorenzo. Not an apology, but the usual attempt to carry on as if nothing happened at all. My phone has stayed quiet. He'll be in the gym by now, hanging out with his hench new friends, painstakingly posting every step of his workout to his Instagram story.

I tap out a quick message to Michaela: *Sorry about earlier, they get a bit carried away sometimes.* I deliberate for a few minutes about adding a kiss but ultimately decide against it because it's obviously a terrible idea.

'It won't be easy,' says Mum, 'but you could really help him.'

'Help him with what?'

'To get through this. To deal with his grief and move on. His mother's worried he's not dealing with it properly. Poor boy.'

I put my fork down. I'm not sure what qualifies me to help Owen through his grief. I still have three out of four grandparents, my nan dying when I was two years old. After my hamster died I refused to sleep in my room for a week in case Tinkerbell came back to haunt me. To lose your dad, and so suddenly . . .

Surely nobody can really know what Owen is feeling.

We finish dinner. Emily hurries out of the kitchen and Dad is running late at work, so I'm stuck with the washing-up. My phone buzzes. I quickly dry off my hands. It's Owen.

Leaving now.

A part of me expected him to cancel. *Hoped* he would. But I'm glad he's coming over. I check the time; it'll take him about fifteen minutes to walk. Hopefully that's enough time to work out what the hell we're going to do when he arrives.

Owen

I put my phone away and shout through the house. 'I'm going.'

'Hang on a minute,' says Mum, emerging from the back room. 'I just had a call from Mrs Walsh.'

My stomach sinks. Mrs Walsh was our neighbour before we moved. We looked after her little dogs whenever she went on holiday.

'She said she saw you at the train station today. In Maywood.' Mum crosses her arms so that the bones in her shoulders threaten to push through her skin. 'I told her she had to be mistaken, but she was adamant.'

'Must have been somebody else,' I say. It's not a convincing argument, but she can't prove me wrong. 'I was at school.'

Mum nods. Looks at her feet like she's biting back tears. 'We left Maywood so you could move on. So you could be happy. Isn't it easier . . . now he's gone?'

'He's dead but he's not *gone*. One way or another, he's staying with us for ever. You think pretending everything was perfect *before* makes it easier *now*. Then you can just grieve the way you're supposed to, and eventually you'll forget what he was really like.'

'I know he wasn't always easy to live with. I'm doing

everything I can,' she says, voice quivering, 'to make this easier for you.'

Her words seem to reach out directly to the pain inside me. It lifts its head, no less intense for its familiarity now. I want to run before it properly wakes up. Instead I look her straight in the face.

'What you're doing is making it easier for yourself,' I say. 'Did you ever think you might be making it harder for me?'

I open the door before she can reply. Slam it behind me. The cold air sears my throat. Every breath grows shorter, until it feels like I'm suffocating. I keep my feet moving and wrap my arms around myself. Beg for this to pass.

When talons grip my shoulders and pluck me from the ground, I decide there's no point in struggling against them.

River Hymns

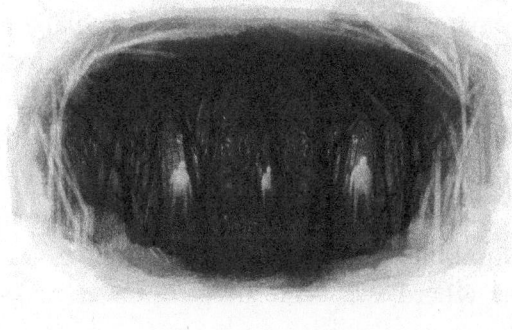

The waterfall obliterates Owen's senses, roaring in his ears, filling his eyes and nose with moisture. The air is draped with it. It beads on his skin and fogs his glasses.

'There's no way down,' Luana shouts over the thunder of the water.

He takes off his glasses and peers over the lip of the falls. It's a sheer drop, the river freefalling into a basin some hundred feet below. The water shimmers and flexes in the darkness like a muscle pulling taut.

'How did we get here?' Owen asks.

'We've been following the river,' says Luana.

He scrapes strands of wet hair out of his eyes. 'We?'

'Do you remember what I told you about the water?'

'It carries spirits.' Owen watches the lip of the fall, imagines souls leaping like silvered fish into empty air.

'Every river flows out to the Sunday Water,' says Luana. 'If we can follow it, eventually we'll get to where the spirits begin their crossing to the afterlife.'

It is impossible to count how many times Owen has wished he could believe in an afterlife.

Although this is only the second time he has met the Forest woman, Owen senses that she has changed. After she danced with the devil on the water, she proclaimed herself a witch. The transformation is more profound than the fresh streaks of grey in her orange hair, the new lines etched into her face. She is animated with purpose, driven by newly discovered knowledge, as tireless as a boulder tumbling downhill.

'Is that where we need to go?' Owen asks. 'The afterlife?'

Luana curls a lip into a wry smile. 'Not quite as far as that, I think.'

There is no choice but to leave the clamouring water behind them and find another way down. They follow the ridge until it begins to slope away. A long while passes before the sound of the falls is dampened by trees. Luana picks out a steep path in the underbrush that carries them stumbling over rocks and fallen branches, sliding through mud and leaves as they zigzag lower. Owen has never been more grateful to have shoes on his feet.

The Forest is real. He knows it now. It does not frighten him as much as it should. He will follow, and see where it leads him.

The dark is an impenetrable blanket by the time the Forest floor levels out, as if they have strayed too far from the sky. This time there are no luminous insects to guide their way. Luana does not stop. They double back towards the river, battling the thickly grown trees, until Owen becomes too tired to worry if anything lies in wait behind the blind spots of trunks and branches.

'I don't understand,' says Luana after a long while, finally halting. 'We should have picked up the river again by now.'

Owen knows what it feels like to be lost; he has been lost for a long time.

'We can wait until morning,' he says.

'We would be waiting a tremendously long time.'

Owen scrutinises the darkness bunched around them. 'Does it ever get light here?'

'Not that I've seen,' says Luana, pushing on again.

They find a spot where the trees are sparse enough to clear the ground and build a fire. Luana teases it to life, and they huddle close enough to thaw the cold from their bones.

'I have to show you something,' says Owen.

Luana rests her hands on top of her folded legs and nods for him to continue.

He turns and hikes up the back of his T-shirt, high enough to reveal the black feathers underneath. A sharp intake of breath, and then he feels fingers brush against them. He shudders, the touch seeming to tug at his skin, his flesh, deeper. Luana snatches her hand away.

'The Forest is claiming you,' she says.

Owen lowers his T-shirt. 'This happened to you?'

Luana shakes her head. 'Not like this.'

He shuffles closer to the fire. 'You said the Forest would test me.'

'I fear it already is.'

Luana sniffs hard, wipes the back of her hand across her nose, and then takes a bundle of dried leaves from her pack. They crumble in her grasp as she packs them into a sewn pouch of animal skin.

'Witchcraft suits you,' says Owen.

She huffs a laugh. 'It's already made me a self-important fool.' She binds the pouch with a length of brown twine. 'I never even knew how to cook. Anything I tried would burn, or crumble, or spill. They were always asking . . .'

Her hands still for a moment as her words trail off. She frowns, as if admonishing herself for an unwelcome memory, and then ties off the pouch.

'Some spirits get lost on their way to the Water, become tangled in the trees or reject death and flounder from the river,' she says. 'They don't know how to find their way or seek the homes to which they can never return, and wander the Forest.'

The flickering profiles of the trees seem to stand taller around them. Owen shuffles as close to the flames as he can bear. 'Exactly what kind of power did that devil give you?'

'Let's find out.' Her eyes flash as she drops the pouch on to the fire. The flames devour it, hissing with delight, and the eddying orange glow blazes suddenly stark white. Owen rears away from the supernova brightness. The light of the pale fire doesn't spread beyond the clearing, instead sealing them in a pillar bounded by impassable darkness. Its flames emanate waves of cold instead of heat.

'A ghost fire,' says Luana, and points behind him.

It takes all his courage to turn and look. Three dimly radiant shapes move through the trees from different directions, converging on the makeshift camp. A phosphorescent pallor blurs human features: the curve and bend of arms and legs, the gait of a walk, rough sketches of faces. Whenever Owen tries to focus on a detail it slips away.

'Spirits,' he says, scuttling around the ghost fire to put it between him and the approaching wraiths.

'Don't be afraid,' Luana tells him. 'You're just going to talk to them.'

'*I'm* going to? About what?'

'They can show us the way to the river. The water calls to them. But not all spirits want to answer. They will be deceptive. You must decide who tells the truth.' She clears her throat and calls out to them. 'Come, join our fire. You are welcome here.'

The spirits reach the haggard flames and hover, like night sentries pausing to hold their hands over the heat, forms flickering restlessly.

'It doesn't warm,' says the tallest spirit in the voice of a grown man. Owen is sure he recognises it. 'It doesn't warm.'

The heavy darkness at their backs frames the ashen figures. The spirits seem to have already slipped half out of this world, but the fire's austere light picks out their features a little more clearly. Owen peers closer at the tall spirit and gasps.

'Mr Hartley.'

Luana frowns. 'You know him?'

'He was my neighbour,' says Owen. 'He died when I was small.'

The old man had never been anything but exactly that, stooped and grey-haired, ancient enough that he was terrifying to be around, as if children would shrivel like fruit in his presence. He walked everywhere, his frame *click-clicking* along the pavement to the shops or the park. If anybody offered him help to cross a road or carry a bag he would wave them off, growling with incomprehensible bad temper.

Owen looks to the next spirit, a little shorter and broader than the first, and squints at its face. 'Uncle John.' Perhaps it would be exaggerating to say that Dad and his brother were estranged, but whatever caused them to fall out when Owen was young was never resolved before his uncle's unexpected death from cancer.

The third spirit is smaller still and has the softer features of a child. 'Ellie Renwick.' A girl from his primary school who died. There was an assembly and they all went home early.

He has never thought about how many people died around him when he was small. Really, he should have been better prepared.

'Talk to them,' says Luana.

What should he say? He hardly knew these people in life, had all but forgotten them in death.

The Forest is testing him. He must pass.

'Tell me about your lives,' he prompts. 'Before—'

The two taller spirits talk at once, voices tumbling over

each other. Luana quietens them with a stern 'Hush!', and then nods for Owen to try again. He gestures to the tallest spirit, Mr Hartley, inviting him to speak.

'I was walking,' he says, like it is an idea to be relished. 'They pushed me and I fell. Broke.' His voice falters. 'I never stood or walked again. It wasn't fair, what they did to me! I didn't deserve it!'

The fire crackles and spits, gnawing on the bones of the story.

'I'm sorry,' says Owen. He remembers Mum and Dad whispering in the kitchen, back when arguments remained quiet. They sat him down at the kitchen table. *Mr Hartley fell on his way to the shops. He won't be coming home.* They had never mentioned any kind of attack, just an old man tripping on a loose paving stone.

Owen points to the second spirit. Uncle John. 'Tell me about your life.'

'They misunderstood,' he wheezes, like he has spent every moment since death trying to draw a single breath. 'They checked, and checked, until I felt like a ruddy pin cushion! I knew something was wrong, but they said they found nothing. 'Til it got worse, and they found something. Too late. I left home and didn't know it was the last time.'

The ghost fire crackles again, sucking the marrow from the story. Owen searches for a memory of his uncle, remembers only his father putting down his phone and slamming a fist into the wall. *Stubborn bastard!* Uncle John had known he was ill, and refused to do anything about it.

The third spirit, smallest of them all, patiently waits her turn.

'Tell me about your life.'

'I liked trees the very most,' Ellie Renwick says in a sing-song voice, as if she isn't enclosed by them now. 'And the clouds in a summer sky. I liked every single blade of grass, and the smell of rain. I liked biscuits. Most of all I liked my mum and my dad and my brother and . . . I can't think of anything I didn't like.'

Owen's throat squeezes tight, and the faintest shade of that familiar pain stirs inside him. It seems to hold less power here in the Forest. Ellie Renwick's death was an event, the little girl at its heart lost to the drama and confusion of facing the unthinkable. He realises now that he never learned how she died.

'It's her,' he says.

Luana watches closely. 'Are you sure?'

When asked about their lives, the other spirits had spoken only of their deaths. Their denial – or perhaps their outright lies – about what brought them to the Forest proves they are not yet ready to leave it.

'It's her,' he says again.

Luana rises to her feet. 'I can't give you back the trees or the grass, the rain or the sky. But I can tell you where to wait for your family.'

The spirit of Ellie Renwick glows brighter. 'Where?'

'You must find a river. You must cross the Sunday Water.'

The other spirits gutter, candles on the cusp of going out, and steal away into the shelter of the Forest. Owen watches them dissolve into the darkness, wishes he could have done anything to help them.

'You must wait there,' says Luana. 'Where all rivers end.'

74

The flames blush orange again, released from the spell. Ellie Renwick's spirit rushes away from the camp. Luana grabs her pack and gives chase into the trees. 'She'll lead us back to the river!'

Owen hurries to keep up. 'She was just a little girl.'

'And yet she remembered her life, instead of raging against her death. She remembers who she was before this place,' Luana says. 'She was lost, and so were we; together we'll find the way.'

The sound of rushing water pushes through the trees ahead of them. Ellie Renwick's spirit slows to a halt on the bank of the river. She does not look back as hazy arms come together in a point above her head. She laughs, the precious chime of a bell, and dives into the water.

All at once the river is a conflagration of surging spirits, threading downstream in an undulating ribbon, its brilliant glow peeling back the night.

'Was that really my neighbour? My uncle?' asks Owen.

Luana doesn't reply. Owen is surprised to find a hot tear rolling down his cheek. As if she has sensed it, Luana glances back over her shoulder.

'I know how it feels,' she tells him.

In the last four months so many people have told him exactly that. This is the first time he has believed it.

'Who did you lose?' asks Owen.

'My husband and my son.' Luana watches the river. 'It's been a long time, I think. I can't let them go. The Fisher of Souls has taken their spirits. I won't find peace until I set them free to cross the Sunday Water.'

'We can get there,' says Owen. 'If we stay together.'

She smiles, and points along the river. 'You might be right. You passed your first test. Now we know the way.'

Before he can say anything more, talons sink into his shoulders and whisk him away.

Chapter Six

Owen

Streetlight on my bedroom wall.

I blink. The light of the river still plays across my eyelids. A cold breeze trickles through the open window, ruffles something on my back. Goosebumps course along my arms.

It must be late. The house is dark and quiet. I tiptoe through to the bathroom and tug the light cord. Take off my T-shirt and turn my back to the mirrored doors of the bathroom cabinet.

The feathers have multiplied. They sprout from underneath my shoulder blades in downy clumps. The original feathers are longer now, shining with health.

I reach under my arm and grip the longest. Pull. Pain lances across my shoulders. The feathers are lodged deep inside my body, as if they have grown from the loose ends of veins and arteries.

At school, we once grew weeds covered by an

overturned cardboard box with a single hole punched through the top. After a week we lifted the box away to find the plants grown tall but deathly pale, reaching like skeletal arms for the lone source of light.

Perhaps the feathers belong to the pain that lives inside me, forcing its way out. Determined to make itself known in the world.

Rooting around inside the bathroom cabinet, I find some scissors. Open them wide and *snick* the blades at the empty air. I reach under my arm again, close the blades gently around one of the feathers. I imagine it bleeding, draining black oil from my body. My fingers tighten on the handles.

There's no point. It wouldn't change anything. The Angels will come for me again, borne on wings of their own. I put the scissors back inside the cabinet and close the doors.

In the mirror, trees envelop my reflection. I blink, and they're gone. The bathroom is restored.

I might have passed the first test, but the Forest isn't finished with me yet.

I switch off the light and hurry back to my bedroom.

Chapter Seven

Duncan

The buzzing phone interrupts my regularly scheduled programming of lying in bed and staring at the ceiling instead of sleeping. An *actual call*, not a message. I fumble at the bedside table and knock my phone on to the floor. I squint against the brightness of the screen.

I'm expecting Lorenzo; he also doesn't sleep well, and occasionally he calls about schoolwork or because he's had too many of his dad's beers, like it's totally normal to call me at 2am on a school night. The only reason I don't put my phone on silent before bed is because it would be worse if he stopped calling altogether.

My eyes adjust to the light. The call is from Owen.

I *should* drop the phone and roll back over. Not showing up to an arranged meeting is definitely punishable by ignoring. I was worried for a while, even thought about calling his mum, but he was probably just messing with me. Petty revenge for the night before or whatever. Even though I hardly know him, it felt like rejection.

Except he's calling now . . .

I swipe to answer.

'You know what time it is?'

I hear him inhale, like he's just checked and he really *didn't* know. 'Sorry. I'm about to watch the first episode of *Battlestar Galactica*.'

'Are you serious?'

'I can't sleep right now.'

I shift so I'm sitting on the edge of the bed, cold nipping at my bare legs. 'You know the first episode is, like, three hours long, right?'

'Yeah, I know.' He sounds exhausted, fragile enough that I forget any anger towards him. 'I need something to keep my mind occupied.'

I know how that feels. 'Is everything okay?'

'Will you watch it with me?'

'It's a bit late for me to go out.'

'You could go out the window.' He huffs a laugh. 'Or we can switch to Skype.'

'Uh, okay.' I flick on my bedside lamp, flinching at the light. 'Give me a minute.'

He hangs up, and I cross to my desk to open up my laptop. I pick it up to bring into bed, but that might be weird. Intimate. But this whole thing is weird. If Lorenzo found out I was Skyping a guy in the middle of the night he would never let it drop. I should just go back to bed, stand him up like he did to me.

Except Lorenzo will never find out. And there was

something in Owen's voice. A *need*. He needs me right now. Watching *Battlestar* is just an excuse.

I leave the laptop on the desk and wrap myself in my dressing gown. The screen's pale light floods the room, and I switch off the lamp just in case Mum or Dad get up for the toilet and spot it.

There's an add request waiting from Owen. He answers my call immediately, face filling the window, screen reflecting brightly off his glasses.

'Nice bed hair,' he says.

'Some of us were pretending to sleep.'

'You don't sleep well either?'

'Not often.' I could tell him why – that my anti-depressants, which are generally brilliant, have made regular sleep a bit of an abstract concept – except that would lead to another conversation I'm not sure I'm ready to have.

'So, three hours long,' Owen says, pushing a strand of long hair out of his face. 'What the hell were they thinking?'

I mean-mug the camera. 'If we're going to do this, I have to make one thing absolutely clear: *Battlestar Galactica* is not just a distraction, it's a life-changing experience. It won't cure insomnia – it *causes* insomnia because it's so awesome.'

'Wow, do you have shares in a Cylon factory or something?'

He already knows the name of the cybernetic organisms in the series. That is a *very* promising sign. I minimise his window and cue up the pilot episode. 'I just want you to be ready for what's about to happen to you.'

'After the last few months, I think I can handle anything.'

I decide to barrel through that. 'We need to start the episode at the exact same time. Hit play on three.'

Owen raises his finger dramatically. 'Three . . . two . . .'

'You can't start on three when I said hit play on three.'

'I thought you'd get the idea.'

'All right, fine. Three . . .' I start, at the exact same moment as Owen begins again at 'one'. 'For God's sake, just hit play . . . now!'

We both slam the spacebar, and the episode begins to play.

'So what's *Battlestar Galactica* about?' he says.

'Oh, come on, we're literally—'

'Relax, I'm joking!'

I glance at his face in the chat window. His eyes are playful, like he's testing how far he can push me. It makes him seem . . . different. Less guarded.

I've seen the opening of the first episode countless times, but I never get sick of it. It's a political meeting between human and machine, the first in years. It's low key and a little weird, the scene ending in a brilliant 'Oh shit!' moment guaranteed to get anybody hooked.

It's difficult to concentrate. My gaze keeps drifting to Owen's face instead, waiting for his reaction. For some reason it's unimaginably important to me that he likes it.

'Oh shit!' exclaims Owen as an explosion engulfs the space station, and I can't help but break into the widest smile.

We watch for nearly an hour without talking much. When Owen notices my eyelids drooping, he calls for a toilet break. My parents' light is off and Mum is snoring as thunderously as ever. I don't flush, just in case. Yellow can mellow.

Owen is already back at his screen, eager to keep watching.

'Ready?' he says.

A sense of loss hollows out my stomach for a moment. This is something I have missed. Hanging out all night with Lorenzo and the guys, playing video games or watching movies, not wanting the night to end because it felt like those hours belonged only to us. It's hard to think that those times probably never meant as much to the others.

I don't want to ruin the moment, but I also remember what my mum said about trying to help him.

'What happened to you earlier?' I say, settling back into my seat.

He jolts, like I've caught him out. Any trace of the humour I saw before is gone and he's back on guard. 'What do you mean?'

'You were supposed to come over.'

'Oh, yeah,' he says. He scratches awkwardly at his back. 'I wasn't feeling up to it.'

It doesn't take a psychiatrist or a telepath or whatever to work out he's not telling me the whole truth. I don't know whether to push him or not. If I'm going to help, I don't want to get this wrong.

'Was it because of what you saw on the high street earlier?' I say.

He pauses briefly, as if he's forgotten. 'I was just buying some noodles and walking home.'

From where? I swallow the urge to ask. 'I was trying to stop them, you know. The guys. When they came over and started acting like that, I was embarrassed. I'm not supposed to be embarrassed of them. I'm supposed to be *like* them.'

I didn't mean to voice what my brain has been asking on repeat instead of sleeping, but cradled in the light of my laptop screen it somehow seems okay. Safe. In the corner of my screen, Owen frowns.

'You mean you're supposed to be harassing girls in the street?'

'Not *that*. We grew up together, and we've always been friends. So why does it feel like they're outgrowing me?'

'Maybe they're not outgrowing you,' he says, resting his chin on his fist. 'Maybe you're just growing in different directions.'

Even if he's right, it still means losing my friends. The only friends I've ever had. Still, somehow, it makes me feel better.

'What direction are you growing in?' I ask.

'These days I have no idea.'

His face in the chat window is washed out by the light of his screen, so I can't read his expression. It would be so much easier just to go back to watching the show.

'I can't pretend to know what it's like,' I say. 'But you can talk to me, if you want.'

He looks directly into the camera, like he's considering shutting the lid, shutting me out. He shifts position to reach the touchpad and the video feed drops, but I can hear him typing. I open the chat window.

Owen is typing . . .

A few minutes pass before the message comes:

I had a couple of friends before we moved. After my dad died, I think they tried to do their best. But it was like they had preset ideas of how it should go. I would be all torn up, depressed, moody, and it would be their job to coax me back to life by buying me chips or playing football or whatever.

He doesn't start typing again, so maybe he's expecting a response.

'There's no way you play football,' I say.

Straight away he's typing.

Ha, no, but you know what I mean, he replies. *So when I just tried to carry on like everything was normal, they didn't get it. They did their bit to defend me against a few people at school who took the piss, but I could tell they expected more. And I didn't know how to give them what they wanted.*

After he sends the message he immediately begins typing again, so I wait to reply. I try to imagine what it would have been like if Lorenzo's mum died now. We knew each other back then, but were too young to know we knew each other. It's hard to imagine how Lorenzo would deal with it. How I could help him to deal with it.

Then there was this time, like the other night, when I just broke down in front of my best mate. Crying, snot, the whole works. Exactly what he should have wanted, right? He freaked out and tried to call an ambulance. I had to pull myself together and stop him. After that they all avoided me.

'Just like that?'

Yep.

It's no wonder he wanted to escape when it happened again in front of me. I could have told everybody at school and made the same thing happen here.

Owen is typing again.

I feel like all I can do is get it wrong. Like I've been letting people down ever since.

'I'm no expert,' I say. 'But I think in the circumstances you can feel however you fucking want to.'

I hear him laugh, and then his fingers on the keyboard. *Can you tell my mum that?*

'I'm a bit scared of your mum now, to be honest.'

Another laugh. *I think I am too. It hasn't been the same between us since. Or maybe it's been too much the same despite this MASSIVE thing being different. She's definitely crying for the right reasons. I'm not sad just because of Dad. It's something to do with me. I don't feel like the same person after he's gone.*

We sit together in silence for a long moment. Long enough for me to make a decision. He has dropped his guard, and it makes me want to do the same.

'Can I tell you something?' I say. 'It seems only fair now you've told me all this.'

Sure.

'Around a year ago I was diagnosed with depression.'

Silence. Nothing changes. Owen simply waits for me to say more.

'It started a while before that. It was really weird, making me tired and sad for no real reason. For a while I didn't tell anybody about it. I was too scared,' I say. 'Then I decided I had to tell my mum and she took me to the doctor, and they prescribed medication.'

Owen is silent, but I know he's listening. Nerves flicker in my belly, but it's a relief to be telling somebody who isn't my family.

'It's actually helped me a lot. But I'm still too scared to tell my friends about it in case they don't believe me, or they treat me differently all of a sudden. It's like, I need them to *prove* that won't happen first.'

How can they do that? he types.

'I don't kn—'

I stop short, because I've just had the most brilliant, ridiculous, possibly catastrophic idea in the history of the world.

On the other side of the screen I hear him fumble at the touchpad, and Owen's face appears in the video window again. 'Hi,' he says. 'You look like you've just discovered a lost season of *Battlestar Galactica*.'

'Did your last school ever have a talent show?'

He narrows his eyes. 'No?'

'Never mind,' I say, trying to wipe the smile from my face and glancing at the time. It's nearly 3.30am and we still have half the episode left. 'We should keep going.'

Owen nods. 'Ready when you are.'

So I shift in my seat and position a finger over the space bar. 'On three . . . two . . .'

Chapter Eight

Duncan

There's probably a real skill to lying about your success with girls, and I'm certain Lorenzo doesn't have it.

'And I swear, she's waiting for me outside the toilet,' he says, grinning from ear to ear. 'And she's like, batting her eyelashes, all *so you gonna buy me a drink*?'

I swear that this never actually happened. I mean, it's not impossible. When I checked his Snapchat this morning it was all videos of him out at some bar with his new gym mates. A bunch of guys in tight T-shirts doing shots that definitely won't fit in with any kind of clean diet.

Saeed, of course, is hanging on every word. 'Did you get IDed?'

'Obviously not.' Lorenzo rolls his eyes. 'They go there all the time, so it's no problem.'

Lorenzo is the size of a porta-toilet, so if he was with a group of older people there's no way he would stand out. If I was being really low, I'd point out that he can hardly drink half a pint before he starts singing One Direction songs.

There's one way I can really get at him about his new friends. 'And they still haven't worked out you're still in school?'

Lorenzo freezes with his mouth open. I shouldn't have said that, but it's so satisfying to see him worry.

'Oh man, this girl's cradle-snatching and she doesn't even know it!' says Saeed.

They both laugh, but Lorenzo glares daggers at me. I've caught him out. The only way for him to keep his new friends is to pretend to be somebody he's not. It's precarious, desperate, and he knows it.

'We'll see what happens with her,' he says, throwing a knowing glance at Matt, as if they're sexual peers. But Matt's been looking at his phone during the whole conversation.

I yawn extravagantly before I can stifle it. By the time we finished the first episode of *Battlestar Galactica* last night there was barely time to pretend to sleep. I'm probably supposed to be spending my nights sneaking into bars and chasing girls. Usually my suspicions over the details of Lorenzo's stories don't quite keep me from feeling jealous. It's obvious he'd rather hang out with his new mates than us.

This time, I don't care at all.

'Am I boring you, Spunk?'

'No, sorry. I didn't sleep well last night.'

My phone vibrates in my blazer pocket and I reach for it instinctively. Lorenzo narrows his eyes in suspicion, like he's deciding if I'm a threat, before resuming his dirty talk with Saeed.

Two messages. The first is from Owen, a string of emojis: woman, robot, stars, explosion . . . it's the opening of *Battlestar Galactica*. A surprisingly accurate tableau. I respond with a gif of Commander Adama chanting 'So say we all!' to an adoring crowd. (Finally, my painstakingly curated collection of *Battlestar* gifs is paying off.)

When I glance up, Lorenzo catches me smiling. His eyes narrow again, just a little – he knows that, if we're all here, there should be nobody else left to message me.

Last night was . . . strange. By the time I got into the shower this morning I felt vaguely embarrassed about the whole thing, about being so open with somebody I hardly know. The late-night ambience tore down my guard. What's even stranger is that I don't regret it. It was a relief to tell somebody about it all – and listen to their feelings in return – without worrying it would change something between us, or make me lose them. I always worried that I wouldn't be able to make new friends if I lost those I had. Maybe that doesn't have to be true.

It isn't right that I can talk about those things with almost a total stranger, but not feel comfortable telling my best friends.

The second message on my phone is a reply from Michaela. I fumble it open: *If you have to make excuses for how your friends behave, you're no better than they are. Maybe it's time you grew out of them.*

I re-read it several times, trying to understand why she's being so harsh. I begin typing an indignant response – *You don't know anything about . . .* – before I delete it. There's no point. She's wrong. It's my friends who are growing out of *me*.

Or are we just growing in different directions, like Owen said?

Last night, I had an idea to test if our friendship is really doomed. At 3.30am it seemed completely ridiculous. Now . . . well, it still seems completely ridiculous, but I'm totally going to do it anyway.

'Guys,' I say, interrupting their conversation. 'I need to ask you a favour.'

They all look at me warily, like I'm about to ask for close-up pictures of their genitalia. I take a breath, knowing it's my last chance to back down and save myself the humiliation.

'My sister's dance group dropped out of the talent show. It's in a week and a half.'

Their expressions only grow warier.

'She needs to find people willing to step in.'

It takes a moment for any of them to realise what I'm suggesting.

'You mean us?' says Lorenzo.

I smile, and spread my hands, a little more pleadingly than intended. 'It might be fun?'

Matt snorts derisively, while Saeed waves his hands in front of him. 'No way, man. No way you're getting me dancing in front of the whole school.'

They all turn to each other, smiling and laughing, like I've gone mad. All it does is make me more determined.

'We used to do stupid stuff like this all the time! None of you ever cared before,' I say. 'My mum would love you for it.' This is a direct appeal to Lorenzo, who still has a soft spot for my mum after all these years. 'It's important to my sister. And that means it's important to me. So why can't you be mates and help me out?'

There is exactly three seconds where I'm convinced my impassioned speech has won them over.

Narrator: It hadn't.

'Not going to happen.'

'No way I'm dancing in front of the school.'

Only Lorenzo stays quiet, though he stills wears an expression like I've asked him to star in a homemade, though tastefully shot, pornographic movie.

'At least come and talk to my sister about it,' I say. I haven't actually *asked* Emily yet if she would accept us as her replacement dance crew, but they don't need to know that.

The bell sounds, and everybody on the playground begins traipsing towards morning registration.

Lorenzo sighs. 'Fine.'

The others look at him like he's just thrown up a basset hound, but there isn't any time left to argue.

We're heading for the main entrance when Owen shuffles through the school gate. His hair is loose around his face, and there are heavy bags under his eyes. As he passes, he glances up at me and smiles. When I nod in return, it's like we're sharing a secret.

I turn back to my group, just in time to find Lorenzo watching me again.

Owen

Nobody knows who I am yet, so I sit alone in every lesson. Or they've all heard so many rumours they *think* they know who I am, and it's not somebody they want to sit near if they can help it. It makes sense. It's only another few months before half the people here move on. No point making new friends.

They've mostly stuck me in the bottom set for every subject, which means I don't share any lessons with Duncan. I didn't think about it at the time, but telling him so much last night was a kind of test. He was supposed to make an excuse and run for it. Or try desperately to fix me. Instead he stayed. Listened. Opened up to me in return. More than anybody else has managed.

Morning break is short enough to ride out by walking slowly around the few corridors left open to students. Afterwards, on the way to maths, I risk a peek at the sky. The Angels remain, turning their tireless circles. I flex my shoulders, feel the feathers chafing under my shirt. I hurry inside.

'Who are you?' asks a teacher I haven't seen before. The lower sets seem to be taught on rotation by teachers that know less about the subject at hand than I do.

'I'm Francis,' I say, plucking the name out of thin air. 'I've just started.'

The lie doesn't matter. As far as anybody here is concerned, I could be anybody.

And, really, I *can* be anybody. I just haven't worked out who yet.

By the time lunch rolls around, I'm itching to get away. Despite the head teacher noticing my escapes, there's nobody standing guard at the staff car park. I wait for a teacher I don't recognise to get into their car and light a cigarette. Then I walk calmly behind them and out of the gate.

The Angels follow. They always follow.

Duncan

Saeed is copying my maths work again. I should stop him, but half of my answers are probably wrong anyway.

'Is that a 4 or a 7?' he whispers.

I squint at the page. 'It's a Y.'

'Oh.' He scrubs out his answer. 'What do you make of Lorenzo's new friends?'

'I haven't met them.'

'You know what I mean.' Saeed glances up at Mrs Keita, but she's focused on the work on her desk. 'It's weird he's hanging out with people way older than him. I mean, if they knew he was a kid, they wouldn't be interested. Look.'

Under the table, he shows me the Instagram profiles of some of the guys Lorenzo's hanging out with. They're all huge, flexing their arms in gym mirrors, posing in huddles with T-shirts as tight as cling film and cans of energy drink clutched in their gigantic hands.

'How did you even find them?' I ask.

Saeed shrugs. 'It's not that hard.'

I pick up my eyes so it doesn't look like I'm staring at his crotch. Saeed has always done everything he could to be like Lorenzo. When we were younger, he'd make his mum buy him the same T-shirts and trainers, then pretend it was a coincidence. Over time, Lorenzo must have started doing more and more that Saeed couldn't imitate. If Saeed tried to do a single press-up I think his arms would snap. Though he must have pretty strong wrists by now . . .

Genuine worry creases Saeed's face as he scrolls through the Instagram profiles. It's hard to tell if it's for Lorenzo or himself. Maybe it isn't just me wondering where I fit into our friendship group these days.

As soon as the lunch bell rings, I pretend to rush for the toilets, leaving Saeed behind. It gets me ahead of the usual crush and out on to the playground before it's too hectic. I look towards the gates, and sure enough I see Owen heading for the staff car park.

Bunking off school is not in my nature. From a young age my parents drilled it into me that it's one of the greatest sins I could ever commit, right up there with punching a teacher or not wearing underpants in public. I don't even believe in the concept of sin any more, but dragging my feet across the playground to the exit is like wading through treacle.

I *need* to know where Owen escapes to every lunch break. It's the only way I can really understand what he's going through.

As soon as he's made it out on to the road, I crouch low and sort of waddle across the car park, no doubt looking twice as conspicuous as if I walked normally, but also feeling a bit like a ninja. Nobody challenges me before I reach the gate, and I set off towards town in pursuit of Owen.

I zip up my jacket so nobody can see my school blazer. Just call me the master of disguise. At first I'm ducking behind lampposts and cars, scuttling between cover and keeping a careful distance. After a few minutes it's clear that there's no point – Owen only looks up, never back. It's like every few seconds he needs to confirm that the sky is still there. I keep back anyway, but otherwise walk normally. Everybody else out at this time – mostly older people or parents pushing prams – is too busy to pay any attention to me.

Just before he reaches the top of the high street, Owen hurries across traffic lights flashing orange. I'm left stranded on the other side, hammering the button as the traffic gets moving again. Owen heads straight towards the train station and through its doors, before I lose sight of him in a crowd of people.

As soon as the green man pops up I give pursuit. I reach the station, but there's no sign of him in the ticket office.

The guard must be on lunch because the barriers are open, so I rush down to the single platform without getting a ticket. A train is waiting on one side, doors open. They beep in warning, and I leap onboard at the nearest set just as they thud closed behind me.

While I catch my breath, the train begins to move. It was on the side of the platform that means it's heading south, towards the coast. Maybe Owen just prefers hitting the beach over staying in school.

Unsteadily, I make my way through the train, clinging to the backs of seats to keep my balance. It's quiet at this time of day, a few men and women in suits working on laptops at the tables, others tucking into packet sandwiches or watching TV on their iPads. I've moved through a few carriages before I see a familiar figure hunched alone against the window.

All at once this feels like a mistake. I've only just met him, and now I've followed him like a crazy stalker. The best thing I could do is hide in another carriage and get off at the next stop.

Instead, I move forward and drop into the seat beside him.

Owen

'So this is where you've been going every day?'

I jump, banging my head against the glass. I turn around to find Duncan sitting sheepishly beside me.

'What are you doing here?'

'I *might* have followed you.'

I return my gaze to the window. We're already outside of town, peripheral housing estates giving way to fields stitched together by pylons. 'You already know you shouldn't have done that. So I guess I'll ask why.'

'I was worried about you.'

'It gets quite boring, having everybody worry about you.' I should be angry with him, but I can't quite find the energy. 'You could have just asked me where I was going.'

'Hang on,' he says, clearly thinking carefully. 'I did, didn't I?'

I can't help but smile at that. This time yesterday I wouldn't even have considered telling him the truth. Last night, he proved he might be able to understand. It would be a relief to have somebody know about it who isn't from my old life. Somebody who hasn't been convinced by proximity that they know it all already.

'I think I know the answer,' Duncan says, unzipping his jacket. 'You're an amateur train spotter.'

'You can't spot trains from inside the train.'

'I have literally no idea what train spotting actually is.'

'I'm going to tell you the truth,' I say, making the decision as I speak. 'I sprung it on you last time, so this time you get a warning.'

He sits up a little straighter. Clearly makes a conscious effort to look serious. There's something genuine about it that encourages me to continue.

'My dad died on this train.'

Duncan stays quiet. There's nothing awkward about it. He's taking his time to think about it instead of instantly reaching into a shallow pool of sympathy and stock responses.

'Not this train exactly,' I continue. 'This is the time-tabled train. He was travelling home from a conference.'

'Is this where he was sitting?'

'I don't know.' I usually pick a two-seater to make sure I stay alone. I think Dad would probably have done the same. He wasn't the type to work at a laptop while he travelled. 'I just know he was by himself.'

Again, Duncan takes his time before replying. It's not the usual walking on eggshells. The hurried calculations to plot the fastest escape from the conversation. He wants to say the right thing. Ask a question that will have a meaningful answer.

'What do you feel by coming here every day?'

Before I can answer, the doors at the far end of the carriage hiss open and the ticket inspector steps inside.

'Shit,' says Duncan. 'I don't have a ticket.'

'Nor do I.'

He looks at me incredulously. 'What do you normally do?'

I tell him to follow me and we hurry to the other end of the carriage. There's a toilet here. I press the button and the semi-circular door slides grandly open. We bundle inside and close it behind us.

'What if he knocks on the door?'

'I don't know. Make diarrhoea noises.'

The toilet smells like the previous occupant had a severe stomach complaint for real. We cover our noses as the train slows to pull into the next station. On the other side of the door, the guard makes the arrival announcement. When the train departs again, we hear the rattle of the buffet trolley arrive, its server striking up a conversation.

'Guess we're staying here,' I say.

There's enough room for us both. Duncan puts the seat down and perches on the toilet. I lean against the wall beside the buttons.

'I think you staged this so you wouldn't have to answer my question,' says Duncan.

'Yes, this is significantly less awkward.' I take a moment to think. He waits patiently, undaunted by the silence. 'After we were notified of what happened, I went on Twitter to see if anybody was talking about it. It happened in public, so somebody must have seen something, right? Instead I just found people complaining about the train delays it caused.'

Duncan grunts in disgust. 'People are the worst.'

'I suppose I hope riding the same train might bring me closer to the truth,' I say. 'Not about why he died – I know there's no rhyme or reason to that except he ate too much processed meat and didn't exercise.'

Duncan smiles, and then wipes it guiltily off his face. I smile too to show him it's okay.

'I think I'll find the truth in what came before,' I say, struggling to find the right words. 'Before he died.'

We both listen to the murmur of voices outside the toilet door for a few minutes. The train jolts and sways underneath us. Begins to slow as we approach the next stop. Maywood. My home town.

'I'm sorry,' says Duncan. 'I don't understand what you mean.'

I smile again, though it's harder to pull off this time. 'Probably because it doesn't really make any sense. I'm still trying to figure it out.'

The train stops. We wait until we hear the outer doors open, and then I hammer the button to unlock the toilet. Together we barrel out past the trolley and the guard on to the platform.

'Hey!' he shouts.

'We've just committed a terrible crime,' says Duncan as we hurry towards the exit.

'We're home-free now. Maywood is too small and quaint to have ticket barriers.'

As usual, there's nobody to check for tickets either. We pass through the office and on to the street, where a couple of taxis wait on the kerb.

'You didn't move very far from home,' says Duncan.

'I don't think it mattered much. Mum just wanted to be somewhere else.'

Duncan takes an exaggeratedly deep breath, like he's bracing himself for a big adventure. 'Okay, then. Show me all the places you used to live.'

Chapter Nine

Duncan

The town of Maywood has always been just fifteen minutes from home, but I've never had any reason to do more than pass through on a family trip to the coast. As I follow Owen out of the station, it's strange to think he was here all along, and yet never existed for me until just a few days ago.

Directly opposite the station, almost hidden behind the queue of optimistic taxi drivers, is what looks like an old village green. At this time of year it's mostly a bog, a lone dog splashing across on a mission to pee against the gnarled, ancient-looking tree at its centre. They probably hold summer fêtes here with the sacrificial burning of a virgin as the headline act.

Narrator: Making him an eligible candidate.

'So, where are you taking me?' I ask.

Owen nudges his glasses up his nose. 'Usually I just sort of walk around, hoping not to run into anybody I recognise.'

'Let's have a signal – if there's anybody you want to avoid, whistle three times and I'll cause a distraction.'

'So this is what it feels like to have found the brains of the operation.'

He glances at me uncertainly after making the joke and looks relieved when I grin back at him.

It's a short walk into town. Maywood is smaller than Westleigh, and looks like the kind of place you usually see printed on a tea towel. The houses are all tall and dark-bricked. Dormant flower baskets hang from cast-iron lampposts. You probably need a knighthood and/or a double-barrelled surname to even consider living here.

'I didn't live in one of these,' says Owen, a little self-consciously, as if he's read my mind.

'This is the kind of quintessential English town that Nicolas Cage would love.'

'He did own a castle just outside.'

'Oh, for God's sake.'

The high street is similarly idyllic, shops appearing to lean forward into a narrow channel, the leaded windows of the flats above practically meeting in the middle. They've probably been here for centuries, passed down through inbred generations of sickeningly wealthy people, modernising with only the utmost reluctance. The few people about are dressed like recreationists from a time that never existed, all flat caps and green farmer's jackets, leading hearty-looking dogs splashed with mud. It's like stepping into one of the glossy period dramas my parents love to watch on a Sunday evening.

Also, there's a Tesco Express.

'There's the post office,' says Owen as we pass it on

the corner of an alley, before he points across the way. 'That chocolate shop is nice.'

The street grows a little wider, leaving space at its centre for a life-size stone sculpture of a horse, head proudly held high. We stop at its base.

'It's been here over a hundred years. I think it was a famous horse in the war?' Owen reaches out to stroke its hoof. 'There's a town legend that if you sit on its back, you'll never leave Maywood.'

'Have you ever sat on it?'

He glances sideways at me. 'Evidently not.'

We trail to the end of the street. Owen points out the town hall, a pub with a funny name (The Pilgrim's Hole), a shop that sells medieval contraception or whatever. I stop listening because my belly is rumbling.

'I don't suppose there are any chicken shops here?'

'There was going to be a KFC, but the tourist board protested it.'

'Right. Still, there must be somewhere to eat.' I point to the nearest café, an independent place that looks suspiciously vegan.

'Not there,' Owen says quickly, and leads the way back up the high street, on to a side road, and into a café with shaded windows.

We order at the counter – a ham and cheese toastie for me, a black coffee and a muffin for Owen – and find a table near the front window.

'This place a favourite of yours?'

'Only since I started coming back.'

Our food arrives. One eager bite of the toastie sends molten cheese oozing over my fingers. Owen picks at his muffin with significantly less enthusiasm. Nibbling at a crumb, his gaze drifts automatically out of the window and up at the sky. Whatever he sees there makes him clench his jaw, look sharply away, and reach for his coffee. Only a sliver of cloudy blue is visible between shops. It's not the first time I've caught him monitoring the sky. Before, I didn't know him well enough to ask. Now I've stalked him to his hometown I guess all bets are off.

'Are you worried about government surveillance or something?'

He tenses, spilling a little of his coffee. His hands shake as he lowers the cup to its saucer. 'I was just checking the weather.'

It's the least convincing excuse I've ever heard, but I know better than to push it.

We sit in silence while I polish off my toastie and Owen neglects his muffin. His eyes keep straying back to the window. There's something more to these visits that he isn't showing me. On one hand it isn't my place to pry, but on the other he could have told me to leave him alone before we ever got off the train. I want to help him, if I can.

'Have you seen that traffic barrier by Asda car park?' I say, using a paper napkin to mop cheese from my fingers.

'In Westleigh?'

'Yeah. I got my head stuck in it when I was a kid.'

Now I've got Owen's attention. 'How did you manage that?'

My cheeks grow hot. Maybe I shouldn't have volunteered this story. 'Lorenzo told me it wouldn't fit.'

I wouldn't usually fall victim to such blatant reverse psychology, but I knew Lorenzo had regular nightmares about getting his head trapped in things (his ears stick out a bit and he's surprisingly self-conscious about it). I wanted to do something he would never dare. Also, he bet me a quid.

'I realised pretty much straight away I was stuck, but I didn't want any of the guys to know, so I keep laughing along, you know? It didn't take them long to figure it out. Then they start filming it and taking photos,' I say. The footage still resurfaces every now and again when they fancy a laugh. 'They started trying to pull me out, but I was proper stuck. After a while, Matt went into Asda to ask for some butter.'

Owen's smiling now. 'This all happened on the high street?'

'Oh yeah. I attracted quite a crowd.'

I remember Lorenzo seeing how embarrassed I was – seeing me literally live out one of his nightmares – and trying to shield me from view. It didn't work, obviously, but I've always been grateful he tried. I wonder what he would do if it happened now. He'd probably run away before I could embarrass him in public.

'They put the butter all over my neck and ears and started pulling. It looked like it wasn't going to work, and then *pop!* My head comes loose so fast that it slams Matt right in the face. At least the amount of blood deflected attention from me.'

'It was that bad?'

I take out my phone and scroll through my pictures until I find a close up of Matt and Becky smiling together.

The straight, white scar above his left eye makes it an incident we can never forget. To his credit, he's never held it against me.

'Is that his girlfriend? She's pretty.'

He sounds genuinely interested in my friends. I get a little warm glow of pride, like I'm showing off photos of my kids.

'Yeah, she is. We were a bit surprised when we found out, to be honest. Matt was always the quiet one. Plus, you know, she's way too cool for him.'

In the photo her hair is dyed jet black and shaved to stubble at one side. She wears dark eye shadow, a silver stud glinting from her eyebrow.

'I bet she has good taste in music,' says Owen.

I shove my phone back into my pocket. 'Everywhere in Westleigh is like that for me. I can show you the basketball court where I knocked out a tooth, or the fence Lorenzo threw my brand-new Kung Zhu Hamster toy over because he was jealous. It's probably still over there somewhere. It's memories like that which make a place part of you.'

'I have those too,' says Owen. 'They're what I think about every time I come back.'

'So instead of post offices and chocolate shops, give me that tour. If you don't mind sharing?'

He takes a moment to think about it, and then stands up from the table.

Owen

I lead him back on to the high street. There's no sign of anybody who might recognise me. I point back to the café I refused to visit.

'We had to stop going there because Dad made a waitress cry,' I say. I remember the shame that burned hot in my cheeks, Mum quickly gathering up our stuff. The cold sense of dread every time I had to walk past afterwards. 'They'd put the wrong kind of sauce on his sandwich, so he threw it at them.'

We head further up the high street. It's not exactly like seeing it all through new eyes. These aren't memories I had forgotten. Instead they had begun to feel as if they belonged to somebody else. Sharing them with somebody new gives me a chance to remember who that person – who I – was when I experienced them.

'That charity shop is really good. I used to get old toys and junk so I could build them into new stuff. Dad didn't like the clutter and threw it all away. So I stopped.'

We pass the statue again. 'There's a photo of my dad sitting on the horse. It's from before they had me. You're not actually allowed to climb it. He looks really proud of himself.'

Instead of turning towards the station, we go up the short hill that leads to our old church. From this side, only the stone spire is visible above the trees. Before we reach it, there's a small playground. Swings and a climbing frame. A toddler plods across the woodchip floor, shadowed closely by her mother.

'We always came here after church. I loved the monkey bars,' I say, reaching up to feel the cold metal between my fingers. 'I could never make it across a single bar without letting go. Dad used to joke about my weak warms, told me to lay off the ice cream.'

'If it makes you feel any better –' Duncan reaches up

to hang from the bars. When he reaches for the next rung he immediately loses grip and drops awkwardly on to the woodchip – 'I can't do it either.'

'We're both equally pathetic.'

We share an ironic high-five. Although I will probably never forget it, the memory loses a little of its power. I'm glad I decided to share it.

A gate at the far side of the playground leads directly into the church grounds. An overgrown path winds through the cramped graveyard. Although the church is old, different parts have been repaired and rebuilt over centuries. It looks cobbled together from mismatched brands of children's building blocks. We stand outside the closed main door.

'My earliest memory is here,' I say. It's surprisingly clear, and most of what I remember was probably embellished later. 'It was a wedding, and Dad got me a suit that matched his exactly. I remember being so proud whenever anybody noticed. I must have been about five.'

'That sounds absurdly cute.'

'Church was a bit of a show for him, I think. I'm not sure he actually believed in any of it. Unlike my mum.'

'My parents are really happy your mum is joining their church,' says Duncan. 'Do you, like, believe in it?'

I peer up at the church spire, try not to see the great, imposing Angels circling around its pinnacle. 'I believe in . . . something. Right now I think I have to.'

Behind me, the gravestones are arranged in haphazard rows. A few are well tended. Fresh flowers arranged neatly at their bases. Toys and trinkets faded by the weather. Who do people bring them for? Who are they really trying to remember?

I don't know what makes me think of it. I set off down the first row of stones, scanning the names I will promptly forget. It was here. I'm sure I remember the floral letters from the hearse spelling out her name.

The gravestone is in the third row I check. Smooth black stone engraved with gold letters. *Eleanor Renwick, 2004 – 2011.* A wilted bouquet of flowers is propped against a faded patchwork doll. Somebody has come here and tried to remember.

'Did you know her?' asks Duncan.

I can feel the Angels circling overhead, but I force myself to keep my eyes on the grave. 'Not really,' I say. 'I wish I could visit myself in the future. Like, drop into my adult body, just for second. Just to check that everything's okay.'

'But if you saw, it might stop you ever becoming that person.'

'Maybe that would be a good thing. Who knows what mistakes my future self has made?'

Duncan plucks at my ponytail. 'I bet he has better hair, at least.'

'Hey! You think you're going to grow up to become a style icon?'

'You never know, right?' He stares at the grave for a long moment. At the name of a dead person he never knew. 'There are probably better versions of me out there. In alternative universes or whatever. Looking fashionable. Leading better lives.'

'You believe in alternative universes?'

'Probably not. It's a nice thought though. Like an infinite number of chances to get it right.'

'It kind of seems like a lot of pressure,' I say. 'It's hard enough working out who I am here and now. Who I'll become next. That's all I have, whether there are a billion other versions of me out there or not. If you think there are, you're always going to feel inferior. And you're not. You can't live like that.'

He thinks about that for a second. 'If you want to know who you'll become, why are you looking for it here?'

'I can't work out where I'm going until I know how I feel about where I was.'

We stand in silence for a moment. After a while, Duncan asks, 'Is your dad buried here?'

The question is so direct that I turn to him in shock. He almost winces, but I smile to show him it's okay. I'm just not used to anybody asking so plainly.

'He isn't buried anywhere yet. I'm waiting. Though I don't know what for.'

At the edge of the graveyard, tucked into a corner of the low wall, is a dilapidated shed that was probably once used for groundskeeping equipment. The inside is nothing but leaves and litter now. The door hangs off its hinges where it used to be so solid.

'There was a bar you could use to seal the door.' I point to the piece of sheared metal, broken off in the intervening years. 'During the service once, me and this other boy who was new snuck outside to play. Dad caught me, threw me inside here, and locked the door.'

Duncan leans down to peer inside. The shed has no

110

windows. The memory is mostly of darkness. It was like I had been thrown out of the world and would never make it back. I think of the satellite in my dream, suspended impossibly far above the Earth. The glass cracking under my weight.

'I cried and clawed at the door, but he didn't let me out until the service was finished. I've been scared of dark spaces like that ever since.'

'That's horrible,' says Duncan.

'He wasn't horrible all the time,' I say, surprised at how defensive I sound. 'Sometimes I don't think he meant to be. Other times, he was only mean when it suited him. Not everybody saw it. That's what's so confusing now everything is in hindsight. Nobody will ever learn something from being with him, only *about* him. Second-hand. Which means people can recreate him however they want.'

Before Duncan can respond, another voice comes from behind us. 'Owen?'

We both spin around. For a moment the Forest appears in front of me, trees looming high before they shrink down into gravestones.

A woman has approached us, clutching a bunch of flowers and some clippers. It's Miss McDaniel, a teacher from my old school.

Duncan

It's too late for me to cause a distraction. We shuffle closer together, like we'll look less suspicious pressed shoulder to shoulder.

'It's good to see you,' says the woman. Her voice is

111

so thick with condescending sympathy that I want to vomit, and it's not even aimed at me.

'You too, Miss McDaniel.'

A teacher, then – somebody who must have worked with Owen's dad. No wonder his voice is shaking.

'You've been a great loss to my class, you know.'

Owen's sideways glance suggests this is highly unlikely to be true. It also turns her attention in my direction.

'Hello . . .?'

'Uh, Duncan,' I say. 'I go to Owen's new school.'

'We had a free period. I thought I'd show him where I grew up,' Owen says quickly.

The doubt on her face is clear. It fades quickly though, in favour of regarding Owen like an injured puppy.

'I really was sorry about what happened to your father,' she says.

Owen nods, like it's all he can do.

'He was such a good teacher. We all miss him so much.'

'I miss him too, miss.'

'Of *course* you do.'

The silence that follows could be entered into the all-time hall of fame for awkward silences.

'I just realised something,' says Owen, meeting her eyes properly for the first time. 'I don't have to justify myself to you any more, Tracey.'

The teacher gasps at what I assume is her first name. It's like finding the only weakness of a superhero.

'And I can just leave without trying to make polite chit-chat, because you're not my teacher any more,' he continues. 'I'll probably never see you again.'

He turns and begins to walk away between the grave-stones, back towards the playground.

'It was, uh, nice to meet you, I guess?' I offer, before running to catch up.

Owen kicks hard at the wood chips, leaving deep furrows in the ground, covering his shoes with dirt.

'Well, that was kind of amazing,' I say. 'Maybe a little harsh.'

He sits on one of the swings, and I take the other beside him. 'Dad wasn't a good teacher,' he says. 'I mean, he was fine. But he got in trouble for being late and swearing at kids.'

'So she was just saying all that?'

He drags his toes along the ground. 'It's like my dad dying has left this vacuum, right, and they've created this whole new persona to fill it – the person they *want* to remember, or feel like they *should* remember. And it's not the same Dad who's in all my memories. If nobody remembers the truth, it's like he never existed at all.' Owen kicks out at the woodchip. 'Am I just supposed to accept the revised version of him? Because if I do – if my memories become invalid somehow – it's like *I'm* being eroded too. My life here, everything that made me who I am, will be gone. So what's left?'

We swing in shallow arcs, chains creaking above our heads.

'You are,' I say. It's probably a stupid answer, but it sounds good.

He sniffs hard, taking a hand from the swing to wipe his nose. Again, I see him glance up at the clouds. 'Dad always made it clear he wasn't happy with who I was.

113

He wanted to let me know what I should have been instead.'

'Who did *you* want to be?' I ask.

'I wasn't sure about that, either,' he says, smiling weakly, before reaching a hand up to waggle his ponytail. 'This could be me, or it could be a painfully clichéd attempt to get back at him.'

'Either way, it has great body.'

Owen pulls out the band holding the ponytail in place and tosses his hair like a shampoo model. 'I know he hated it. Hated the music I like too. I had an electric guitar that I used exclusively for down-tuned power chords. I played it all the time. The week after he locked me in the shed, he invited the new kid from church over to play. This kid *loved* my guitar. No idea how to play it, but wouldn't stop. My dad gave it to him.'

My mouth practically drops open. 'He what?'

'The kid protested, like you're supposed to. But my dad said that I never played it, so he might as well take it.' Owen shakes his head. 'I didn't have the courage to stop him.'

'What about your mum?'

'She didn't either.'

'And you never got it back?'

'Nope.'

I stand up from the swing, chains creaking overhead. The story has made me angry in a way I don't quite understand – I just know I have to try and fix it.

'Does this kid still live here?'

'Uh, yeah, I think so? Why?'

114

I grab the chain of his swing and shake it until he hops off. Then I begin marching towards the street. 'We're going to get your guitar back.'

Chapter Ten

Owen

We only visited the Davies' house a few times before we all stopped pretending to be friends. There was no dramatic moment that ended it. I think the kid – Joseph – always knew he shouldn't have taken my guitar. After that, he rarely spoke to me. Dad took against Mr Davies for some reason I never understood. We kept going to the same church, but quickly moved on to rigid smiles and nodding terms only.

This means they might not still live in the semi-detached house on the corner. A Range Rover sits on the driveway, so somebody must be home. Duncan and I stand on the other side of the road, like we're casing the joint for a robbery. Maywood isn't the kind of place you can hang around for long without somebody getting suspicious.

'It was six years ago,' I say.

Duncan bounces on his heels, psyching himself up. 'That guitar meant a lot to you, right?'

It was my most prized possession. Even if I was – how did Dad put it? – *execrable* at playing it. I nod.

'Right. We're going to get it back then.'

He marches across the road. His hands ball into fists and then open, again and again, betraying his nerves. I shouldn't let him do this. I also want to see just how far he'll go.

The wooden front gate opens soundlessly. We follow the pink-and-black brick path, on to a porch bordered by a fallow flowerbed. Duncan reaches for the metal door-knocker. Hesitates. I don't know him well, but this behaviour is clearly out of character. I think he's trying to impress me.

'You really don't have to,' I say. One last opening for him to back down.

He seizes the knocker and slams it three times – *rap, rap, rap*.

Instinct tells me to run. Knockdown ginger. Kids playing a stupid game.

Footsteps approach the door. It opens wide, no caution about who might be on the other side. A middle-aged woman in a high-necked floral dress regards us with blank expectance. Probably primed to turn down our sales pitch at the first word.

'Hi, Mrs Davies?' I say, hardly recognising her.

'Yes?' She shifts her weight, one arm remaining stretched to cling to the door.

'I used to be friends with Joseph? We went to the same church.'

She blinks and shakes her head as if dislodging cobwebs, big earrings clicking against her cheeks, before breaking into a smile. 'Of course! It's Owen, isn't it?'

A statement, not a question. A part of me had hoped she wouldn't remember. She'll have heard about Dad. It would have been announced in church, even though the funeral was held elsewhere.

'Joseph's at school, I'm afraid,' says Mrs Davies, frowning slightly because she knows we should be too.

'Oh yeah, of course. We were just—'

'Does he still have his guitar?'

Duncan's face is set with deliberate determination. He's psyched himself up and now he can't stop, like a car careening down a hill. Mrs Davies' frown deepens.

'Up in his room. Can I help with anything?'

'That guitar belonged to Owen.'

'Oh, that's right!' Mrs Davies smiles. 'He was so thrilled when he came home with it, he—'

Duncan cuts her off. 'He'd like it back.'

She smiles uncertainly. 'I don't understand.'

'Your son shouldn't have taken it. It was Owen's.' His voice shakes. 'So we're taking it back.'

Mrs Davies pulls the door a little closer. 'He's had the guitar for years now. He's really getting quite good.'

Despite everything, I'm pleased to hear it's still being played. Joseph is probably better at it now than I ever was.

'It doesn't matter,' I say.

'It *does* matter!' shouts Duncan.

Brittle determination is crumbling into stubborn petulance. That suits him even less. I take his arm firmly and pull him off the porch. 'I'm sorry, Mrs Davies.'

At least I can still blame any erratic behaviour on grief. She watches until we reach the pavement, and then shuts the door hard.

Duncan

I didn't know it was possible to feel this angry and helpless at the exact same time. It's like realising you've been short-changed when you've already left the shop, or the sequel to your favourite movie being a terrible disappointment.

(I haven't led a very difficult life.)

Owen tries to keep me walking away from the house, but I glance back one last time. On the far side, it's attached to the house next door. Closer to us, there's a tall side gate and fence that must lead into the back garden. I don't know what Owen is feeling, but I don't want him to see me giving up. So I hurry to the fence, grip its top with both hands, and begin scrabbling up.

'What are you doing?' says Owen.

In my head, climbing the fence would be fairly easy, but either it's higher than I realised or I'm significantly weaker.

Narrator: He was significantly weaker.

I sort of sling my arms over the top and swing my legs up to try and find purchase.

'I'm getting your guitar,' I grunt.

'No, you're *not*.' He grabs my belt and tugs. It both dislodges me from the fence and dislodges my trousers halfway down my arse. 'Just stop, okay?'

'I thought . . .'

My righteous anger evaporates while I pull up my

119

trousers. What *was* I thinking? I wanted to help. Or, at least, *show* that I wanted to help.

'I know what you thought. And I appreciate it. I just don't need a big gesture or whatever. We've had my life-story tour and the emotional-graveyard talk. That can be enough.' He leads me away from the fence. 'You don't have to prove anything to me. I'm not like your other friends.'

I straighten up. 'What does that mean?'

'It means . . . nothing.' He grips his stomach and glances up at the sky again, and then away down the street. 'Look, do you think you can find your own way home?'

'Oh. Yeah, probably?'

'I don't want to argue or anything. I think you coming here has helped. A lot. But I just need a little more time here alone.'

I can hardly complain after I followed him here uninvited. Before I can ask him if he'll be okay, I remember how that teacher sounded. The last thing he needs is to be patronised again.

'*Battlestar Galactica* later?' I say instead.

He nods, and I leave him there alone on the street corner.

Owen

As soon as Duncan has set off towards the station, I go back to the playground. It's still empty, so I take a swing and push off the ground. The momentum seems to flow from the grief inside me, urging me closer and closer to the sky. In moments I'm kicking my feet at the clouds. Zooming back only to surge forward higher.

The descent of the Angels is imperceptible. They move lower, closer with every swing.

Breath ragged in my lungs, I shift my grip on the chains. One more swing forward. At the peak of the arc I let go. My body flies into empty space. Before the ground can rise to meet me, feathers wrap me up tight. Grateful, I am borne into perpetual night.

House in the Shadows

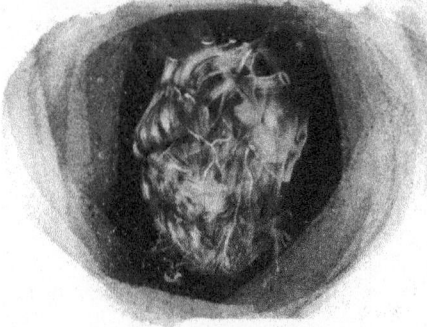

The house in the shadows of the Forest is an unexpected relief. Owen has been walking for days – he feels the ache deep in his muscles, the blisters chafing on his feet, the sting of scratches inflicted by low-hanging branches – even though he has only now returned. He will give anything for a rest.

'There,' says Luana, sounding tired to the bone. 'We can ask to spend the night.'

Night reigns here always, but Owen doesn't argue.

The last of the trees fringe a bare, muddy yard. A house at its far edge is built on a firm platform of stacked flat stones, patterned in pale lichen. A rotten fence skirts a wooden stoop covered by a sloping wood-tiled roof, sagging under a heavy carpet of sodden brown leaves.

Green paint peels freely like hang nails from doors and window frames.

'Was I gone?' Owen asks.

Luana does not answer. If they have been journeying together for a while, they won't have shared much small talk along the way.

Owen sinks to his ankles in mud as soon as he starts across the yard. A firm hand on his shoulder holds him back.

'Something has happened here,' says Luana, glowering across the yard.

Looking closer, he sees the house's windows are broken, boarded with mismatched scrap wood. A single deep set of footprints trails across the yard, steps oddly irregular, as if whatever made them grew longer legs as it went. They lead to a lopsided outbuilding close to the tree line. Rusted tools hang outside it, a wood axe leaning close to the door.

The ache in Owen's bones is replaced by a chill. 'We should keep going.'

Luana ignores him – again – and begins wading through the mud, leaving him little choice but to follow. The wet clay sucks and slurps at his shoes, like a mouth picking meat from the bone. Chicken feathers litter its surface. Around the first set of footprints are darker splashes, the mud turned the colour of pomegranate.

'Is that blood?' he asks.

Face set hard, Luana finally reaches the steps that lead up to the house. The boards sag and sigh under her feet. When she bangs a fist against the door, the house answers with a timorous creaking, as if speaking to itself.

'Let's just go,' says Owen, still standing in the mud. Dread has long since displaced his desire to rest.

'We mean no harm,' calls Luana. 'We seek shelter for the night.'

Movement inside, a shift that must be bodies creeping closer. Eyes appear at a narrow gap in the nearest boarded window, wide and wet with fear.

'Leave us alone.' A trembling woman's voice. 'My family wants no more trouble.'

'We don't bring you any,' Luana says softly. 'Perhaps we can help deliver you from whatever trouble you already face.'

An exhalation, close to a laugh. The eyes retreat from the window.

The spaces between the fir trees are growing darker, as if the night is draining from the sky and filling up the world. The night may never leave the Forest, but perhaps it can quicken, a tidal ebb and flow. They have travelled deep into the Forest on a trail no living person should follow. Who can know what lurks between the trees here?

A noise like bones popping painfully into misplaced sockets sounds from the outbuilding. Owen hastily tugs his feet from the mud, topples backwards on to the stone steps.

The eyes reappear at the window. They watch the yard, waiting for trouble. A moment after they slip away again there is a click of a lock and the door is opened.

A woman hurries them inside and slams the door. She wears a long, white blouse tied at the waist with a bright blue belt of soft cloth. Blood, dried and darkened like a scab, stains her front, and her dark hair is caked with mud. She heaves a wooden block into a bracket to seal the door.

Inside, the house is lit by handheld gas lamps, low flames burning steadily inside round chambers of iron and smoky glass. Two big rooms flank the entrance hall, as well as another smaller room opposite the front door that appears to be a pantry. Strings of tough-looking sausages hang from the ceiling, giving off a musty, spicy smell. The pantry still has its door, but the rest have been removed and used to barricade the windows. The walls are draped with thickly woven carpet, the colours of flowers faded and worn.

Owen stamps the mud from his shoes and follows Luana deeper into the house. A family huddles in the room that must serve as a kitchen and living space. An unlit fireplace houses a small metal stove. Mismatched chairs and tables have been set with meticulously clean plates and utensils. As well as the woman, there is a younger girl and an even younger boy. A daughter and son, grubby, wide-eyed and on edge.

'What haunts you?' asks Luana.

'Monster,' says the boy, chewing on his knuckle.

'Their father – my husband – died three nights ago,' says the mother. 'Ever since, we have been terrorised by some creature.'

'What kind of monster?' asks Luana. 'Does it carry the shape of a man?'

Outside, footsteps press into the mud. Regular, rhythmic, but landing abnormally far apart, as if whatever makes them is taking long, loping strides through the bog.

The mother's eyes flick to the barricaded door. 'Sometimes.'

Owen crosses to a boarded window. Through a sliver of space he sees an empty yard, the darkness profound enough now to blot the trees from sight.

'There's nothing,' he says.

Luana jerks her head to beckon him away from the window. 'It comes after nightfall?'

The family nods as one.

'We have a little time then. Can you spare any food?'

They are served shallow bowls of oily meat and vegetable broth, offered with a crust of stale bread. The food smells hearty, homely. Owen finishes it in moments, hardly tasting it, simply relishing the heat in his belly. Luana lingers longer over it, all the while peering around the room. At first he thinks she is assessing the house's strengths and weaknesses as a stronghold. Then, when he has finished mopping up the last dregs of broth with his bread, he realises she is watching the children. She follows every move they make, every yawn and tremble, as if trying to remember if she has met them before.

When they are finished, the bowls are stacked, and they sit together in the glow of the faintly hissing lamps.

'The first night, it killed our chickens,' says the mother. 'By the time it came again we had already boarded up the house.'

'You did well,' says Luana. 'It couldn't get inside?'

'It could, if it wanted.' She looks to her family. 'It tried to lure us out. It sounded like . . .'

When she trails off, Owen asks a question that has been playing on his mind. 'Why did you stay here?'

'Just in case he's still—'

A board creaks on the stoop. They freeze, and listen as it prowls slowly around the house, as if prying for a way inside. A shadow moves across the boarded window and the little boy whimpers, his sister pulling him close for comfort.

'Get away from here!' shouts Luana.

A wheezing, keening peal, almost like laughter. Fingers slip through the gap in the boards, too long and with too many joints, teasing at the wood. The mother picks up a fire iron and cracks it across the bony knuckles, forcing the hand to withdraw.

Wife.

A man's voice, hoarse as gargled fir needles.

I have come home, just as you prayed.

The mother whimpers and squeezes her damp eyes shut, but doesn't move, as if this is a test she has faced before.

'How did your husband die?' asks Luana.

'He was attacked by the wild. It left him for us, but the damage was too severe.'

'Where did you bury him?'

The mother glances at her children, and then back towards the window. 'The church is too far and I couldn't . . . we left him in the chicken house.'

A thud rattles the front door. The sealing bar holds firm, but the old wood around it flexes under the blow.

'Into the pantry, quickly.' The mother ushers her children into the cramped space beneath the sausages.

'You too,' says Luana. 'I will do everything I can to protect your family.'

The woman refuses, closing up the pantry and brandishing her fire iron at the front door. 'He died protecting us. I won't let anybody else do the same.'

'Can you use your witch powers to stop it?' asks Owen.

'Not in a straight fight. You must find a way help me.'

Another test of the Forest, Owen realises, so much more frightening than the last.

The next blow against the door splinters the wood. A split appears, and another strike cracks it wider.

'We have to cut out its heart,' says Luana.

'What—?'

Long fingers snake through the wood and prise pieces of it loose, opening a window on the night. Owen expects to see a monster. Instead, the lamplight picks out the face of a man, streaked with dirt and blood. Claws have opened his cheek in three perfectly matching lines, the wound bloodless, days old now.

Wife.

'No,' says the mother.

You left me to die, when all I wanted was to come inside. The words seem to churn in his throat. **Welcome me inside now.**

The woman has begun to cry. 'I'm sorry,' she says.

'That is not your husband,' says Luana firmly. 'You saw him die.'

The man's eyes consider her for a moment, before flicking to Owen. When he smiles, there is mud between his teeth.

Guests in my home. It's rude to leave me outside.

'It doesn't matter how much you want him back, or

how much guilt you feel about his death,' says Luana, voice less steady now. 'Your husband is gone.'

The mother moves too quickly to be stopped. She swings the fire iron sideways, hitting Luana in the stomach and doubling her over. Owen lunges to try and hold her back, but she is already at the door. The thick wooden bar clunks to the floor.

Another wheezing laugh, and the door explodes into pieces. The mother tumbles backwards. Splinters of wood shower the entrance hall. The shape of a man stands silhouetted in the empty frame. His proportions are wrong, neck stretching too tall and arms hanging too long. The wheezing gives way to the sharp pop and crack of bones shifting, assuming new structure, cartilage flexing and reforming. Its jaw lengthens and its legs break inward at the knee. Grey, waxy skin shines dully in the lamplight.

Luana unsheathes a long knife from her belt. The creature pounces, its animal legs allowing it to spring impossibly quickly. It collides with Luana and slams her against the wall. The impact jars the knife from her grip and it clatters at her feet.

Owen scrabbles to reach it, brings the blade up and slashes at the creature's back. It doesn't even draw blood. When he brings the knife down in a vicious stab, the skin is tough enough to break the blade. The creature snaps at Luana's face, only her firm hold on its throat keeping the teeth at bay.

'The axe,' says the mother from where she is slumped against the wall. Owen remembers it, leaning against the outbuilding. He runs for the door, and the creature lets go of Luana to pursue him. As it springs, the mother raps the fire iron against its legs, causing it to sprawl clumsily across the floor.

The opening allows Owen to tear down the steps and into the mud. His feet are swallowed up to the ankle. Every step is slow, painfully at odds with his racing heart. The outbuilding seems impossibly far away. As he pulls one foot free for another step, the creature appears on the stoop. It snarls, crouches and launches itself to land in the mud just a few steps behind him.

It tries to leap again, but its weight has pushed it too deep into the bog. Owen takes another laboured step and the creature flounders after him, swiping and clawing at the air. The outbuilding is just a few agonising steps away. Owen's muscles burn as he forces a leg clear, throws it forward, tries to ignore the hot, rank breath on his back.

The rusty head of the axe rests on a tuft of grass. If the edge is too dull, it will fail to penetrate the creature's thick hide. One step away. Owen reaches for the long handle.

Claws slash across his back. The pain is like being branded. Owen screams out, dives for the axe. In one quick movement he wraps his fingers around it, turns and drives the axe into the creature's chest.

The blade bites deep. Black blood gushes from the wound. The creature howls, staggering sideways so that the axe comes free. Its bones are already popping, limbs shortening, body returning to its human template. Owen readies the axe to swing again, but the creature stumbles past him into the gloom of the outhouse and falls quiet.

Breathing hard, holding the axe ready at his shoulder, Owen approaches the doorway. It is no longer a creature. Lying on a mound of straw is the pale corpse of a man.

Luana banishes Owen to watch over the children as she cuts out their father's heart. Inside the house, their mother busies herself lighting a fire.

The crude surgery only takes a few minutes. Luana returns to the house holding a small cloth-wrapped bundle. There is no more blood.

'I thought it was my husband,' says the mother, fire now crackling hot under the stove.

'It happens when a family can't bear to bury a body. The creature takes it and uses it to torment the people they loved most in life. It twists the person you knew into something else.' Luana unwraps the heart – a sad lump of foundered muscle – and places it in a shallow stone dish. 'It looked like him, but that's all.'

'I'm sorry I let it inside. I wanted . . .'

Luana gently shakes her head. 'You wanted him back. I understand. Your husband has already crossed the Sunday Water.'

The mother leads her children into the other room. The air quickly grows clammy and warm.

'A witch can't fight such a creature,' says Luana, sliding the dish inside the stove so the flames consume it. 'But she can vanquish it.'

'A spell?' asks Owen.

She shakes her head. 'Merely the proper procedure.'

Beside the sticky heat of the fire, Owen peels off his tattered shirt to reveal the damage from the creature's claws.

'The feathers?' he says.

'It missed them, though barely.'

The relief he feels is almost enough to numb the sting when Luana cleans the wounds with cool, clean water. It drips on to the feathers, runs oily down his back.

'This happened because they weren't ready to grieve,' says Owen, quietly enough that the mother won't hear.

'It's no easy thing,' says Luana, dabbing at his back.

'They're not spirits like we saw before. Are they like the people who lived in this place when it was a kingdom?'

She wrings the cloth into the basin of water. 'They could be. Even they might not remember any more. They are trapped here by death as much as I am. Like you will be, if we do not reach the Fisher of Souls.'

'How did your family die?'

Luana drops the cloth into the basin with a splash. 'It was my fault. Or at least it feels like it. You cannot grieve when you feel you need to atone. Cannot accept support or sympathy. So you are alone.' She looks into the house. 'I know why they could not bury him.'

'You're not alone any more,' says Owen.

She smiles and hands him the remains of his shirt. 'I know that too.'

The heart has been reduced to ashes by the time it is removed from the fire. Luana heats clean water on the stove and pours four steaming cups.

'Can you bring the children?'

Owen fetches the boy and the girl. They settle warily around the fire to watch Luana deposit a pinch of the heart ashes into each cup.

'Drink,' she says. 'It will send the creature away.'

'For good?' asks the boy.

Luana smiles and strokes his cheek. 'For good.'

The mother drinks first, draining her cup of ashen water, before encouraging her children to do the same.

'Bury him in the morning,' orders Luana, before turning to the children. 'Remember your father as he was in life, not what this creature made him in death.'

They nod, and their mother pulls them close to her.

'My son was his age, or thereabouts,' says Luana, picking up the fourth cup. 'He meant everything to me. To us.'

She takes a long gulp and hands the cup to Owen.

'Why do I have to drink it?' he asks.

'We both do.'

The heat tickles his throat as he inhales the rising steam. He brings the cup to his lips and drinks. It tastes of little more than dirt. When he swallows, his head begins to spin. He casts around for a chair.

The world changes as he sits. The house in the shadows is gone. Darkened fields trail past the train window, seat juddering gently underneath him. Owen lifts a hand to his lips, where the taste of ashes lingers, before resting his head against the cool glass to watch the night pass him by.

Chapter Eleven

Owen

It's late by the time I make it back to Westleigh. It still registers in my mind as going *back* rather than *home*. Neither place feels like home now. I am transient – fallen somewhere between. In the Forest, a splinter of myself is leaving that shadow house and once again delving deeper into the trees. My spirit may already be trapped in that place, remaining behind to continue its journey while I return as an empty shell.

When I'm there – when *all* of me is there – do I still exist here? A doppelganger play-acting in my shoes?

I have been divided in two. But along what line?

Terror threatens to choke me. Under my school shirt I feel my feathers grown larger, fuller. The Forest wants to keep hold of me. Yet it's also leading me somewhere, begrudgingly offering me a way out. The truth is there, not in Maywood. The Forest is a test that I must pass.

I take three deep breaths before putting in my

earphones and blasting music at full volume. Battling guitars bludgeon all thoughts into silence.

Westleigh High Street is alive at night. Pubs ring with the sound of football matches on TV and dance music thuds from a nearby door. Illuminated chicken-shop signs wash across the tarmac and the day's bin bags are piled around streetlights. It's easy to be anonymous here. Nobody pays me any attention as I walk between the closed shops. I slow down to enjoy it. I've already messaged Mum to tell her I went to Duncan's house after school.

Shit. Duncan. I abandoned him in a strange town. I realise I'm passing the Asda road gate, and I stop to peer at the tight spaces between bars.

'No way he got his head stuck in there,' I say to myself.

When I get moving again, I fire off a quick message to him. *Sorry about earlier. Still on for Battlestar?*

It's strange, to *want* to speak to him, just hours after seeing him. After bringing him so close to the person I used to be. Until now it felt easier to keep all of that stubbornly hidden.

Luana believes we need each other to find our way through the Forest. Perhaps it's not so different here.

My phone buzzes. *No need to apologise. Let me know when you're ready.*

Christ, he's a good guy. I'm not sure he even realises it.

The sky is too dark, the glow of the streetlights too bright for a glimpse of the Angels. I close my eyes. For a moment I feel leaves against my face, branches scratching at my skin, the deep ache in my calves. My spirit is still there, pushing its way forward through the trees. Laughter on the other side of the high street snaps me out of it. A couple emerges from a side street, walking awkwardly with their arms wrapped around each other. I recognise Lorenzo straight away. Duncan's friend who's broad as an Ikea bookshelf. There's a gym bag clutched in his free hand. He's grinning ear to ear as the girl strokes his chest, lifts her face to kiss him. Streetlight catches her face, the shaved side of her black hair, and I recognise her too. I saw a photo of her earlier today – Becky, the girlfriend of another of Duncan's friends.

I shouldn't be seeing this. Before I can put my head down, Lorenzo glances up and spots me. The smile drops from his face and he snatches his arm away from her.

'What's wrong?' she says.

I turn away down the nearest street and speed up to leave them behind.

Duncan

There's no easy way to ask your younger sister if you and your mates can join her amateur dance group. If she refuses, I'll never live it down. If she agrees, I actually have to convince my mates to join her amateur dance group.

I'm fully expecting her to reject the idea out of hand. That's why I wait until Mum and Dad have gone to bed. Her room is right next to them so she can't laugh at me too loudly.

'Oh my god, that's an incredible idea!' she shrieks before I can even finish my carefully rehearsed pitch.

One of our parents bangs on the adjoining wall.

'Seriously?' I whisper.

'I mean, it's a *ridiculous* idea, but incredible.' She throws her laptop from where it was resting on her knees in bed. 'Have they actually agreed to it?'

I sit on the edge of the bed. 'They haven't *not* agreed to it.'

'I can work with that. Your friends are pushovers.'

'Maybe don't call them that while you're trying to convince them.'

I'm getting up to leave when she calls me back. 'Seriously though, thank you. I really didn't want to do it alone.'

'At this point I'm pretty sure I owe you more than one. Plus you haven't seen any of us attempt to dance yet.'

My phone buzzes in my pocket. It's a message from Owen. *Home now. Ready to go to space?* I smile before I can help it.

'Who's that?' asks Emily, smiling suggestively.

'Nobody,' I say, slipping out of her door. 'Goodnight.'

We take a toilet break at 1am because we're simul-watching the episode where the entire fleet's water supply blows out of the ship and it always makes me need to pee. I idly check Lorenzo's Snapchat while I'm in the bathroom. Usually it shows him with his buddies at the gym, lifting heavy things and testing the physical limits of tank top shoulder straps, before going to a pub or whatever. Tonight, it's oddly empty.

'I think Boomer is my favourite character,' says Owen from the small window in the top corner of my screen.

'She is my number four *Battlestar* crush.'

'I meant because she's interesting and conflicted. But one day I'll be asking for that complete list.'

'Number one will *shock* you.'

He does one of those laughs where you blow out a little breath through your nose, more an acknowledgement of humour than an actual laugh. That's okay, it wasn't a particularly good joke, but it's also clear that he's distracted, and by more than Boomer in her flight gear.

My phone vibrates. A message from Lorenzo, outside of the group chat.

You still talking to the new guy?

There's no way he can mean right this second. These late-night sessions are strictly secret. I should just ignore him, except he'll see I've read the message and must therefore still be awake.

Yeah, sometimes, I type back. *Why?*

Message seen. He doesn't begin a response.

'Who're you texting at this hour that isn't me?' says Owen.

I'd forgotten that he can see me. 'Oh, it's just Lorenzo.'

He seems to think about that for a moment, opening his mouth to say something before changing his mind. 'I thought it might be a girl.'

'Yeah, right. I'd have a better chance with a Cylon.'

Owen shifts in front of his screen, settling back in his seat and keeping his eyes on the episode, even though it's clear we're both distracted now. 'What about that girl from the other night?'

'You mean Michaela?'

'I probably do,' he says. 'I assume she isn't a Cylon.'

'Is it weird that I'd like her more if she was?'

'A-ha!' he says, leaning triumphantly towards the camera. 'So you *do* like her?'

Once again I see that spark of humour in his eyes. It's almost like somebody else looking at me. This time he doesn't immediately stamp it back down.

I slump back into my chair. 'I think so? It's hard to tell these days. She's pretty much the only girl I know outside my family, so it could just be a proximity thing.'

'You're such a romantic. Do you think about her when you—?'

'No, mostly just the Cylons.'

'I was going to say wake up, but okay.'

I unlock my phone and find the last message Michaela sent me. Usually I'm a black belt at reading too much into literally anything, but even I have to admit there's no romantic subtext here. I read it aloud to him.

If you have to make excuses for how your friends behave, you're no better than they are. Maybe it's time you grew out of them.

Owen is quiet for a second before he says, 'How do you feel about that?'

I look at the laptop screen, at his face occupying the chat window. Every cliché about only knowing someone for a week but it feeling like a lifetime applies here. This whole thing is different to any kind of friendship I've ever known. And I like it. It's a paradigm shift or whatever.

'If this was a book I'd prove her wrong through a series of non-consensual but nevertheless elaborately romantic dates until she gave up and fell in love with me. Unfortunately, I think she's right,' I say. 'And I think it's for exactly that reason I won't hear from her again. She's not the same person I knew two years ago, but I still am.'

Owen takes another of his long, ponderous pauses. I'm used to them now, which means I can wait patiently instead of desperately filling them with inane banter. Finally, he leans forward and pauses the episode.

'Do you mind if I switch to typing?'

The video window goes blank. I pause the episode on my end and listen to his fingers move across the keys.

After what we talked about in Maywood earlier, I've been thinking how nostalgia can be a form of mourning. It's how we grieve for the people and places we miss, the periods of our lives that are gone. Nostalgia is how we mourn the person we used to be.

I read it through twice before responding aloud, trying to think of anything I can say that doesn't just sound stupid. 'If that's the case, I haven't got anything to mourn. I've lived here and had the same friends pretty much my entire life.'

Another long pause, and then the sound of typing. Before any message appears, my phone rings. It's set to silent, so Owen won't hear it. The screen says *Lorenzo*. He must have got drunk with his new friends and decided to give me one of his late-night calls. I decide not to answer. It rings off just as Owen's message appears.

I don't think it's as simple as that. When you told me about getting your head stuck in that gate, or losing your new toy, it was because you miss how things were back then. You're still friends with those same people, but it isn't the same any more.

'We haven't messed around like that for years,' I say. They were all too conscious of growing up and becoming men. Lorenzo got obsessed with the gym. Matt, against

140

all the odds, got together with Becky. Saeed has a full masturbation schedule he must keep to at all costs. 'That's just growing up though, isn't it?'

That doesn't mean you're not allowed to miss it, he writes. *All those things made you who you are now.*

My phone screen lights up again. *One voicemail received.*

'Then maybe nostalgia is dangerous,' I say, looking into the camera but unsure if he can still see me. 'It's like you said earlier. We should focus on who we're supposed to become so we don't get left behind.'

There's another long pause before Owen begins typing again.

My dad didn't like who I was, says Owen's eventual reply. *So I always tried to hide it from him. After a while I was doing it with everyone.*

That explains the other side I see of him sometimes, before he hides it away inside.

'You don't have to do that with me,' I say. 'You can be yourself.'

I want to try. After everything that happened, I've lost so much sense of who I was that I don't know who I am now. This fresh start I'm supposed to be having is like pulling a new existence out of thin air.

'Can I be totally honest with you for a second?' I say.

Yes.

'I'm more my actual self with you than I am with the friends I've known for years. And you're right, it's sad.' My cheeks burn hot, and I keep my gaze away from the camera. 'But I'm grateful too. You shouldn't have to lose everything that came before to find a way forward. I'll help you figure out who you are now, if you want.'

141

After another moment of silence, the microphone fuzzes as he switches it back on. Light flares in the chat window and resolves into Owen's smiling face.

'Thank you,' he says. As simple as that.

'Also, I might have done something stupid.'

His brow crinkles. 'What?'

'I asked my friends to join a dance group.'

Owen laughs so suddenly that it quickly collapses into a cough. He thumps a fist against his chest, strands of hair coming loose around his face. Again, it's almost like he becomes a different person.

'You mean with your sister?' he asks after he's recovered.

I wince and nod. 'It seemed like a good idea at the time.'

He considers this for a moment. 'Want me to come along?'

'Would you mind?'

'Frankly, I'd be annoyed if I missed it.'

'All right. Thanks.'

We finish the episode in possibly the most comfortable silence I have ever experienced.

Chapter Twelve

Duncan

I only remember the voicemail from Lorenzo when I'm half asleep on the toilet in the morning. I set it to play on speaker.

Answer your fucking phone! Lorenzo's voice booms.

The words are blurred by a loud shuffling, heavy footsteps hitting the pavement, music playing in the background. He must have been somewhere outside when he called.

I swear it's 'cos of you, the message continues. *Fuck sake, man.*

He sounds tired, his words slurred and weary, which probably means he was drunk. It sounds like he's blaming me for something but I have no idea what.

It's like, you never . . . you never had to worry. You're just the same. You don't have to try like me. A long sigh, and then, *I guess I'm stuck with you now.*

The message cuts off after a moment of fumbling.

I stay on the toilet long after I'm finished, trying to work out what he meant, but it doesn't get any clearer.

If he remembers leaving the voicemail, he pretends otherwise at lunch. We line up together in the rehearsal room like a bunch of criminals, while Emily looks each of us up and down and shakes her head disparagingly.

'Please stop shaking your head disparagingly,' I say.

'What do you expect, when you bring me such poor excuses for men?'

Beside me, Lorenzo ostentatiously clears his throat. 'What about me, babes?'

Emily cocks an eyebrow. 'Don't worry, I've got plenty of time to make a man out of you.'

Saeed nudges me suggestively with his elbow and I die a little inside.

While my sister pokes at Matt's curiously solid boulder of a stomach, I glance back towards the door. By the time lunch break arrived I had 87 per cent convinced myself that Owen would show up here instead of performing his usual disappearing act. It's a good thing I'm not a gambler.

'Okay, okay, I was trying to do the whole mean-but-inspiring mentor thing,' says Emily. 'I know you don't really want to be here and I, like, really appreciate it. So let's see if this is going to work.'

The far wall is covered in smudged and smeared mirrors. We don't look much of a dance group: Matt manages to be both tall and round, Lorenzo's muscles give him the flexibility of a two-finger Kit-Kat, and Saeed is so skinny he practically disappears inside his school blazer.

As for me . . . well, in loads of the books I read, the teenage boys have a habit of reaching up for something above their heads so their T-shirts ride up to reveal the unexpected but highly alluring chiselled abs underneath. The last time I saw my abs was when I had diarrhoea for the entire week of my eleventh birthday and was convinced I was going to die.

Narrator: He didn't.

'Let me play you the song,' says Emily.

She grabs her phone and plays a dance track I don't recognise. It's worryingly fast, high-pitched synth notes swirling over repetitive drums. While she listens, Emily shifts slightly in her chair, hinting at the moves she'll expect us to perform. We meet each other's eyes in the mirrors, all of them looking at me like I've signed them up for an amateur testicular examination.

'We have to dance to that?' asks Matt when the song ends.

Emily nods enthusiastically. 'What sort of music do you usually listen to?'

Matt looks baffled. 'I don't.'

'*O*-kay . . . what would your talent be if you were going to enter the show by yourself?'

He considers for a moment. 'I can eat a packet of chocolate Hobnobs in less than a minute.'

'I can eat your mum in less than a minute,' says Saeed.

'Crude, ladies present,' adjudges Matt. 'Two out of ten.'

My sister glances sideways at me like I've set her up on a disastrous blind date. This was my idea, and despite the keen sting of regret stabbing at my gut I have to try and make it work.

'Let's try running through some of the moves really slowly,' I suggest.

Emily positions herself in front of us, facing the mirrors, and demonstrates the first move. It involves reaching above her head with both arms, before gripping the top of her head and turning her neck in a circle, like she's trying to massage out an ice cream headache.

Before I can even begin to try it for myself, Matt accidentally elbows me in the side of the head.

'Sorry, mate.'

Head ringing, I step away from him so I have more space. We practise the move a few times, each of us wrenching our necks at different speeds in different directions while Emily watches on in horror.

'Okay, from there we go side to side . . .'

She shoots her right arm into the air and back down, and then the left, alternating sides like she's playing table tennis with both hands. In the corner of my eye I see Saeed start on the wrong side and stumble to correct himself. This time Matt accidentally hits Lorenzo, earning himself a hard thump on the arm in return.

'You've got the coordination of a drugged baby giraffe!'

'Okay, better!' calls Emily, like she's coaching pre-schoolers. 'This next one is a bit more complicated.'

This time, instead of turning only her body, she shifts her chair to one side and reaches a hand towards the ground, before deftly switching to the other side to do the same. It really looks like it shouldn't be *that* difficult.

Narrator: It was.

Saeed tries first, reaching low too eagerly and losing his balance. He topples into me, sending me staggering across into Matt just as he's straining towards his toes. There's a short, sharp *rip* and Matt straightens up, clutching at the seat of his trousers. Lorenzo collapses into laughter.

'My trousers!' shouts Matt.

They're split all the way from the crotch around to the belt line at the back, offering a gaping window on to his baggy Spider-Man boxer shorts.

Behind us, somebody begins to clap. We all spin around (the first time today we've been perfectly synchronised) to find Owen watching us from the doorway.

Owen

They freeze like I've caught them in the middle of a shameful crime. Scatter like there's still a chance to escape with their fragile reputations intact.

'Where are you going?' says Duncan's sister as they each begin collecting their bags from against the wall.

'Forget this,' says Lorenzo. 'I'm sorry, but it was a stupid idea.'

'Everybody's going to laugh at us,' whines the skinny guy, Saeed.

'My bloody trousers!' cries the big guy, Matt.

Emily chases after them pleadingly. 'You can't just give up already.'

The three of them shoulder their bags and glance at each other guiltily. None of them wants to be the first to leave. Duncan looks frozen beside them, fumbling for a way to make them stay. Emily beats him to it.

'Just wait a minute!' She grabs Saeed's sleeve and spins him around to face her. 'Saeed, you're already the least cool person in the entire school, so it's not like you have to worry about this ruining your bad-boy reputation.'

'Harsh,' he mutters, rubbing at his arm where she pinched him.

Next, she turns on Matt. 'You've never cared what anybody thinks about you, so why are you starting now?'

He keeps his hands protecting his modesty but nods mutely.

'And you, future husband,' Emily says, squaring up to Lorenzo. 'Not only are you putting our engagement on the line, but you're proving you're not the man I thought you were. If you're so comfortable with your raging masculinity, prove it by being comfortable doing this.'

'Babe—'

She silences him with a finger. It's impressive to watch her play them so easily, but the hardness set on her face is brittle. Already beginning to crack. 'This really means a lot to me, okay? And I don't have a lot of other options right now.'

The three of them exchange uncertain looks. They clearly want nothing more than to run for it. Whatever delicate thread ties them here is fraying. Duncan watches them closely, waiting for it to snap.

'I have an idea,' I say.

They blink at me like they had forgotten I was here. Emily gratefully nods for me to share.

'How many other dance groups have entered this talent show?' I ask.

'Three.'

'And I'd guess they're doing the same kind of *Britain's Got Talent* dance routine.' I hold my hands up placatingly

148

before she can protest. 'Nothing wrong with that, but you should do something to make sure you stand out.'

She doesn't look convinced, like standing out is the last thing she wants to do. 'Okay, so what?'

I take out my phone. Untangle the earphones and offer them. Emily wipes them off on her leggings before inserting them into her ears. I find a reasonably tame song – Iron Maiden's 'The Trooper' – and set it playing.

She flinches as the intro kicks in at full volume. I turn it down. Within a few seconds she's nodding her head to the classic galloping melody. She takes out an earphone.

'Metal is your suggestion?'

'It's not everybody's cup of mead, but it's *different*. And these guys wouldn't have to do anything too energetic,' I say, turning to them. 'The thing about metal is that it's all a bit ridiculous. So you go the whole way: costumes, lights, dry ice, all that.'

Emily looks unconvinced but listens until the end of the song. 'Do you have a playlist or something?'

'Of course,' I smile.

'Plug your phone into the speaker.' She turns to Duncan. 'I already like him more than your other friends.'

It's hard not to laugh at how utterly flummoxed he appears by this comment. He looks at me and smiles gratefully, before dropping it as soon as he catches Lorenzo's eye. I realise Lorenzo has refused to look directly at me ever since I came into the room.

I dock my phone and find a classic metal playlist. 'There are loads of choices.'

'I'll need your help,' says Emily. 'I don't know anything about this music.'

Finally, Lorenzo turns to me, sneering. 'What do you know about choreography?'

'About as much as you know about dancing.'

He falls sulkily quiet as I set the music playing, tinny guitars and drums fuzzing from the speaker loud enough to drown us all.

Duncan

The song is hard and fast, crunchy guitars duelling over frantic drums. It sounds like the soundtrack for a particularly preposterous anime fight scene. Lorenzo recoils like the music might physically hump his leg, while Matt and Saeed simply look bewildered, but Emily grins and begins banging her head, swinging her long hair in circles.

The music is loud enough to fill the room, so I can't hear what Lorenzo says when he grips Owen's shoulder and speaks close to his ear. As ever, Owen's face remains unreadable. He simply nods, meets Lorenzo's eye undaunted for a moment, and then leaps into place beside Emily just in time to air-guitar a screeching solo. They windmill their hair in unison, and she drums along (horribly out of time) on the arms of her chair. I can't help but grin stupidly at them both. It's the most animated I've ever seen Owen, almost like he's throwing down a challenge. It's so different to his usual reserved calm, but it doesn't seem forced. It's still undoubtedly him.

'I've decided I like metal,' pants Emily when the song is over. 'Also I might be sick.'

Owen retrieves his phone before the next song kicks off. 'It makes you feel powerful, right?'

'It just sounds like noise to me,' sniffs Lorenzo.

'We can choose something a bit slower,' says Owen. 'It can be just as powerful though. Epic. Maybe a song that tells a story.'

Emily nods enthusiastically, beaming at the idea, completely sold. It makes me smile too, and I turn it on Owen in thanks. He smiles back, humbly dipping his head. Lorenzo spots the exchange, but the bell rings to signal the end of lunch before he can say anything. We quickly set about packing everything up, Emily hurrying to the front of the room to fetch her stuff.

'There's a new pub near the station that doesn't ID,' says Lorenzo, handing me my bag. 'We're heading there tonight. Fancy it?'

Whether deliberate or not, he's excluded me from that *we*. They made these plans without me, plans that will happen whether I'm part of them or not. It shouldn't make me feel so hollow, so desperate to somehow make it right.

'Yeah, definitely,' I say.

'Owen?'

We both jerk around to look at Lorenzo, like it might be a joke. He smirks slightly in what can only be provocation. He might as well slap a glove across Owen's face.

'All right,' says Owen, pushing hair out of his face. 'Sounds good.'

'Cool.' Lorenzo heads for the door. 'Meet at the station about eight.'

As soon as he's gone, Matt and Saeed trailing behind, Owen turns to me. 'Come to mine first and help me look eighteen?'

'Only if you can work the same miracle for me.'

Chapter Thirteen

Duncan

Although I've never been on a first date, visiting Owen's house must be approximately what it feels like. Palms sweaty. Arms heavy. Mum's spaghetti. I'm *nervous* (and if I do vomit, it'll actually be Mum's potato waffles reappearing).

Making new friends as a sort-of-almost-adult, it turns out, is completely different to when you're a kid. Back then, you just stuck to the boy who had the best toys and/or games console and worried later about whether or not you actually liked each other. Lorenzo was the first kid in school to have a Nintendo Wii, so the rest of us competed to be his friend. Only a few survived.

Doing it now, as a roughly fully formed *person* rather than an opportunistic bundle of pre-pubescent vigour and snot, feels like really putting myself on the line. The first house visit could make or break it.

Is this what growing up is like? It's *terrible*.

'Do you want picking up later?' asks Mum as she pulls the car over outside the house. I suspect she only offered the lift in the first place to escape doing the washing-up.

'I'm not sure what the plan is,' I say. This is partly true. An ill-advised underage raid on a dodgy pub is definitely not going to go as intended. 'I'll let you know.'

'Okay. Not too late, please.'

I cross the road in front of the car (whispering a quiet prayer that she won't accidentally run me over) and then wave her off. The houses here are terraced, tall and narrow like they each house a detective agency or secret magical society, front doors opening on to the pavement.

Owen answers the door almost immediately, as if he was waiting behind it. 'I wanted to get to you before Mum,' he explains.

It must have been a close race, because she's right behind him. It's still a shock just how fragile she looks, like a fall would shatter her like the mug she's drying with a tea towel. 'Duncan! Welcome. It's nice to see you here.'

For one terrible moment I think she's going to hug me, but instead she awkwardly pats my shoulder with a damp hand. The way she smiles at me is grateful, like my presence is granting her a favour.

'What have you boys got planned for tonight?' she asks.

'Not much. Just hanging out.' Owen leads me up the steep staircase and we leave her behind. 'Don't worry, she's going out soon,' he whispers to me.

The house feels oddly cramped, the space between the upstairs doors and the banister just wide enough to squeeze through, the doorframes lower than they should be. Instinct tells me to duck when I follow Owen into his bedroom.

'This isn't exactly what I imagined your room would be like,' I say.

Empty. A single bed is pushed into the corner, the small desk beside it completely bare except for his laptop. Moving boxes are stacked two or three high against the walls, a couple open with clothes spilling over the flaps. There has been no effort to make the room his own. He could have moved here yesterday, could be moving out tomorrow. I hoped it might give me a better idea of who he is, bring out that other side of him I've seen a few times, but there's nothing here.

'You've been imagining my room?'

'The little glimpse I get through the computer screen was too tantalising to resist.'

Owen starts some music – noisy guitars, of course – playing at low volume on his laptop.

'I've been giving this whole trying-to-look-older thing some serious thought,' he says.

'And what conclusion did you reach?'

'Several.' He sits on the edge of his bed. 'At first I thought it was all a bit pointless because I don't even want to go to the pub. But then I quite like the idea of dressing up.'

I frown at that. 'When you say dressing up . . .?'

'Well, show me what *you've* done.'

I unzip my hoodie. Underneath is literally the only smart-ish non-school shirt I own, a pale blue number Dad thought I should have for reasons that remain

unclear. Job interviews? Court appearances? It hasn't
been ironed in quite some time.

Owen looks sceptical. 'My plans might seem elaborate
in comparison.'

He stands up and whips a leather jacket out from
under his bed covers. It looks old, white and brown
cracks circling the arms like tiger stripes, and when he
shrugs it on it's just a *little* too big at the shoulders.

'It belonged to my dad, but he hadn't worn it for ages,'
he says. 'I also nicked some of my mum's eyeliner.'

I gulp. 'I might just stick with my shirt.'

'I'm going now, love!' Owen's mum shouts from
downstairs.

'Bye!' he calls back. As soon as we hear the door slam
he turns the music loud enough to make my eardrums
wince.

'Don't you have anything a bit less antisocial?' I shout
over it.

'Hang on a minute,' he says, and changes the song.
The fuzzy cacophony of guitars ceases, replaced by a
steady *chugga-chugga-chugga* and rumbling bass. He
turns it up even louder. 'Nothing makes you feel more
powerful than metal!'

He tips his head back and then slams it forward in time
with the riff, hair arcing over to hit his face like a wave.
Again, the music gives me a glimpse of that different
Owen, patiently biding its time until it's allowed to take
over.

'Is there a mirror in here?' I shout.

'Downstairs!'

He scoops up the laptop and the noise carries us

through to the kitchen. There's a mirror in the hallway just outside.

'Have you eaten?' Owen asks, finally turning the music down.

I nod. 'Potato waffles.'

'Nice.' He opens a kitchen cupboard and takes out a packet of instant noodles. 'You remember I went to the Chinese supermarket?'

Beside the large Chinese characters on the packet is a picture of steaming noodles and a cartoon boy with flaming red cheeks spooling them on to chopsticks.

'These look like they will kill me,' I say.

Owen switches on the kettle. 'These aren't too hot, and I promise they're a million times better than any noodles you've had from Asda.' He empties the block of noodles into a deep bowl and pours out the bright red flavouring powder. When the kettle boils, he fills the bowl with steaming water and breaks up the block with a fork. 'The shop here sells a flavour that's so hot you can only order it online in China.'

I recoil from the bowl. 'This isn't that, is it?'

Another packet is brought out from the cupboard. This time the cartoon boy has smoke pouring from his mouth.

'Maybe another time?'

Owen grins, and returns his attention to the bowl. The noodles have absorbed most of the water and softened into red strings. Just the smell is spicy enough to sting my nose.

'You first,' I say.

A huge clump of noodles clings to the fork, forcing him to slurp them loudly into his mouth. His hair doesn't instantly catch fire, which I suppose is a good sign. He hands me a clean fork.

I make sure to snare significantly fewer noodles, and hold my breath as I bring them to my lips. The taste arrives first: rich and savoury, definitely better than any noodle I've eaten before. It lulls me into a false sense of security before the heat roars up like a fireball.

'Oh no,' I say, as I swallow and my mouth becomes a furnace.

'Whatever you do, don't lick your—'

In my panic, I lick my lips. The heat spreads instantly, tingling and throbbing. Panting at the air only seems to stoke it hotter.

'Water,' I gasp. 'Or kill me.'

Owen yanks open the fridge and thrusts a bottle of milk at me. I fumble off the cap and gulp it down. My eyes brim over with water and tears stream down my face. After a few seconds, the cool milk brings me back from the brink of noodle-induced insanity.

'They were quite nice,' I say, wiping my eyes. 'Until I wanted the sweet release of death.'

He laughs, and shoves another massive bundle of noodles into his face. 'Can I interest you in that eyeliner now you've stopped crying?' he says around the mouthful.

'Lorenzo would actually ex-communicate me. I've got some hair wax though,' I say, taking the pot from my pocket.

We stand side by side in front of the hallway mirror, me massaging a white blob of wax into my hair and Owen carefully tracing his eyes with a black pencil.

'I've never actually been to a pub,' he says. 'At least not when it isn't Sunday lunch with my parents.'

'Lorenzo claims he's been doing stuff like this for months, but we've never gone together like this.' Under my clumsy hands, my hair stands greasily on end at the front, while the back flops sadly against my scalp. The only sensible solution is to add more wax. 'Usually he or Matt goes to the off-licence while we hide around the corner, and then we drink in the park.'

'Now drinking in the park I *have* done.'

'Lorenzo's been a bit weird recently,' I say. 'What did he say to you earlier, in the rehearsal room?'

Owen finishes one eye, shrugs and starts on the other. 'Nothing much. Just asked what the music was.'

That seems unlikely. I try and catch his eye, but he's too focused on lining it. 'We don't have to go,' I say. 'We could just stay here and watch *Battlestar*.'

'And waste this makeover? I think not.'

'Just be careful around him, I guess.'

It's not like Lorenzo's going to ambush us from around a corner and hit him with a steel chair. Despite a lot of recent evidence to the contrary, he isn't a *total* dick. Still ... something about this whole situation doesn't seem right.

Owen finishes off his eyeliner and steps back from the mirror. He takes a breath, as if bracing himself, before he turns to me. 'What do you think?'

I should automatically hate it, because boys categorically do not wear eyeliner, but actually, 'It looks surprisingly good,' I admit. 'Is this what the real Owen looks like?'

He looks confused by the idea. 'I don't know, I've never worn it in public before. I guess we'll find out.'

'How about me?' I ask.

My hair looks a bit like I've been dragged backwards through a hedge, standing up in every possible direction.

'We need to leave in two minutes, so it'll have to do.'

Owen puts on his leather jacket, releases his hair to flow free around his shoulders, and then spoils the effect a little by adding his glasses. We probably look sort of eighteen?

Narrator: They definitely didn't. Like, at all.

We head towards the front door. 'Have you always lived in the same flat?' he asks.

'Since I was little. As soon as they knew Emily would need a wheelchair my parents moved somewhere with better access. I don't remember the old place at all.'

'I'd lived in our old house my entire life. It's really weird not having the muscle memory of this place.' The hallway is dark, and Owen has to fumble at the wall before he finds the light switch. 'In our old house I could walk around in the pitch black because I knew where everything was. Every switch, every door, every step. It was programmed into me. If I did that here I'd walk into a wall and break my nose.'

To close my bedroom door properly I have to lift the handle slightly and then push. There's a sweet spot for latching the bathroom window open, and I know exactly how loud I can have the volume on my laptop before Emily hears it next door.

'You'll learn it all for this place after a while.'

'Oh, I know. I just never thought I would have to.'

He pauses for a moment and then appears to make a decision. 'Can I show you something?'

He takes me to a closed door at the back of the house. Inside is a small, cold room, light from a sliding glass door showing furniture covered in dust sheets, more boxes stacked against the wall and a fireplace. A single framed photograph sits on the mantelpiece, alongside a white cardboard box.

I step closer to examine the photo. A family portrait. 'Is that . . .?'

'My dad, yeah.'

He's smiling. All of them are smiling. I point to the cardboard box.

'And is that . . .?

'My dad, yeah.'

'Shouldn't ashes be in a vase or an urn or something?'

'We're not keeping them,' Owen says. 'We just haven't worked out what to do with them yet. My mum thinks it should be my decision. Anyway, that's not what I wanted to show you.' He picks up the framed photograph.

'It's a nice photo,' I say.

'It is.' Owen flips the frame over and takes off the back. Another photo is hidden inside. Owen takes it out and shows it to me. It's his dad again, this time by himself, sitting in an armchair with a glass of wine in one hand and delving a finger deep into his nose with the other.

'He used to eat whatever he found up there,' says Owen.

So did I, but I'm not admitting to it now. 'Does your mum know it's there?'

'My mum wants to remember him one way,' Owen

says, turning the frame to look at the first picture. 'I'm actually trying to remember all of him. I just don't know if it's possible.'

He replaces the hidden photo and returns the frame to the mantelpiece. We stare at it and the cardboard box for a few moments. Eventually he turns to me, leather jacket creaking.

'I've put a downer on the night a little bit, haven't I?'

'Nothing pretending to enjoy the taste of beer won't fix.' I check my phone. 'We should go. Last chance to stay here and watch *Battlestar Galactica*.'

'No, not now I know how much you *enjoy* watching it by yourself.'

'Dude, I told you that in good faith.'

We head back to the front door and put on our shoes.

'Ready?'

Owen takes off his glasses and shoves them into a pocket. He blinks at the world, and for a moment he does look older.

'Ready.'

Chapter Fourteen

Owen

The group's attempts to look older are a mixed bag. Lorenzo could easily be early twenties, a dark curl of chest hair peeping from the top of the low-cut grey T-shirt that strains over his muscles. Matt is large in a different way. The polo shirt (collar popped) he's wearing could cover my entire bed. He makes me think of hanging clothes on a snowman. Saeed is wearing a trench coat that makes him look like he's sitting on another kid's shoulders.

'You came,' says Lorenzo. I can't tell if he's surprised or disappointed.

'That's what your mum said,' adds Saeed.

'Five out of ten,' mutters Matt.

Lorenzo frowns and doesn't respond. I smile uncertainly. Duncan throws me a sheepish look. 'It's a thing they do.'

It's busy outside the train station, commuters coming home and others heading on nights out. In the low light it takes a moment for anybody to notice my eyeliner. Lorenzo spots it first. My heart judders a little as he leans close to gawp.

'Is that what I think it is?'

I reach out and squeeze his rock-hard shoulder. If my spirit is still in the Forest, I can make this left-behind shell into any version of myself that I want. One that says things like, 'Try not to get too turned on.'

The others laugh, and I relax a little. Lorenzo pushes my hand away. When I turn to Duncan he's watching us anxiously, like we're two sides of his life careening towards a head-on collision.

'Just don't fuck this up for me, okay?' says Lorenzo, striding away from us.

We follow him down a sloping street parallel to the train station. On the other side of the fence a southbound train sits at the platform. Its open doors tug at me. I could make it if I ran. Be home in less than an hour.

Not home. There's nothing left for me in Maywood now. I have to try and find the way here instead.

'So what's this pub, then?' asks Saeed.

'The Railway Sleeper. It's got new management so they're not fussy who they let in,' says Lorenzo. 'You ever been drinking before?'

Apparently, the question is aimed at me. 'Not like this.'

He slings a thick arm around my shoulder. 'It's all right, man, we'll look after you.'

For a moment I see Luana walking on my other side. She glances at me, eyebrows lifted questioningly, teasingly. Then she's gone.

Lorenzo's bicep squeezes tight against the back of my neck. Heavy enough that he could drive me into the ground like a post. Anyone watching might think he was marching me to the pub against my will.

In the rehearsal room earlier today, under the cover of the music, he told me: *You can't tell anybody what you saw, yeah. Me and Becky. You haven't told him?*

I shook my head. It's not my place to tell anybody.

You can't tell him. I had expected a threat. Instead he said, *Please.*

That means I have no reason to be scared of him.

Still, Duncan sticks close at my shoulder. Protective. I give him a small nod to show my appreciation.

'What if we don't get in?' asks Matt.

'We're going to get in.'

'What if we don't?'

'When we get there, just walk straight inside like we do it all the time,' says Lorenzo. It's beginning to feel like we're planning a heist. For some reason, our success really matters to him. 'No hesitation or looking nervous.'

It's him who looks nervous. I can tell Duncan sees it too.

'I've only got £3.70,' says Saeed. 'Is that enough?'

The pub sits at the bottom of the road. It looks like a converted Victorian house, overlooking the railway line across the road. The lower windows have been painted black so we can't see inside. The lights underneath the pub sign flicker exhaustedly. A banner above the doors reads 'Under New Management!' Underneath it, a bouncer stands with his chin tucked into his coat, stamping the cold out of his feet.

'Are you sure about this?' whispers Duncan.

Lorenzo doesn't stop. 'Don't be a pussy all your life.'

The words seem to land like a blow. Duncan misses a step, then catches himself as his expression hardens. He follows as Lorenzo approaches the door and gives the bouncer a nod. The big man steps across to block their path.

'Got any ID, fellas?'

Duncan

I am 99 per cent certain it's not an arrestable offence to try and get into a pub while underage. That single percentage of doubt makes me scan the bouncer and make the easy decision to run instead of fight. Or maybe if we surrender immediately and beg for mercy he'll leave my face intact?

Apparently, Lorenzo has other ideas.

He pats a series of imaginary pockets as if this happens all the time. 'I think I've left it at home, mate.'

'Then I can't let you inside,' says the bouncer.

Lorenzo scoffs like it's a bad joke. 'I was here the other night. We just want a quick drink.'

The bouncer peers past him to where the rest of us are gathered like beggar children hoping for an extra serving of gruel. It might be my imagination, but I swear his eyes linger specifically on my painstakingly sculpted hair, a smile flickering at the corners of his mouth. Plainly, it doesn't convince. He looks Lorenzo square in the eye.

'It's illegal to serve minors.'

Lorenzo tenses. 'I'm not a minor.'

'But you can't prove it.'

Lorenzo squares up to him, pushing his face unsociably close. 'Call me a minor again.'

Behind me, Matt huffs a sigh, like he's bored.

'Hey, come on,' I say, gently taking his shoulder. He whips around to throw me off, and for a second I'm sure he's going to hit me. I hold up my hands in surrender. 'It doesn't matter. Let's just go.'

'I'm not a fucking minor!'

I remember the first time I noticed Lorenzo was changing into somebody who didn't quite resemble the person I knew. He came second in a two hundred metres race in PE, when usually he easily came first. Instead of letting it go and making sure he won big at whatever event came next, he stormed off and wouldn't speak to anybody for the rest of the day. A few days later, in front of the entire class, he tripped up the kid that beat him.

The bouncer does nothing to hide his boredom at Lorenzo's display. He plucks a phone from his pocket. 'Do I need to call the police?'

'Oh, shit,' says Saeed, backing away.

Lorenzo finally yields, throwing his hands up and skulking away back up the road. We follow behind, struggling to keep up. It's only when we're nearly back at the station that he wheels around to face Owen and me.

'It was fine coming here with my other friends,' he shouts. 'It's because you two look like children! What do you think you're doing coming out in *eyeliner*?'

'I've been told it gives my eyes depth,' says Owen.

I flash him a warning look. 'Lorenzo, we tried—'

He shakes his head at me. 'I don't know why I bother with you sometimes.'

I remember his voicemail from early this morning. *I guess I'm stuck with you.*

The hurt is there, quicksand in my gut, but this time it doesn't quite have the strength to pull me down. This shouldn't matter so much. Our friendship shouldn't rely on being served in some stupid pub.

'Not getting in doesn't mean anything,' I say.

'It would mean I could have got some chips,' mutters Matt.

Lorenzo jabs a finger at me. 'We would have got in if you weren't here.'

He starts walking again. It's tempting just to let him go. I really would rather be at home getting a little too worked up over supermodel Cylons. The night is young, after all.

Instead, I go after him while the others stay behind. By the time I catch him we're back at the station.

'Come on, man,' I say when he finally stops. 'Why's it such a big deal?'

Lorenzo throws his hands up into an exaggerated shrug. 'I was in there just the other night.'

'So you know exactly what we're missing.'

'That's not the point.' He kicks a toe against the ground. 'My mates at the gym found out I'm younger than them.'

'Oh. I guess that didn't go down well?'

'They messaged me last night telling me to leave them alone. I think somebody told them.'

'Don't look at me,' I say, putting a hand against my chest.

Lorenzo shoves his hands into his pocket. 'I don't know, man. It was humiliating. I liked hanging out with them.'

I know what he's really trying to say – he liked being the person they thought he was. He liked the life it gave him, so instead of letting it go he tried to recreate it with us. I wonder if he felt the same way with them as I do with him, like I'm desperately trying to keep up but always falling further behind.

Somebody steps up beside me, and I'm surprised to find that it's Owen.

'Why don't we just get some drinks from an off-licence and go to the park,' he says in an appeasing voice. 'It's basically the same, and we'll get more for our money.'

Lorenzo sighs a cloud of breath, as if the idea is beneath him. The corner shop we usually visit is only a few minutes away. It's next to a kebab place, which will keep Matt happy.

'All right, fine,' says Lorenzo. 'Give your money to Matt and don't let anybody see you. You know the drill.'

Owen

We hide around the corner for a few minutes, outside an estate agent where a guy working late eyes us warily through the glass. Lorenzo's phone chimes, and he takes a few steps away from us to check it.

'How do you get it so neat?' asks Saeed, peering closely at my eyes.

'I used to practise in secret. I can show you some time, if you want.'

He considers the offer for a moment, then shakes his head.

Matt eventually comes back, swinging a carrier bag bulging with cans in one hand and holding a polystyrene box of steaming chips in the other. He offers them around so we're all chewing as we set off for the park.

'How come you're not balls deep in Becky tonight?' asks Saeed.

Matt scowls. 'Don't talk about her like that. I don't know. I think she was doing something else.'

I haven't lived here long enough to know the best drinking park yet. I follow behind as we head away from town. Duncan trails back with me.

'You all right?' he says once we're out of earshot.

I know he means well, but the protective act is getting tiresome. 'Remember how I said I don't need people treating me like I can't cope?'

I try to say it lightly, but it comes out sharp. He looks shocked and nods apologetically. Shoves his hands into his pockets.

'I didn't mean it like that.' Although maybe I did. 'I'm supposed to be out on a limb here. That's kind of the point. So don't worry about me.'

'It just seems like . . .'

'What?'

He wipes his nose on the back of his hand. 'Nothing.'

A dark iron fence that skirts the road marks out the park. The gates stand open, a dimly lit pathway cutting past bare flowerbeds and across a darkened field. Goalposts stand empty. A single light bobs across the grass like a lifebuoy out at sea, a lone dog off its lead. We claim a cold bench for ourselves beside the toilet block and Lorenzo breaks out the beer. It's cheap. Tastes like licking a two-pence coin.

'Last to down the can does a dare,' says Lorenzo.

We set about gulping the warm fizz as fast as we can. It dribbles over my chin. I jut my face out to try to stop it running on to my jacket. Beside me, Matt finishes in a few gulps, exhaling triumphantly and crushing the can in his fist. I tip the can higher, bubbles burning on my tongue, and force the rest of it down. Me and Lorenzo finish at the same time. Next is Duncan, leaving Saeed to cough and gurgle like he's drowning.

'Lie on the floor,' Lorenzo orders him.

'Why?' questions Saeed, but he's already obeying.

Once he's laid out shivering on the path, Lorenzo and Matt open fresh cans of beer. Hover them over his mouth.

The corner of Saeed's mouth quirks into a smile. 'I've seen both your mums in this same position.'

They tip the beers, pouring them over his face. He gasps and tries to sit up to escape. Lorenzo pins him down, forcing him to choke and splutter.

'Stop the mum jokes, all right?' he says, voice deadly serious. 'It's not funny.'

When he lets him go, Saeed sits up so sharply that he headbutts Matt in the mouth. Dual roars of pain. 'Why does everybody keep headbutting me in the face?' It breaks the tension because the rest of us fall about laughing. The beer has already gone to my head. My vision swims slightly, the cold leaking out of my bones.

Across the field, the dog is caught by its owner and attached to a lead. The dog walker is a middle-aged woman. Sensible boots, bulging poop bag dangling from her wrist.

'Your turn, Spunk,' says Lorenzo. He nods at the woman. 'Tell her how much you like her dog.'

Duncan looks pained. 'Do I have to?'

Saeed is still wiping off his face. 'I just got water-boarded, so you're not getting out of this.'

He glances at me. Like he's seeking my approval. Like he's worried he'll disappoint me if he does it. I shrug a shoulder to tell him it's not up to me.

The dog walker has cut a diagonal track across the field to avoid us. As she rejoins the path and passes under a lamppost, Duncan calls out, 'Excuse me?'

The woman stops and turns.

'You have a . . . lovely growler.'

She huffs – actually *huffs* – and tugs on the lead before hurrying away. While the others laugh, Duncan looks at me like he's being held hostage. I show my teeth in a silent growl that convinces him to smile.

Lorenzo juggles his beer between his hands to make space for his e-cigarette. Blows a cloud of smoke over his shoulder. 'Now it's your turn, new boy.' He watches me. Waiting to see if I'll back down. I'm playing into his hands by accepting the challenge. Right now, I don't care.

He points to the toilet block, a low, dark building at the edge of the field. 'Shut yourself in there for ten minutes.'

My heart stumbles and trips over. I try to keep the panic off my face. 'That's it?'

'It's haunted,' says Saeed.

Matt sighs. 'It's not haunted, it just smells.'

'It is, man, I swear.'

The path to the toilet block door is covered in weeds and litter. I take a few steps closer and peer inside. It's almost too dark to see anything. A metal clasp on the door has no lock, but it doesn't stop a stab of fear that they might push me inside and seal it.

I turn back and catch Duncan's eye. He looks almost as scared as me. He remembers what I told him on our visit to Maywood, the shed in the church graveyard.

'Come on, you can do better than that,' I say, puffing myself up as I shift my gaze back to Lorenzo.

His eyes flick between Duncan and me, like he's trying to work out what passed between us, before they light up with a new idea. 'There's a house on the other side of the park,' he says, and tips his head back to laugh.

I move so I'm standing right in front of him. 'What do you have in mind?'

Chapter Fifteen

Duncan

A painstakingly rectangular hedge at the end of the short driveway hides us from the house as we scan the windows for signs of life. It's bigger than most of the houses around here, two wide floors, an extended garage jutting from the front. Above the extension is a window out of sync with the others, tall and thin, almost exactly in the centre of the house. Through it we can see the stairs curving up to the top floor, a dim light glowing somewhere deeper inside the house.

'That window?' asks Owen.

Lorenzo pops a fresh beer. 'You should be able to climb up on the garage.'

They explained the dare as we crossed the park. I expected Owen to refuse straight away. Instead he just kept walking.

Beside me, Saeed lets out a high-pitched giggle, like a drowning hyena. It means he's both tipsy and nervous. I am firmly only the latter, but I'm doing everything I can to hide it.

If Owen is hiding the same, he's much better at it than me. He scans the front of the house one last time, before tying his hair back into a ponytail. When he catches my eye, I try to make my expression say everything I'm thinking: *You don't have to do this. Lorenzo is just flexing. He's not really this much of an arsehole – or he never used to be. We're all going to get caught and tortured in a hidden sex dungeon.* It's unclear how much of this translates, but when Owen quirks an eyebrow I'm sure he's saying, *Fuck it.*

'I'll try and spare you seeing too much,' he says aloud, before slipping around the side of the hedge.

The Owen I watch approach the gate is one I haven't seen before, entirely separate from the reserved and cautious Owen and the more relaxed version that sometimes breaks through. He's *trying* to be somebody else – somebody that doesn't quite suit him.

The gate creaks slightly when he pushes it open. The rest of us shrink back from the sound and watch the house for movement. Owen dashes across the driveway into the cover of the garage, into a narrow space that cuts between the wall and another hedge. The bush shudders, and we hear feet scraping against brick.

'He's actually going to do it,' says Matt.

Lorenzo takes a slug of beer. His phone chimes again but he ignores it. 'We'll see.'

He frowns at the can of drink, like an old drunk blaming booze for his troubles. Owen has called his bluff. The muscles in Lorenzo's jaw squeeze tight as he grits his teeth. Everybody here knows he wouldn't dare do this himself.

There's a hint of another expression on his face too. He looks just a little too pleased with himself.

'Who lives here?' I ask.

Lorenzo shrugs and smiles, takes another sip of beer. Again, his phone buzzes.

Owen's face appears over the edge of the garage. He's lying on his belly, hair loose and hanging in his eyes. He pushes it away and grins down at us.

'He's nuts,' says Saeed.

Owen shifts into a crouch and creeps towards the vertical window. It reminds me of a window from some old movie, where an oppressed housewife would stand and gaze out over the wreckage of her life, plan her violent escape. Or something. I can't imagine the kind of person who would install it on their house in Westleigh.

'You're really going to make him do this?'

Lorenzo's gaze is fixed on the house. 'I'm not making him do anything.'

Saeed takes out his phone and begins to film, giggling to himself like this is the funniest thing he's ever seen. On top of the garage, Owen peers into the window. There's still no sign of any movement inside.

The coast clear, Owen stands up and begins to fiddle with his belt.

'Get ready for a full moon,' mutters Matt.

I silently will him not to go through with it. Not to bow to this ridiculous peer pressure. To be better than I would be.

Belt unbuckled, he pulls down his jeans, followed by the back of his boxer shorts. He takes a steadying breath, and then backs himself into the window to press his bare arse against the glass.

'No way!' squeals Saeed.

Owen yelps – it must be freezing – before rubbing his butt side to side, grinning down at us. We all splutter with laughter, trying and failing to keep quiet.

Until the shape of a person appears in the glass behind him.

Owen

It's like pressing my bum against a block of ice. After the initial shock, my skin goes numb. I imagine the window melting under the heat of my body, every sideways swipe of my cheeks carving deeper into the glass.

A satellite cracking open into empty space.

The laughter below has stopped. I start moving in luxurious circles, my skin squeaking against the window. There's no dignity in this. I might as well wring as much laughter from it as I can.

The hedge shakes. Saeed goes tearing away along the road. Duncan's head pops up, eyes wide, desperately gesturing for me to stop.

'Get down!' he hisses.

The light from the window behind me dims slightly. My shadow is blotted out. As if something has moved in front of it.

I stop moving my bum. Slowly turn around.

A familiar face glares out at me from just above where my behind meets the glass. A man who doesn't look too happy about the view. A man who is the head teacher at my new school.

My bowels shudder. This is Mr Spencer's house.

The fury etched across his features is tempered only by confusion. It offers a head start that I'd be wise to accept.

I jump away from the window, forgetting that my jeans are around my ankles. My feet catch and I sprawl face-first on to the tar-papered roof. Roll on to my back and fumble my jeans back up. As soon as they're roughly fastened I scoot to the edge of the garage roof and hang my legs over the side. Glance behind just in time to see Mr Spencer turn away from the window and thump down the stairs.

Weight forwards. Bend my knees when I land. The impact jars through my body but I manage to roll rather than crash. I'm up and running for the gate by the time I hear the front door thrown open.

'How dare you?!' he bellows.

The temptation to shout back *You should have just given me detention!* is almost irresistible.

I reach the others and we run for it. They all waited for me – well, all but one. I would have expected Duncan to stay, but the others owe me nothing. Our feet thunder on the road.

'Is he chasing us?' says Duncan.

Nobody risks a glance back. We run like we'll never stop, legs at full stretch and lungs ready to burst. Lorenzo and Matt aren't built for sprints and fall behind, leaving Duncan and me to lead the way across the corner of the park and into a narrow alleyway that cuts between houses. He's slightly ahead of me, laboured breaths echoing around the walls.

Invisible branches whip against my arms and cheeks. My feet stumble over unseen rocks and roots.

When the air shifts, I almost lose my balance. I just have time to glance up and see the wings opening, the talons reach for me from the darkness, before my aching feet are relieved of the ground.

Duncan

Running was invented by masochistic egomaniacs intent on showing off how much pain they can inflict on themselves before they melt into a puddle of sweat. My threshold is incredibly low. After thirty seconds – surely a new record – my lungs burn and a stitch bites deep into my side. At least a marauding Mr Spencer angered by partial underage nudity and the necessity of a large tip for his window cleaner proves strong motivation to fight through the pain.

The alley turns almost ninety degrees and I crash into Saeed. He screams and holds his hands up in pitiful surrender before realising it's me. We lean on our knees and heave as much air into our bodies as they'll take without floating away.

'Where. Are. The. Others?' he asks.

'They're just . . .'

I fling a tired arm behind me, expecting to find Owen on my heels. He was right behind me when we reached the alley. Instead I see Lorenzo's bulk arriving, Matt panting close behind. No sign of anybody chasing them.

'Where's Owen?' I ask.

Lorenzo leans against the wall. 'No idea.'

'Did you know . . . it was Mr Spencer's house?' asks Matt between breaths.

Lorenzo wipes his forehead and flashes a grin.

I can be angry about that later. Right now I push past them both and peer down the length of the alleyway. There's nowhere else he could have gone. 'He was right behind me.'

Owen has disappeared into thin air.

The Prince's Empty Armour

The air is even colder in the Forest, and the moonlight has scant strength to shoulder through the close press of trees. There should be no comfort in this perpetual night, in the branches that rake at his cheeks and scalp, the biting breaths in his lungs. Yet here, at least, he is himself, doubtless moving forward.

Instead, it is Luana who looks troubled. She stops on the cusp of darkness a few metres ahead. Her eyes are bloodshot, ringed with shade. It's as though she has been walking for days without a break. Owen shares that fatigue, deep in the fibres of his body, but it is only an abstract concept. It will not stop him.

'I can't remember how far we've gone,' she says, folding at the waist to catch her breath. It pours out of her in reams of cloud. 'I don't know how much farther we need to go.'

We.

Owen tries to remember the journey. He, or some part of him, was here to experience it. The river – they returned to it from the house in the shadows and followed it for what might have been a day before it burrowed underground. They have lost their way.

He remembers.

'The Forest is fighting us,' says Luana. 'It wants to trap us. Lose us.'

'We won't let it.'

She doubles over again. 'I've been searching for so long. Did it take my family this long to make it to the Water? They must have been so tired.' She sniffs. A tear reaches the end of her nose, hangs, drops silently on to the browning pine needles under their feet.

Owen hovers. He has been comforted so many times, yet still does not know how to comfort others in need.

'I came as quickly as I could,' she whispers, as if breathing the words into the earth. 'I thought I could catch them up and carry them there. I lost them once. If I don't find them now, we'll be apart for ever.'

Owen rests a hand on her back. Bones strain close to her skin. 'We're going to get there. We'll find them.'

She looks up at him and tries to smile. 'I'm tired.'

'We should rest.'

Straightening so that his hand falls away, Luana glances around warily. 'Not here.'

The Forest is interminable. Even if daylight existed there would be no clear path, no way to discern a route between the trees. Owen did not know so many types of darkness existed until he was brought to the Forest: darkness silvered by the moon and stars and reflections on the water; darkness that blossoms and decays like the passing of seasons, that flows like liquid to fill any space or vessel; darkness that is so absolute it hides his own hands and feet from sight. The darkness of the Forest is an organism that pursues them, deviously changes its form to hinder their progress or draw them deeper into its clutches.

Their feet crunch on the fine layer of pine needles that crisps the Forest floor. 'We need a divining rod,' Owen says.

Luana stops. 'A what?'

'You know.' He scoops up a pair of sticks and sweeps them through the air. 'It helps you find flowing water.'

'Hokum,' she snorts, and sets off again.

'Yeah, *that* would be crazy,' he mutters.

The carpet of pine needles grows deeper as they walk. First it kicks up at their toes, and then creeps over their feet to the ankle. Owen shakes his trainers clear and peers around at the looming trees. By rights they should be barren, but instead they bristle, thickening the gloom. The fallen needles climb towards his knees.

'Luana?'

She has waded ahead, almost out of sight in the darkness. 'Just keep moving.'

It reminds him of pushing through freshly fallen snow. In the dim light it is as if the ground itself shifts, their bodies etching tracks through the earth, the smell of festering damp rising like vapour from the tomb. Soon

182

the needles are prickling around his waist, itching inside his clothes, jabbing at his skin.

'Luana!'

There is no longer any sign of her ahead. The needles have closed over her tracks. Owen casts around, trying to return to the shallows, but the needles are up to his throat now and still drawing him down. He stumbles another step and plunges out of his depth.

It is like being nicked by a million miniature blades, a vast wire brush flaying him alive. No matter how much he kicks and thrashes, trying to swim, he can find no purchase on the ever-shifting tide. One breath and needles fill his mouth, choke off any chance to scream.

Perhaps he will sink all the way down to the subterranean river, where his spirit will ebb to the Sunday Water, and that is how he will complete this journey. He imagines his body back in the real world, excavated, hollow for the rest of his days.

He makes his body limp, arms trailing above his head.

A firm hand grasps his wrist. It heaves him upwards, strong enough to defy the clawing needles. Owen's face breaks the surface and he gulps at the frozen air, choking on the spikes in his throat. A rock juts above him like an island, and Luana pulls him on to it, both falling flat in exhaustion.

'Thank you,' Owen gasps when he has breath enough to speak.

Luana sits up and presses a dirty finger to her lips.

Their island is more than a rock. It is a chunk of masonry, broken from a much larger whole. More lies around them, stepping stones of ruin strewn throughout the needles, as if scattered here by storm or blast. Luana climbs wearily to her feet.

'Come on,' she whispers.

There is no apparent need for quiet. Nothing could possibly live here. Any reticence seems born more of reverence than fear.

They jump between the stones, taking turns to catch each other over the larger gaps. Soon the trees peel back and the stones fall closer together. The shape of the building they belonged to makes itself clear: a length of shattered wall, the hollow of a lost room, a protruding column of bricks. Whatever stood here was ruined decades ago. Centuries. Thick green moss grows like a tapestry, weeds and saplings prising open cracks in the stone.

'What is this place?' Owen asks.

Luana lifts a hand for them to stop. In the absence of their footsteps they hear another sound: rasping breath, like a tide drawing forward and back over a pebble beach.

Now Luana rushes ahead, feet tracing the ruined foundations. Owen follows until they reach a stretch of square, stone floor. A wall looms ahead, broken like everything here, but still reaching high into the trees. Luana halts a few steps from it.

A man is slumped at the base of the wall. At first he appears as a magnified sculpture, limbs outsized and hulking, chest swollen out of proportion. Only when Owen steps closer does he realise the man wears a heavy suit of armour. The dark metal is scratched and buckled, rusted at the joints. Ornate etchings in the breastplate are too tarnished to make out – a coat of arms, perhaps, or the outline of an animal? – but still they seem to glow with a feeble light.

The head of an old man pokes from the armour like a tortoise trapped inside its shell. Strands of thin, grey hair trail down on to a sallow-skinned, hollow-cheeked face. Every breath rattles and gurgles, as if his lungs are full of thawing ice.

'A ruin,' he wheezes. 'How long was I away that my home has become a ruin?'

Luana drops to her knees beside him and bows her head. 'My Prince.'

The old man attempts a laugh, a choking huff that leaves a mist of condensation on his armour. 'I surrendered that title a long time ago, even if I did not realise it until now.'

Owen stands a few paces away, unsure if he should recognise this man – this so-called Prince. He seems impossibly ancient, as old as this twilit Forest.

'I thought you were only a story,' says Luana, gazing around at the ruins.

Owen remembers a story she told him the first time he arrived in the Forest; of how it used to be a flourishing kingdom until its Prince disappeared.

'This is him?'

She nods solemnly, reaching for his papery hand. 'What happened to you?'

'Fear,' he breathes. The cloud of his breath spirals up and out of the ruined hall.

Luana shuffles closer. 'The King and Queen were happy. Their people considered them fair and just. The land was prosperous. What were you scared of?'

A piece of stone falls from the wall above, shattering with a thunderous boom on the hall floor. 'That it would end,' rasps the Prince.

He takes several stuttering breaths before he speaks again. 'You cannot enjoy happiness if you live in ceaseless fear it will be snatched away. My mother and father would grow old, as inevitably as the sun sets, and I knew one day I must lose them. I could not accept it. So I dressed in my finest armour, saddled my horse, and set out in search of a way to save them. Immortality. I would gift them eternal life and keep everything as it was. For ever.'

Owen peers around at the ruin, rendered in abstract shapes and shadows by the stubborn night. How much time has passed since it was a palace?

'I searched,' says the Prince, trying to manoeuvre himself to sit upright, the armour too heavy to oblige, 'every corner of the land, and for so long. I found . . . nothing. When finally I gave up, I tried to find my way home. The trees hid it from me. By the time I returned, I had lost my mother and father long ago.'

The Prince looks between the two of them, rheumy eyes growing clearer.

'I let death rule my life, and barely lived at all.'

Luana draws a shuddering breath and stalks away, covering her mouth with her hands. Owen goes to her and, as gently as he can, lays a hand on her shoulder. This time it is easy to do.

'I think of my family every waking moment,' she says.

Owen moves in front of her so he can put both his hands on her shoulders. They are almost the same height, and when her tear-filled eyes meet his he does not look away.

'There is no right way to grieve,' he says.

A tear escapes down her cheek, cutting a track through the dirt on her skin. 'They haunt me. I am not the same person without them.'

Owen nods. He too is different for what he has lost, though he doesn't yet know *how* – if it's for better or for worse. If the difference can be quantified in such simple terms.

She does not need him to share her pain. Only hear it. Acknowledge its power. That is the only real support he can give.

So, lightly, he draws her into a hug. She lets him, pressing her face into his shoulder, and in this they understand each other.

When it is enough, he lets her go and returns to the Prince.

'Is there anything I can do for you?'

The Prince's eyes shine. 'Give me your body.'

'What?'

A gauntleted hand seizes his throat, squeezing with crushing strength that belies the Prince's frail appearance. The Prince pulls him closer, until Owen feels each cold breath against his skin.

'Surrender your body to your Prince so that he might live again,' he says. 'I cannot take hers!'

Luana appears between them, trying to pull the Prince's arm away, but this last gasp of strength is too fierce to resist.

'I will make you strong. I will make you handsome.

I will make you rich,' rasps the Prince. 'All you must do is give your life to me.'

The pressure on his throat makes it difficult for Owen to breathe, to speak. Haltingly, he manages to say, 'Then I would not be myself.'

The Prince releases him, hand thudding to the ground like dead weight, strength spent. He draws one, final, laboured breath, and holds it in his body as if savouring its taste. When he lets it go, he does not draw another.

'Death has found me,' he says, lips unmoving, voice already stronger for no longer needing air.

A figure emerges from a cleft in the ruined wall, wreathed in shadow, stepping soundlessly across the broken hall. Owen and Luana move away, neither daring to turn their back. Death reaches down and helps the Prince to rise, leaving his empty armour on the ground.

'Perhaps I will see my parents again, after all.' His eyes light up for a moment, before he turns away from them.

The armour at their feet begins to tremble and jolt, as if a trapped creature is probing for escape. A split opens in the chest plate, the metal cracking open along the seams of the etching. A green shoot gropes at the air, a sapling growing taller by the moment, leaves unfurling and branches stretching.

A sliver of moonlight illuminates the face of Death. Owen's breath catches inside his throat. It is the boy who first brought him to the Forest; who danced across the water with Luana what might have been days or centuries ago. His dimpled smile is unreadable as he guides the Prince though the cleft in the wall and under the shelter of the trees beyond.

After a moment, Luana follows them, pushing once again into the tree line. Owen catches up quickly, taking her shoulder.

'I need to know we're getting somewhere,' he says. The trees are too familiar now. The night every inch as resolute. The Angels could drop him somewhere different in the Forest every time, hundreds of miles apart, these tests playing out in rehearsed inevitability, and there would be no way he could ever know.

Luana shrugs his hand off and keeps moving, leaves and sticks crunching under every step. 'We're still going, aren't we?'

'But *where*?'

She doesn't answer, striding through the trees more quickly now, forcing him to stumble along behind.

'I've passed every test. The Forest is trying to take me but I won't let it,' says Owen. 'I'm ready to face the Fisher of Souls. We should be there by now.'

'It might not all be about you,' Luana says, releasing a branch she had pushed back from the path so it almost hits him in the face. 'Or maybe you're not as perceptive as you think you are.'

'*You* tell me then!' Owen can hardly keep up. While Luana strides easily across the uneven ground, he trips over roots and fallen branches. His spirit has been here for so long, but it is no better at negotiating the way. They could carry on like this for ever, he thinks, endlessly searching through the trees and never getting any closer to an end. Maybe this is the real test; how far will he walk before he realises it is futile, that the Forest is boundless?

Hopeless.

'Do you really know where you're—'

Luana hushes him and cocks an ear. 'You hear that?'

Owen listens. A new sound wrests control from the silence of the Forest. 'Water,' he says. 'Waves.'

The crashing hush of an ocean reaching up on to land, enveloping it completely before peeling back to come again, never quite managing to cling to shore.

Now Owen rushes ahead, barrelling through branches that snatch at his skin, trying to hold him back while the sound of the water tugs him irresistibly closer.

And then the Forest ends.

Owen staggers into empty space. The trees retreat all at once. He stands on a pebble beach that slopes gently down to a vast, dark ocean shimmering with silver trails of moonlight.

The Sunday Water.

They have made it. He throws his hands in the air triumphantly, turning back to the tree line to welcome Luana on to the beach. Before she can emerge, talons snatch his wrists and lift him up and away from the shore.

'Not now!' he shouts.

The trespassing darkness rejects his lamentations.

Chapter Sixteen

Duncan

Inexplicably, there are no local listings for search parties or sniffer dogs. That leaves us to trail around the nearby streets in search of Owen, like he's taken a blow to the head and wandered off to find a quiet place to die.

Saeed heads home first, already past his curfew. Ten more minutes pass before Lorenzo, who's been on his phone the whole time, gets fed up too.

'He got scared and ran off. Why should I hang around for him?'

That leaves Matt and me to peer between parked cars, cross the park again and strain our eyes into the darkness, hover outside the train station in case he magically appears there. I even phone him – an actual *phone call* – but it just goes to voicemail. It's obvious he doesn't want to be found, but for some reason I can't just leave it.

'You can go home, you know,' I say to Matt.

He shrugs, shoulders almost reaching his ears. 'I don't mind.'

I decide to take his stoicism as a grand gesture of loyalty that will one day be rewarded with a knighthood and fertile lands.

Narrator: Like he'd ever have fertile lands.

We walk towards the high street in silence, huffing out clouds of breath. Matt was always the strong, silent type. It makes people think he's stupid or simple, but I've always thought he's just so *comfortable* with himself that he doesn't feel the need to share much of whatever goes on in his head. He doesn't need anybody to agree with him, or to like him. Matt just *is*. Like an ancient mystic in a mountaintop monastery or a garden gnome that always seems to be watching you wherever you move.

'Can I ask you something?' he says.

'Uh, yeah, of course.'

He frowns, like he's arguing with himself about saying anything more. 'How do you know if a girl is cheating on you?'

We stop at the Asda road gate where my head got stuck. I look at the light scar on his eyebrow while I try and process what he's asked.

'It's not really my area of expertise. You think Becky's cheating on you?'

Matt takes out his phone and opens Instagram. He finds Becky's stories and sets them playing. A few photos go by – Becky posing in front of the bathroom mirror, Becky's dog balefully eyeing her chicken nuggets – before Matt pauses the sequence with his thumb.

'Look,' he says, pointing the screen at me.

It's a selfie from late last night: Becky lying on the edge of her bed, hair tousled, winking at the camera with her lip curled teasingly. It looks just like half the photos she posts every day.

'Behind her,' Matt prompts.

A sliver of bed is visible at the back of the shot. Her sheets are pink, the opposite of her entire aesthetic. The bed is unmade, rumpled and messy.

I shake my head and look to him for help.

Matt shifts his finger to point at a lump of duvet. 'That's a leg.'

I lean closer and squint. 'I guess it could be?'

'It's a leg,' he says, lifting the screen to his face, like he's trying to convince himself.

This is a tricky situation. If I try and reassure him that it *isn't* a leg, I'm essentially accusing him of being a paranoid psychopath boyfriend. If I agree with him, I am aiding him in actually becoming a paranoid psychopath boyfriend.

'Have you asked her?'

He looks at me like I've suggested he becomes a vegan. 'She's probably just finally realised she's way out of my league.'

We all thought the exact same thing when they got together, but it's still a shock to hear him talk about himself that way.

'That's stupid, and also it still wouldn't justify her cheating on you. *If* that is a leg.'

Matt stares at the photo. 'I probably deserve it. You know why I really like being with her?'

'The sex?'

He frowns. 'No. I mean, yeah, obviously. But it feels like it's really *mine*. It's something Lorenzo doesn't have.'

It's typical that as soon as Matt decides to string together more than one sentence and a *your mum* joke rating, I can't think of anything worthwhile to say in return. Luckily he doesn't seem to need me to answer right now.

'We always followed him. It was just normal, right?' Lightly, he kicks at the road gate. 'This is the first thing that felt like maybe I was okay without him. And it was something he wanted so bad. I *beat* him.'

It's never been quite the same between them since, which means it hasn't been quite the same between any of us.

'You like her, though, right?' I say.

Matt turns and sighs out a long breath. 'I'm not stupid. I can't believe my luck.'

Right now I should put a hand on his shoulder or nudge him with my elbow or deploy some other move from the supportive friend handbook. Except we've never really been like that. It would feel like acting.

'It might not be a leg,' I say instead.

'Yeah,' he says. 'But what if it is?'

Owen

The feathers are so thick on my back I'm sure they must show through my T-shirt. A tell-tale bump. A hunchbacked deformity. I feel around my lower back to see if the oily tips protrude from under the hem. Then I fumble through my boxes of clothes until I find my oversized dressing gown – another hand-me-down from Dad –

and wrap it around myself. Nobody will see the feathers through its bulk.

It's just in time. There's a knock at my bedroom door. Mum opens it, but doesn't step inside.

'I didn't hear you come in,' she says.

Even though the feathers are covered up, I keep my back turned away from her.

Mum looks at me hopefully. 'How was your night?'

'I got drunk and mooned my new head teacher.'

She gives me a curious look, as if she can no longer tell if anything I say is the truth or a lie. Simultaneously amused and sad.

'We should spend more time together,' Mum says, leaning on the doorframe, feigning composure. 'I thought we would, after we moved here.'

I stand rigid, holding the dressing gown closely around myself. Unsure what she needs me to say. She watches, waiting, as if I have the power to fix everything. Then she slants her head against the doorframe.

'I don't know when it happened,' Mum says.

For some reason, I'm frightened to move. 'What?'

'He got between us. Your father.' She sighs. 'And I let him.'

A pop-up appears on my laptop screen, accompanied by a tinkling tune. Duncan calling. It startles Mum. She straightens up and peers warily at the screen.

'I should answer,' I say.

Mum nods. Shuts the door behind her.

Instead of answering, I turn to the wall and lean my back against it. Feel the feathers flex like they might spring back and launch me into the air. I push against them as hard as I can, determined to feel the wall against my shoulder blades, but the feathers have grown too abundant. They cushion me from the cool, hard surface.

A minute passes, maybe more, the Skype call still ringing insistently. I close my eyes and, for a moment, the sound turns into waves tipping gently on to a beach. A tolling bell resounding gently on a buoy out at sea. Behind me, Luana steps from the trees and points past me. Out at the expanse of ocean or –

– to the laptop.

I push away from the wall and fumble to answer the call.

Duncan

The Skype call dials for a solid two minutes, far longer than I would usually consider socially acceptable, before Owen answers with sound only. Immediately I feel like an idiot for having my camera on, but it would be too conspicuous to shut it off now.

'Hello?' says Owen, as if my name isn't displayed in big text across his screen right now.

'You made it home, then?' My attempt to sound chilled instead of passive-aggressive is a total failure. Thankfully he doesn't seem to notice.

'Yeah. I just ran for it.'

I frown, before remembering he can see me. 'I went to your house. You weren't there.'

As soon as Matt decided to go home, I couldn't resist. Thankfully his mum wasn't there either. That would have been an awkward conversation. *Your son is missing after mooning the head teacher*. I lingered a while after knocking to see if he would show up. There was no reason to be so worried. It wasn't like Mr Spencer would have wrangled a posse to hunt him down. But the way he just disappeared . . .

'I took the long way home,' says Owen. He sounds amused, like he'd be smiling if I could see him.

'So . . .' I say, trying to match his light tone. 'How do you feel about Spencer seeing your bare arse?'

He huffs a laugh that crackles in my speakers. 'Not brilliant, to be honest.'

'You think he recognised you?'

'I'd be worried if he recognised me from that angle.'

I lean away from the camera, so only the top of my head floats in view. My hair is still an abomination of hair wax, but it's uncomfortable having him watch my face.

'The guys were pretty annoyed you ran off like that,' I say.

This is my cowardly way of telling him I'm a little annoyed with him too. It felt like I took a chance in bringing him with me, introducing him to the group, and then he just left me to torment and death.

'I guess that cancels out any goodwill I garnered with them for taking the dare,' says Owen.

He's so flippant about it that my irritation only grows. I know it shouldn't – I didn't want him to take the stupid dare in the first place. It's just so . . . *dismissive*. Like none of it mattered. They're still my friends, whatever he might think of them.

'Why did you even do it?'

'I thought it would be funny.' I hear the shrug in his voice. 'And I wanted to see if it suited me.'

'Did it?'

A breathy sigh fills the speakers. The ensuing silence is painfully tense. I'm considering pretending to go through a tunnel and cutting the call when he finally speaks.

'Do you ever feel like life slowly whittles away everything that makes you who you are? Until there's nothing left. Like, when I was a kid we used to spend every New Year's Eve at a family friend's house, playing Pictionary and eating cocktail sausages. They moved up north when I was nine and we never saw them again. And then my favourite guitarist died, my old primary school got knocked down . . . this probably sounds stupid.'

I sit forward and prop my chin on my fist. 'It doesn't sound stupid.'

'Every single subtraction makes you a different person afterwards. Maybe less of a person,' he says. 'You try to replace those things you've lost – try to stay the same – but it's just diminishing returns. Eventually, whether you realise it or not, you're this whole different person you don't even recognise. What of you is really left?'

I take a long moment to think before I reply. He can see me; he knows I'm not blanking him. I need to get this right.

'Do you want to know why it took me a while to tell anybody I thought I had depression?' I say.

'Tell me.'

'It wasn't just because I was worried nobody would believe me, or that they'd be weird about it. It was because I didn't want to admit it to myself. If I faced up to this huge *thing*, I thought that was the same as giving in to it. I thought it would immediately make me a different person. People would treat me like I was all broken, the medication might zombify my brain, whatever. It was like I would *become* depression. I was terrified.'

I pause, expecting some kind of response.

'Sorry,' says Owen. 'I was nodding, forgot you couldn't see me. Go on.'

'Okay, well, eventually I realised something *needed* to change. Whether I admitted it or not, depression had become a part of me. If I didn't do anything about it, it really would take me over,' I say. 'By facing up to it, I could keep hold of myself. I guess I, like, evolved. Became the next version of me. Like a Pokémon. One of the cool ones. It was a big change, but it was still me.'

I stayed the same and, at the same time, I changed. It's only recently that I've started to realise how much.

I look straight into the camera, imagine him looking back. 'You're fifteen years old and you're already talking like you've got one foot in the grave,' I tell him.

Owen laughs. 'I know. It's just something I've been thinking about a lot.'

'I'm not trying to replace anything from your old life,' I say. 'I don't think I can or should. But you have me. I'm new.'

A brief fumbling sound, and the chat window opens up with a flare of white light before Owen's face resolves in its centre. His room is dark, the glare of the laptop screen washing him out.

'I think it's going to take me a while,' he says. 'To work out who I am now.'

'It might not be as different from who you were before as you think.'

'I'm definitely not the kind of person who hangs out with your friends.' He looks directly into the screen. 'I don't think you are either.'

'What does that mean?'

'What I did tonight is how you think you should be acting, right, if you weren't growing apart from them? You think that's the person you should be. But it isn't *you*.'

All the irritation from before comes back stronger than ever, boiling over into anger. I lean closer to the screen.

'You've been out with us *once*,' I say. 'You don't know anything about them.'

'I know more about them than you realise.'

'I've known them almost my entire life!' I say, fighting to keep my voice down so my parents or Emily won't overhear.

Owen stays infuriatingly calm. 'You said yourself you're growing apart.'

'So, what, I should just throw them away?'

'You shouldn't stay friends with people who make you unhappy. Not all friendships are meant to last for ever.'

'Like the friends that abandoned you after your dad died?'

Instantly, I know I've gone too far. We each stare at the other on our laptop screens, which means our eyes don't quite meet. I should apologise, but I'm still too riled up to give any ground. After a moment Owen reaches for his touchpad.

'Yeah, exactly like them.'

The call ends and the window goes blank.

Chapter Seventeen

Duncan

We're awkward with each other for almost the same amount of time as we were effortless friends. A few days pass of us both sort of pretending there was no argument while also avoiding speaking or being near each other unless absolutely necessary. I even ran into him on Westleigh high street, coming out of a charity shop with two overstuffed carrier bags of junk. I nodded – actually *nodded* – before ducking into Starbucks to hide.

Ongoing rehearsals for the talent show have, unfortunately, made it necessary for us to be together on a regular basis. We get together at lunch break for Emily and Owen to issue directions that we follow with painstaking lack of coordination. They've chosen slower moves that don't require too much grace or skill; lots of powerful gestures like slashing the air and pumping our fists above our heads. The song we've settled on is heavy but not fast, like a steady march into battle, guitars grinding like tectonic plates and thumping drums mellowed by an atmospheric synth line. Owen calls it Viking Metal but I'm not convinced that can actually be a thing.

What's most surprising is that we're getting better. Everybody remembers the routine and nobody falls over halfway through any more.

I notice that Owen makes an effort never to single me out, instead admonishing the whole group, even when it's clearly me displaying all the agility of a drunk reindeer on an ice rink.

Lorenzo has also noticed that our relationship has changed. He hasn't made any effort not to look pleased about it. He's even been nicer to me, like he wants to take advantage of the fallout. If he wasn't so tired all the time, he'd probably be pushing harder. If Snapchat and his late-night messages are anything to go by, he's been trying hard to get back in with his gym buddies. It's like he's hedging his bets, keeping me close as a fallback option. I guess I have to settle for that, if I've lost Owen.

A few days before the talent show, we get to the rehearsal room to find it already occupied by Emily's (former?) friends. Steph, Renata and another girl I don't recognise are all dressed in gym clothes, practising synchronised moves in front of the mirror while a dance track pounds behind them. They break off when they see us clustered inside the door.

Steph and Renata come across together, standing as a pair in front of my sister. 'Did you book the room?'

'I didn't know you *could* book the room,' says Emily.

Renata wipes sweat from her forehead. 'Soz, we've got it today.'

I can't believe my sister was ever friends with somebody who says *soz* out loud.

They stare each other down for a moment, while the other girl stands awkwardly by the mirrors, snatching lusty glances at Lorenzo. Eventually I nudge Emily's shoulder.

'We'll find somewhere else.'

As soon as we're out the door Emily hurries off to book the room for the next day. 'We have to beat them!' she calls back over her shoulder.

The next day, I get up after another night of hardly any sleep. My head feels like it's brimming with curdled milk. I can't be bothered to take a proper shower so I run my head under the tap to thwart my bed hair, apply a wet wipe to my armpits and crotch (in that order), and douse myself in deodorant.

These are all warning signs that it's going to be a Bad Depression Day (trademark pending). I could probably get away with giving in to it and staying home, but that usually only makes it worse.

Mum and Dad have already left for work, so it's just Emily sitting at the breakfast table, halfway through photographing her gigantic bowl of Cheerios. Cuthbert the cat sits beside her, hoping for a spill.

'You smell like the last day of a comic-book convention,' she says, wrinkling her nose.

'Morning to you, too,' I say, fighting to stifle a yawn.

'I thought you'd been getting more sleep the last few nights.' She smirks over her dripping spoon.

I take the seat opposite her and pour myself a bowl. 'I'm too tired to work out what you're insinuating.'

'It's just that you probably think I can't hear absolutely everything through our bedroom wall.'

The milk sloshes over the rim of my bowl and streams across the table. My chest tightens as I think of all the things I do in my room that I definitely don't want my little sister to overhear, before I realise what she actually means. Surprisingly, the embarrassment ebbs away.

'It's no big deal,' I say, tearing off a sheet of kitchen roll to mop up the spill. Cold soaks through to my skin. Cuthbert licks up the drops that have reached the floor.

'You were talking to Owen every single night,' says Emily. 'And then suddenly not at all.'

'We were just watching *Battlestar Galactica*.'

Emily lifts a salacious eyebrow. 'It sounded a lot more intense than that.'

'You make it sound like we were having grisly phone sex.'

'Ew, no. But I got the impression it was kind of important.'

I fix my eyes on my bowl and munch a mouthful of sugary cereal to give myself time to think. I want to get this exactly right.

'I'm 99 per cent certain I'm not in an amateur rom-com with Owen. It's not like that,' I say, thinking of all the books I've read where this kind of relationship would rapidly become *exactly* that. 'I haven't had a friend like him before. I don't think I realised how much I needed that. But I messed it up.'

'You *are* good at messing things up.'

'Thanks. It's probably for the best anyway. It was making things weird with Lorenzo.'

Emily drops her spoon and huffs. 'All right, I'm going to tell you why my friends ditched me. For the record, I don't *want* to tell you, but it's relevant to your situation and might help you learn an important life lesson or whatever.'

'Okay . . .'

'They thought I was a loser,' she says matter-of-factly. 'They hated my ideas for our performance. And when I insisted – you know I can be very insistent – they slated my taste in pretty much everything. Nothing I liked was cool enough. They were *well* harsh. So I had to make a decision: go along with them and try to keep the friendship, or be true to myself and let them go.'

'And you could just do that?' I say. 'After being friends for so long?'

Emily cocks an eyebrow. 'It wasn't easy. And obviously I'm not over it. Why do you think I'm so determined to do the show with you losers?'

'I'm sensing some double standards here.'

She smiles. 'I'm just saying, you shouldn't worry so much about being somebody Lorenzo will like. He's just a hot idiot anyway.'

'That's your future husband you're talking about.' I stare into my cereal for a moment. 'Owen basically told me the same thing the other night and I bit his head off.'

'Come on, like he's not as sad about it as you are.'

I look up eagerly. 'Did he say something?'

'No, it's just completely obvious to anybody who's stuck being around you both for more than five seconds,' says Emily, waving her spoon so milk spatters the table. 'You guys should just make up or whatever.'

I think of the last few times I fell out with any of the guys. When Saeed put a video of me kicking a football into my own face on Snapchat; when Matt thought I was sexting his girlfriend; when I told Lorenzo his new trainers looked like clown shoes. There were no apologies or heartfelt speeches. We just waited a day or two (or sometimes just an afternoon) before everybody involved pretended it had never happened.

This feels like it deserves a little more than that.

I flick a soggy Cheerio at my sister. 'You're getting wise in your old age.'

'I was always wisdomous,' she says, lifting her nose in the air. 'Now don't forget to take your tablet and let's get to school.'

Owen

The Angels are circling high today, lazing on the updrafts, tracing a hazy perimeter in the sky. They don't frighten me any more. It's clear now that they are necessary. For a moment the playground around me turns into an ocean, saltwater stinging my nostrils. I want to get back there. I *need* to.

All the same, I keep my head down as I cross the playground in case anybody catches me looking. The feathers bristle under my shirt. Thicker than ever. A seemingly solid lump that's growing harder and harder to hide.

Rehearsal has already kicked off by the time I arrive. The familiar music pounds out of the door as I slip into the room. They're lined up two on either side of Emily in the middle. Hands above their heads, fists crossed, before Emily spins backwards as if caught in the chill gusts of a snowstorm. It is both the most and least metal display I have ever seen. At least there will be nothing else like it in the talent show.

Positioned beside his sister, Duncan catches my eye and smiles. It's practically the first time he's looked at me since our argument. I'm so surprised I smile back without even thinking.

They make it through the whole routine with only a couple of small mistakes. The final move, a guaranteed crowd-pleaser, has always caused problems, but they pull it off without a hitch.

'Is it okay that I feel really proud of you all right now?' I say when the music stops.

'As long as you don't want to hug us,' says Lorenzo, cracking his neck side to side.

'We're good, right?' says Saeed uncertainly. 'Like, it's okay to tell my parents to come to this?'

'Anyone might think you're *enjoying* this,' I say.

He affects a shrug. 'I'm not *not* enjoying it. Right, Matt?'

Matt grunts, which is about as enthusiastic as he gets. I knew I would win them over eventually.

'All we really need now is a little stagecraft. I looked into getting dry ice, but Asda doesn't sell it.'

'I could have told you that,' mutters Matt.

I sling my bag off my back. 'But I have started on some costumes.'

They all glance at each other like they had assumed they'd be performing in their school uniforms. Inside my bag is a bundle of clothes I bought from charity shops around town. Black shirts with open collars. Black jeans with unnaturally torn knees. Black hoods that hang low over the face. There is nothing here that isn't black.

I bought some other stuff too. The wings on my back gave me an idea. If I can make it work.

'What the hell are these?' says Saeed, pulling out a clanking carrier bag full of ragged holes. He tips out rolls of studded belts, long bandoliers complete with (fake) bullets, a spiky dog collar and cuffs. 'Is this, like, your fetish?'

'They're all stuff I bought but never had the balls to actually wear.'

Duncan meets my eye. He knows what I'm really saying. Dad would never have let me wear anything like this in public. I'm not even sure *I* wanted to. Maybe I just wanted the option.

Lorenzo drapes a bandolier over his shoulder and across his chest. 'So you'll wear make-up to the pub but not this. Makes sense.'

'Actually, I've got something just for you.' I dig into the bottom of my backpack and take out the leather jacket I wore out the other night. Lorenzo takes it by the collar, studies the worn material appreciatively, and then shrugs it on. It fits across his broad shoulders almost perfectly.

'It was my dad's,' I say.

He freezes, like I've caught him snatching it directly from the grave.

I smile to show him it's okay. 'Except he was mostly fat instead of muscle.'

In the short time I've known him, I've learned that the best way to appease Lorenzo is to pay him a compliment. He pulls the jacket across his chest admiringly.

'Though I think you *should* wear some make-up to go with it.'

'If I get to wear this jacket I might consider it.'

'Feel free to make the costumes your own,' I say. 'Take them with you and do whatever.'

Matt is stuck with a sort of hooded robe, the only outfit that fits him, while Saeed gathers an armful of the studded gear. 'I have a fancy dress Viking helmet at home!' he says.

'What about me?' says Emily, staring at the pile. 'These are all for guys.'

'I'm working on something special for your costume,' I tell her. 'It's not quite finished yet.' It's currently a heap on my bedroom floor, but she doesn't need to know that.

We run through the routine one more time. Even fewer mistakes. Then we begin packing up so we can catch the end of lunch. I go ahead. Duncan catches me up before I reach the canteen.

'What are you doing after school?' he asks.

'I have never had an exciting answer to that question.'

'All right, well, I've got an idea,' he says, smiling uncertainly. 'There's somewhere I want to take you.'

'Is this another one of your grand gestures?'

'Possibly. I think it's a good one, though.'

'Okay. If you're sure, after . . .?'

'Let's get lunch and talk about anything but that.'

By now there's only a queue of a few people left in the canteen. We join the end, and that's where Lorenzo catches us up. Despite the fact that he's still wearing the leather jacket, he hardly acknowledges me before he squeezes Duncan's shoulder and cuts between us.

'So this is where you went running off to.'

'Yeah, sorry, I needed to tell Owen something.'

Duncan changes when he's around Lorenzo. He holds himself taller, but somehow manages to shrink at the same time. It's not as simple as being scared of him. More that Lorenzo's presence drains him of confidence. Makes him self-conscious of everything he does.

I shouldn't have told Duncan what I thought of his friends, but my opinion hasn't changed.

'No worries,' says Lorenzo. 'You getting lunch?'

'He's standing in the lunch queue,' I mutter.

Lorenzo ignores me. 'You shouldn't eat the muck they dish up here. I've started bringing my own.'

The queue moves steadily forward. I should probably leave them alone. That's obviously what Lorenzo wants. Despite rehearsals together every day, it's clear I'm unwelcome.

'Actually, I was wondering if you wanted a revision session tonight?' says Lorenzo, expressly speaking only to Duncan. 'I can come over to yours. It's been a while.'

'Uh.' Duncan shoves his hands into his pockets. 'I already have plans with Owen for tonight.'

Now Lorenzo looks at me, expression turning hostile. 'What, are you two bumming each other now?'

'Would you have a problem with that?' I say.

That makes him look guilty, at least. He turns away,

like he might storm off, before spinning back to Duncan and lowering his voice.

'Come on, I really need your help.'

Duncan squirms. It's unclear if Lorenzo is genuinely hurt or simply expects to be put first. Either way, I'm sorry for him.

'It's all right,' I say. 'We can do our thing another day.'

To my surprise, Duncan shakes his head. Faces Lorenzo. 'We can revise together another time, all right?'

Lorenzo blows a sharp breath through his nose, nods curtly and stalks away. Duncan watches after him. Anxiously at first, before he seems to emerge from his shell. Returns to the boy I recognise.

'You sure that's okay?' I ask.

He smiles, proud of himself. 'Yeah, I'm sure.'

Chapter Eighteen

Duncan

The train station after school is a melee of kids and work evacuees trying to get home before their souls completely wither and die.

'We should definitely get tickets this time,' I say as we push through the crowds.

'Then I'll need to know where we're going.'

Even though it's not the most sensible course of action, I'm firmly committed to the grand gesture, and determined to keep it a secret for as long as possible. I take charge of the ticket machine, Owen peering over my shoulder. When I select our destination he leans closer like I've made a mistake.

'We're going to the beach?'

'Sort of,' I say, effortlessly coy.

'In February. When it's almost dark.'

'*Somebody* isn't beach body ready.'

We stand on the southbound side of the platform.

Owen has got the train here so many times that he knows exactly where the doors will stop. That means we bundle inside ahead of the crowd. I let Owen pick the seats, just in case I choose any that remind him of why he *used* to get this train. We sit opposite each other in a four-seater beside a couple of strangers.

The first twenty minutes of the journey is spent recapping *Battlestar Galactica* (I rather dominate this portion of the conversation). Whenever he speculates about what might happen next I have to keep my poker face firmly fixed. Eventually we're interrupted by the ticket inspector. The sight of him makes us both break out giggling, and he eyes us suspiciously as he defaces our tickets with a biro before moving on.

'Is Lorenzo going to be annoyed with you?' Owen asks.

'Probably.' It's strange to find that I don't care. 'He won't show it though. Not obviously, anyway.'

We both watch the sun setting behind the fields that slide past the window.

'You've known him a long time, right?'

There's a sense that, after our argument a few days ago, we're on dangerous ground. It doesn't keep me from answering.

'Since primary school,' I say. Before that, really, but that's when we became friends. Ever since he was smaller than me, since he used to cry when he fell over in the playground, since before he would freely wield a nickname against me that he knows I hate. 'He probably seems like a bell-end when you first meet him, but he's a good guy. He really does care about his friends.'

'He has a funny way of showing it.'

I sigh. 'Let's not do this again.'

'I don't want to argue,' he says. 'Just . . . when you see him tomorrow, ask him about the girl he's seeing.'

'The one from the gym? I thought that was just fantasy.'

He waves a hand like he's already said too much. 'Just ask him, okay?'

I promise I will, before we change the subject for the rest of the journey to what kind of underpants Commander Adama wears under his uniform.

Owen

It's almost dark by the time we arrive. The streetlights are haloed in the hazy air. Seagulls flash through them on their squawking way home for the night. Haysea is a pretty typical seaside town. A ragtag row of shops slopes away from the station and seems to drop into nothingness when it reaches the ocean. Everybody leaving the station pulls their jackets tight against the chill, salty air. It's strange that I can't remember if I've been here before, just half an hour along the line from Maywood. Maybe I have. When I was too young to remember.

'I love that ocean smell,' says Duncan, taking a deep breath and promptly choking as we pass a pile of bin bags outside a kebab shop.

The waterfront is quiet. Most of the shops are closed for the night or the season. A chip shop breathes greasy steam into the air. We stop to grab a bag to share, the chips piping hot and soaked in vinegar. I follow Duncan down some steps on to a pebble beach. A few people are huddled over cans of drink, and we leave them behind,

214

feet crunching. The waves course on to the shore before chattering excitedly away. Further out, the ocean is glassy darkness.

I let my eyes lose focus and think of the Forest. The darkness lurking between the trees like a living entity. There, I'd been searching for the ocean. The Sunday Water. I found it, came so close to the end of that journey, before I was returned. Being here now is like bringing two sides of myself together. Two iterations standing on the exact same spot in different universes. Idly, I wonder if I could step out on to the surface of the sea, walk away from shore. If somebody would meet me out there.

Above us, I can just make out the shapes of the Angels, swimming through the murky night.

'We came here a lot when I was a kid,' says Duncan. 'And then again when my depression was bad. Being by the sea always seemed to help. It's like it washes out your mind. Though it was never this bloody freezing.'

We crunch along for ten minutes until the town falls behind us and the sea wall turns into a craggy cliff face. The beach turns to rock, jagged teeth jutting from the water that slaps and froths around them. A lone fisherman sits on a folding chair, a tiny light bobbing on his line.

'Please tell me we're here for pirate treasure,' I say.

'Like I'd share it with you.'

Eventually our way forward is cut off by a sharp curve of cliff. A spit of low rock extends into the tide. Duncan begins to climb it. I follow, the rocks slick and slippery underfoot, forcing us to scramble on all fours. Only when we get above the tide line can we stand up and hop easily between the boulders until we reach the end.

'Here we are,' says Duncan. He sweeps his arms in an expansive flourish as if he's presenting the ocean to me as a gift.

Waves drain noisily through the rocks underneath us. Wind tears around the edge of the cliff to tug at our clothes. Far out to sea there's a flash of lightning, too distant for the thunder to reach us.

'You're going to have to be more specific,' I say, raising my voice to be heard over the noise.

'I know it's difficult to tell anybody what you're really feeling because they won't understand,' he says. 'So I thought you could tell the ocean. It won't understand, but it won't judge you either. It doesn't have a memory. In fact, the ocean doesn't really give a shit.'

I laugh at that and peer out across the water. More lightning flickers somewhere near the horizon. 'I don't even know what I'd say.'

Duncan clears his throat, and then bellows at the top of his voice. 'MY BRAIN IS TRYING TO KILL ME BUT I'M NOT GOING TO LET IT.'

The words are snatched away by the wind, torn apart by the breaking waves and strewn across the rocks.

'Go on,' he urges.

I push my hair out of my eyes, take a deep breath, and scream. 'FUCK!'

'Nice. Eloquent,' nods Duncan. 'Feel better?'

This won't fix anything for good. It's a grand gesture he's read in a book or seen in a movie. In a story, we would kiss afterwards. Still, the pressure pent up inside me has eased. Enough to make it easier to carry for a little while longer until I can make it back to the Forest.

I scream again, this time a formless howl, holding it until my throat feels raw. Lightning flashes on the horizon, and a few beats later a rumble of thunder follows like my cry coming back to me.

Duncan lifts his voice to join mine. We roar in harmony. The noise is a surrogate for everything I want to say but can't find the words to express. This is the *emotion* of it, or at least an approximation, that I have yet to learn how to refine.

When our throats hurt too much to continue we stand for a long moment, wind plucking at our clothes, watching the distant lightning.

'I think you *are* you,' says Duncan. 'You always were. It just spent a long time hidden away. Now you have the space and support to let it out again.'

'Maybe you're right,' I say.

'Was this okay?' asks Duncan.

I nod. Close my eyes and enjoy the wind on my face.

'I know grand gestures are easy,' he continues, 'but I want you to know I'm here for everything in between too. The everyday stuff that really matters. When you're ready, or whatever.'

He still doesn't really understand. But that's okay. There's no way he can. Instead of telling me how to feel, he's giving me the space to figure it out for myself. Letting me know that he'll be here for as long as it takes.

The ocean laps around the rocks. It won't be much longer. I have almost made it to the end of the Forest.

'Thank you,' I say. 'It's better not to be facing this alone.'

We stand for a while in silence to watch the storm

moving closer across the water. The lightning flashes grow more frequent, giving away the boats and ships passing by far out to sea.

'We should go before it reaches us,' says Duncan.

He turns and begins picking his way back over the rocks. I delay a moment as words rise unbidden in my raw throat, as if they've been stuck there for a long time and have only now been dislodged.

'I don't miss him,' I whisper to the ocean.

The waves carry my confession away.

Chapter Nineteen

Duncan

The train home is quiet, so I take the opportunity to call Lorenzo to try and patch things up. He's stubborn enough that he would probably never speak to me again if I left it up to him.

It rings a few times before he answers. Pounding music fuzzes through the line, forcing me to hold the phone away from my head. Behind it I can hear the chatter of voices and metallic thuds of gym equipment.

'Yeah?' he says.

It's not ideal that I've caught him mid-workout. He'll be hopped up on testosterone and ready to pull off somebody's head with his bare hands.

'Hey, you still want to revise tomorrow?' I say, affecting the most casual voice I can muster.

'Aren't you seeing your new boyfriend?'

I glance over at Owen. His head rests back against the seat, eyes closed. I hope he isn't listening.

'Homophobia really doesn't suit you,' I say. 'How about after school?'

'Maybe you shouldn't bother.' A thud on the other side of the line makes me imagine Lorenzo dripping with sweat in a stripy Victorian weightlifting outfit, hurling an oversized dumbbell against the wall. 'You've made your loyalties clear.'

I take a breath and fix my eyes on the darkness outside the train window. I can't let him keep doing this. 'I'm not going to apologise for keeping plans I made before I spoke to you. Owen needed me today, so I'm offering you my time tomorrow. Do you want help with your revision or not?'

Several seconds pass of nothing but pounding music and background masculine grunting. I picture Lorenzo squeezing his phone until it disintegrates. Then he says, 'Yeah, fine. I'll meet you in the library at free period.'

He ends the call. I release a breath I absolutely knew I was holding. My hand is shaking. That might be the first time I've ever stood up to Lorenzo. And I didn't die. It didn't reduce our friendship to flaming wreckage.

Narrator: Not yet.

When I turn back, I find Owen watching me through sleepily hooded eyes. He smiles, and I wave him away, embarrassed.

Back home, the town is Thursday-night busy, smokers lining the fronts of pubs and chicken shops luring them with greasy wafts of guaranteed salmonella poisoning. We head down the high street until we reach the point where we need to part ways.

'It's not that late,' I say. 'You want to come over for a while?'

Owen

We sit around the kitchen table, each working on a different part of the costume. Duncan's dad is making black cladding for Emily's wheelchair. His mum is trying to open a packet of sequins without spilling them everywhere.

'So what's this special *thing* you have planned?' she asks.

'It's not a big deal, really,' I reply. I shouldn't have mentioned it until I knew I could get it working. There are only a couple more days to get it ready. 'You know I said I used to like building things? I thought I'd try again.'

Duncan and Emily are roughly reshaping her outfit. They cut the flowing sleeves of an oversized black shirt into billowing strips and rip holes in black, glittery tights. Apparently I have the daintiest hands, which leaves me sewing dark blue sequins on to wristbands like a scaly second skin.

'I think you missed your calling as a seamstress,' says Mr Cyman.

'What's a male seamstress called?' asks Duncan. 'A seamstud?'

'I've got the hair to pass for a seamstress,' I say, shaking my ponytail.

Emily huffs. 'I am *not* happy that your hair is shinier than mine.'

The conversation flows so easily. Even when it lapses

into silence, it isn't uncomfortable. They are utterly at ease with each other. A family that enjoys each other's company. It's . . . really weird.

'Do you know who you're up against in the show?' asks Mrs Cyman.

'Yeah, people way better than us,' says Emily.

I hold up a sequinned wristband. 'But nobody who is going to look anywhere near as badass.'

We take a tea break. Emily produces her phone and sets playing the song they're going to dance to. It opens with an ominous bell tolling before deep chanting voices roll underneath it like waves.

'Absolute classic,' I say.

Emily grins. Her parents look puzzled. The guitar riff starts up, punctuated by the strikes of the bell, before the drums kick in and send the song marching forwards. Everybody around the table instantly begins nodding their heads.

Duncan leans over to me and whispers, 'You're a terrible influence.'

While the rest of the song plays, Emily shifts slightly in her seat as she mentally runs through the moves. Her family watches her with slightly baffled pride.

My family was never like this. We lived with each other because we had to, not because we wanted to. Distrustful. Resentful. I always hoped it would get better. That Dad would find a way to accept us. When I lost him, I lost that hope too. We will never have the chance to try.

I look around the table. Across at Duncan. There's still a chance to make things better.

When the song finishes, Emily and Mrs Cyman go to her room to try on the complete outfit. I take out my phone and do an image search.

'I was thinking about what Lorenzo said about make-up.'

'You mean his total refusal to wear it?'

I select an image so it fills my screen. 'We should do corpse paint.'

Duncan looks at the picture, and then at me like I've gone crazy. I show his dad and his face blanches.

The image shows a man with long, black hair trailing over his shoulders. His face is painted completely white, except for heavy black smears around his eyes, dripping down like oily tears to equally black lips.

'Is this a Satan thing?' says Mr Cyman. 'Because generally we're against that.'

'It's a *metal* thing,' I argue, pulling a palette of face paints from my bag. 'And if Lorenzo is embarrassed about the show, it might hide his identity.'

They both raise their eyebrows at me to make it clear they're not buying that argument.

Emily saves me by returning to the kitchen in full dress. She holds up her arms, the ribboned sleeves flowing and wristbands sparkling in the light. Fixed to her chest is fancy-dress armour plating, painted to look scratched and battle-worn.

'You look incredible,' Duncan and I say at the same time.

She gives a satisfied smile, before she spots the black and white face paints. 'Are we doing corpse paint?'

Duncan turns to me again. 'You really *are* a bad influence.'

Chapter Twenty

Owen

I expect Mum to be in bed when I get home, but the lights are on. The TV has been plugged in, talking quietly to itself in the sitting room. I know exactly where I'm going to find her. She has taken the dust cover off the sofa in the back room and sits in front of the fireplace, facing the white cardboard box on the mantelpiece. Hunched shoulders tell me she's crying but trying to hide it. I crouch in front of her and try to take her hands. They're clasping the framed family portrait too tightly to budge.

'We have other pictures,' I say.

'I know.' She gives the portrait one last look before dropping it on to the sofa and clutching my hands instead. 'Did you have fun tonight?'

I nod. 'I would have stayed home if you'd asked.'

She sniffs and shakes her head. 'I'm glad you've made a friend. They seem like good people.'

The jealousy in her voice is hard enough to detect that

I might have imagined it. It should make me back off. Instead I want to worry at it, like a cut on the roof of my mouth.

'I think they're happier than we ever were,' I say.

Her breath hitches. 'It wasn't always easy there. But it was our lives. And now . . .'

I squeeze her hands tighter as she trails off. Maybe she understands better than I realise. 'Do you miss him?' I ask.

Her gaze lifts to mine, bleary with tears. 'Of course I do.' There is a question in her eyes. One she is too afraid to ask. I answer it by looking away from her.

'I thought we had the chance to start again,' Mum says. 'But it can't be as easy as that. It couldn't be, after everything he did.'

I still don't know what to say. Whenever I've tried to say anything negative about Dad, she's shut down. Shut *me* down. I don't want to push it now when she seems willing to talk.

'It was always a lot of effort to keep your father happy,' she says, looking at the framed photograph. 'I put so much into him because I thought if I handled him, it would make things better for you. Instead you ended up cast aside.'

'That's not true.'

'It is. He had so many hopes for what you might be, and I indulged him, because it was easier than pushing back. Even when I could see you weren't happy.'

She used to talk about Dad's hopes for me like they were the usual ambitions of a father. Dreaming their son can grow up to be prime minister or a superstar

225

footballer. Not the stifling boundaries he set on my life to try and ferry me down the single path he had picked out. The path he himself had failed to walk. I didn't realise she had ever noticed.

'It wasn't your fault,' I say.

She smiles sadly, eyes growing wet again. 'I thought if there was one upside to all this, it was that he wouldn't be able to come between us any more. But somehow he's still managing it.'

'It's not him. It's what you've made him.'

'It was easier,' she says, 'than admitting it.'

For months, life has felt like an opportunity I'm missing because I didn't know how to take it. I thought I had to find a way to carry on alone. Maybe there were more opportunities than I realised, a succession of tiny offerings that start with new friends, my mum, and grow larger and larger to lead me into the future I'm trying to find.

'I always loved you,' I tell her.

A tear runs down her cheek. 'I love you, too. I think your father did too.'

She wants me to say that I loved him. And I did. But it's so much more complicated than that.

'I think you need to decide what to do with his ashes,' Mum says.

'What about you?'

She reaches out to touch the cardboard box but pulls her fingers away before they make contact. 'It should be whatever you want. You need that.'

After a few quiet minutes she goes up to bed. I pick up the framed photograph and return it to the mantelpiece.

It doesn't make me feel much any more. It's a relic. An indisputable memento of my – our – past. It doesn't have as much power over my future as I thought.

I check that Mum's bedroom light is off, and then go quietly into the garden. Look to the skies. Wait for the darkness to coalesce and take me away.

Threnody for the Lost

Owen drops to his knees and feels the pebbles of the beach sink under his weight.

Beside him, Luana offers a wry smile. 'You asked if we were getting anywhere.'

The coastline to his left stretches straight and true, the trees halting abruptly in a uniform line like day-trippers frightened to get their feet wet. To the right, the beach curves inland, the ocean opening wide across the horizon. It reminds him of ink, liquid blackness pooled, as if formed by the dark draining from between the trees. The Forest, endless just moments before, seems dwarfed by the Sunday Water's sheer magnitude.

Owen stands. 'We have to get across this?'

Luana gazes out across the water. 'I can't walk it this time.'

He had thought they were so close to the end. So near to unearthing the truth. And he *is*. So much closer than before. But it remains out of reach. He watches the wavering lines of moonlight on the water and imagines them as spirits trying to skim across.

'So how?' he says.

'Can you swim?'

Owen turns to her in disbelief and is relieved to find her smiling. She lifts a finger to point along the curving coast.

'Perhaps we should ask them.'

Disembodied orange lights are drifting along the beach like sentient fire. Owen shields his eyes to peer closer and realises they are lanterns, carried by a procession of people moving in narrow ranks across the pebble front. It moves away from them, almost out of sight around the curve.

'Come on,' says Owen.

They run to catch up, stones crunching and shifting under their feet. It's strange, wrong, to have this much *space*. Owen swings his arms as he runs, kicks up pebbles, jumps up and springs off a skeletal twist of driftwood.

Trailing the long arc of the beach, he sees what the procession is heading towards – a headland that rises high from the shore and pushes out far into the tide. A lighthouse stands on its highest point, tall and stark against the sky. Its light, a brilliant pyre, burns steadily instead of the intermittent flashes Owen expects. He looks out to sea and tries to find the horizon, any sign of ships or islands that would benefit from the lighthouse's caution.

Slowly, he realises the colossal torch is not aimed out to sea. Its lens faces inland, light labouring to penetrate the Forest's eternal darkness.

'It's supposed to guide lost spirits to the Sunday Water,' he says.

Luana jogs beside him. 'We never saw it.'

Perhaps they were never truly lost.

When they catch the procession it has started up a set of smoothed and pitted stairs carved into the rising headland. Its members are dressed in light linen clothes that billow in the breeze. Their skin is rimed with salt, white and scaly, as if they are freshly risen from a long slumber underneath the waves. The final pair in line glances back at them, faces oddly expressionless, and offers them each a paper lantern. A small flame flickers to life inside. 'What are they doing?' whispers Owen.

Luana simply nods for him to fall in beside her and follow.

The stairs are steep and uneven. At the top of the headland, a worn path leads through scrub grass to the foot of the lighthouse. Up close, it blazes bright as a halo. Surely they should have seen its light inside the Forest, its power sluicing through the trees to chase out the darkness and illuminate this entire world.

Owen glances back at the Forest, and shivers.

A narrow entrance forces the procession to proceed single file. Their lanterns reveal scuffs and scratches on the cold stone walls, inflicted over ages of use, as a coil of stairs winds tightly upwards. After a few rotations of the stairwell they are met by a round room with warped wooden floors and simple furniture, a book propped open on a chair, an unwashed plate and mug on a tabletop. Of whoever calls the lighthouse home, there is no sign.

Up and up, higher than seems possible, until the air in the stairwell glows orange and hot as if molten.

Owen is the last to duck through the low doorway at the top of the stairs. The air is stifling, every breath searing his lungs. The fire is ensconced in the centre of the circular space, contained by two curved lenses of glass that clasp together to enclose it. The flames are tremendous, fierce, leaping up at the scorched black vent high above. Their movement is unusual, seeming to wobble and vacillate, as if the fire is simultaneously tearing itself apart and fighting to keep together.

Everybody has gathered on the far side of the room. Owen moves around the beacon fire and startles when he sees what they are standing over.

A body.

The man lies flat on his back, eyes closed, hands crossed over his chest. His skin is dark and leathery, beard flecked heavily with grey. For a moment, Owen expects it to be his dad in disguise, before he shakes the thought away.

'The lighthouse-keeper?' he says.

Nobody answers. Instead, they set down their lanterns and wrap the body in a sheet, covering his face and binding his arms tight to his sides. When the bundle is secure, half the group gathers around ready to pick it up, leaving a gap for one more person.

'Should I . . .?'

Luana steps forward instead. 'Let me.'

She leans down to take her share of the burden. The group lifts the body up and brings it to their shoulders like pallbearers, before returning to the stairs. Owen waits with the others and watches Luana go, unsure what he should do next.

More blankets are produced, these thicker and rougher, laid out on the ground like dustsheets. A man and a woman wind strips of the same material carefully around their hands until fully bandaged, before reaching up to the curved glass panes. The first dislodges easily, flexing as if deciding whether to break or turn to liquid, glowing red hot. They lay it gently on to the blankets, before removing the other lens and placing it alongside, tucking both snugly together, two halves of a whole.

The fire, free of its cage, swells out to fill the space, as if it might spill into the room and engulf them. It seems brittle somehow, like at any moment the flames will break apart into a million embers and extinguish themselves.

The remaining group gathers around the safely dismantled lens. A space is left. Owen wipes sweat from his forehead and steps up to fill it. Loose handfuls of the blanket are taken in tight grips, the heat of the glass billowing over them as they lift it from the floor. The blankets smoulder. It's heavy, but there are enough of them to guide it quickly towards the stairwell and down.

Owen looks at the faces gathered around the bundle. Although trails of sweat cut through the salt on their skin, there is no sign of strain. They are performing a duty, a ritual, actions they might have performed a hundred times before so they have become routine. He wants to ask what they are doing, the purpose of this ceremony, but nobody else has spoken. Breaking the silence would feel like blasphemy.

Outside, they follow the first group down a second set of steps carved into the other side of the headland. It leads down to the shores of a shallow bay, the coastline curving sharply back outwards to trap a horseshoe of ocean inside.

Two rowing boats bob on the gentle waves. The first group has already reached them. They lay the swaddled body inside the first boat. Luana is the last to step away, whispering words Owen does not hear.

His group sets their bundle at the edge of the water and unwraps it. The glass is still blazing hot, charring the blankets black. They take the corners of the material and lower it steadily into the water. Plumes of steam are thrown into the air, drenching their skin in moisture. It billows across the surface of the bay like rolling mist. The lenses crack and sizzle, the last of their light dying out as they cool.

The group gathers around to push the lighthouse-keeper's boat into the haze. It slips silently away, the tide taking its hand to guide it towards open water. In moments it is absorbed by the steam.

Luana watches it go, her face sombre but serene. When it is out of sight, she beckons Owen to the other waiting boat. 'Quickly.'

'It's for us?'

'The lighthouse-keeper will show the way to two last spirits.'

Owen clambers awkwardly into the boat and sits at its front, facing back towards shore, while Luana takes her place on the central bench and unhooks the oars.

'Thank you,' she calls back to the crowd.

The faces watch them impassively as Luana cuts the oars into the water, cords pulling tight in her neck as she drags them through the waves. The boat glides into the veil of steam, the shore and its inhabitants receding in moments, as if they are slipping through a portal to another world.

'That can't all have been for us,' says Owen.

Luana rocks with the rhythm of her work. 'The ritual is old. It's the only way for the living to cross the Sunday Water.'

'He didn't . . .' The lighthouse-keeper can't have died just for them. Perhaps the beach and the lighthouse, the people caked in salt, had been frozen there, preserved, awakened only when Owen and Luana emerged from the Forest.

The shroud of steam blots everything around them. The shoreline has disappeared. Turning to peer ahead, he sees the first boat and its lifeless passenger, moving easily across the water as if guided by some invisible oarsman.

'His spirit is crossing the water,' says Owen

'And we can follow it all the way there,' finishes Luana.

Emerging from the other side of the mist, he sees that the beach and the Forest beyond it have been swallowed by darkness. Only the lighthouse and its beacon are still visible. The orange glow shudders. The flames break apart into iridescent particles that float up, up. Fireflies, thousands of them, come together in conflagration, now scatter like constellations across the night sky.

'What did you say to the lighthouse-keeper?' Owen asks.

'I thanked him. He will have led my family this way before us.'

Owen nods, knowing there is so much more she isn't saying. 'What was my test?'

'You passed it,' says Luana, heaving back on the oars. 'Just being here makes you braver than you know.'

Owen's eyes are fixed on the dispersing lights when an Angel swoops through them, snapping its beak at the smouldering particles. His fingers tighten on the rails of the boat.

'Not again!'

He wants to stay and see this through. They're so close! He ducks low, but there is nowhere for him to hide, to run. Wings beat against the air, dispersing the last of the mist. Owen reaches for Luana to try and hold on. Before he can touch her, talons close around his shoulders, their sharp grip all too familiar. He is plucked into the sky, the boats reduced to specks below as he is borne up to soar through the shining fireflies.

Chapter Twenty-one

Duncan

These are the peace-offering snacks I buy for the free period revision session with Lorenzo: Pink 'N' White wafers (his favourite since childhood), pre-cooked chicken bites (protein!), and a packet of snack-sized scotch eggs. I keep that last one sealed because the smell reminds me of unwiped gym equipment.

As I've told myself about a hundred times today, I don't have anything to apologise for. It just seems safer to make sure he isn't hungry.

Lorenzo arrives in the library twenty minutes late, undoubtedly calculated as a fair punishment in his eyes. He throws his rucksack on to the table and takes out an A4 pad, the pages crinkled with their scrawl of Lorenzo's illegible handwriting.

'I think I dreamt about the talent show last night,' I say, trying to break the ice. 'I went on stage and realised I'd forgotten to put any trousers on.'

I can't believe it's tomorrow. *Tomorrow*. We're actually going to get up in front of the school and *do this thing*. Our last rehearsal is right after this.

'Can you help me with science?' he asks, thrusting a handful of pages at me.

I take the notes and settle back into my chair. Lorenzo perches on the edge of his seat as if this is a make-or-break interview.

'I bought snacks,' I say.

He glances at the food on the table with utter contempt. 'I'm good.'

Among the notes are some practice questions he's printed off. Only half the words make any sense to me. Science is probably my worst subject after maths. And history. And maybe Spanish? I'm not good at many of the subjects. Thankfully the answers are written on the back, so I can at least read them out and pretend to understand.

'What is two times two?' I ask.

He gives me a withering look. 'The amount of times I'm going to punch you in the dick if you don't take this seriously.'

I hold my hands up in mock surrender. 'All right, all right. How do antibiotics prevent the growth of bacteria?' I read.

Lorenzo leans forward on his knees and frowns, like the question doesn't make much sense to him either. 'Say it again.'

I repeat the question. Usually he'll answer anything like this immediately, like even a moment's hesitation would be a stain on his reputation. Now he stares at a fixed spot ahead of him and lets out a long breath through his nose.

'They destroy the bacteria controllers?' he says.

I flip the page. 'No, they prevent cell-wall formation.'

Lorenzo bites off an admonishment, tips his head back, and then asks for another question. When I read the next on the sheet it's met with the same blankness. He clenches his eyes shut and massages them roughly, like he can push the knowledge forcefully into his brain.

'I swear I knew this last night,' he says.

'Do you want me to—?'

'Ask me the next one.'

This time he manages to mumble the first half of the answer, before trailing off uncertainly.

'Are you all right?' I say. 'You normally know all this stuff front and back.'

He leans back in his chair. 'I'm just tired.'

I know an excuse when I hear one – *I'm just tired* has long been my way of avoiding saying *My head feels like it's full of cotton wool and also I cried for no apparent reason this morning*.

For the first time since he arrived, I look at him properly. He's pale, and there are heavy bags underneath his eyes. The sheer size of him almost hides the exhaustion, like a sleight of hand trick. If he's looked like this for a while now, I would have noticed. I'm sure I would.

'I prescribe a scotch egg,' I say, reaching for the packet.

He waves it away. 'Nah, I'm on this new plan.'

'Mate, I don't think you want to get any bigger. You'll have to start dressing in props from the Harry Potter movies.'

It's just a joke, but Lorenzo glowers at me like I've insulted him. 'I was at the gym late last night, then spent a couple of hours revising. That's all.'

'It's no good revising late if you're too tired to remember any of it.'

'What else am I supposed to do?' he snaps.

I wave the scotch eggs at him, hoping I can tease out a smile. Instead he turns away and sighs, almost like he's disappointed.

The way it usually works with Lorenzo is that we skirt around any issue or grievance for as long as possible, framing it in the language of jokes for fear we might accidentally stumble into a serious discussion. I always assumed that was the way he wanted it, because boys – *men* – aren't supposed to talk about their feelings. Maybe I was wrong. Maybe it left him with nobody he could really talk to.

I got to know Owen by talking without any bullshit pretence, and it was a huge relief. It was something I needed. Lorenzo might need it too.

'Do you think you might be doing too much at once?' I say.

He keeps his face towards the door, like he might make a run for it at any moment. 'Too much what?'

'I mean . . . you're revising like crazy, working out like crazy, and you've got these new mates at the gym. That girl you like.' That last one is supposed to massage his ego a little, but I swear I see him flinch. 'Maybe you could cut down on the gym a little. Just until exams are over.'

He shakes his head. 'I can't do that.'

I lean forward and speak as softly as I can, trying not to turn this into some kind of impromptu intervention. Getting through to Lorenzo is like untying a wet shoelace – you have to gently tease it open, or you'll only pull it tighter.

Narrator: You are really full of shit sometimes.

'Why not?' I say.

Lorenzo pauses for a moment, staring past me, and for a moment I'm sure he's about to spill whatever's bothering him. Then he stands up sharply and starts shoving his notes back into his bag.

'Ten minutes 'til lunch. I promised Emily we'd grab the rehearsal room.'

He makes for the door before I've even packed the uneaten snacks away.

Owen

The last rehearsal before the show tomorrow begins badly. Matt hasn't shown up, and Saeed is struggling to remember the moves without someone beside him to follow. They look lopsided, a ship with too much weight at one end.

I stop the music again when Saeed pumps a fist in the air instead of pretending to swing an axe at an invisible marauder. The others groan with frustration.

Saeed scratches the back of his head. 'Sorry.'

'It's all right,' I say. 'Should I step in until Matt gets here?'

'You're secretly thrilled to get the call, aren't you?' teases Emily as I take up my position beside her.

I shake out my hair. 'I'm *half* the man Matt is. Literally.'

The routine goes smoothly this time, all of us

transitioning easily from the intro, through the snaps of the snare drum and into the grinding guitars, the actions growing increasingly aggressive. We're almost at the halfway point, the song building in intensity, when we're interrupted by laughter from the door.

Emily's friends have snuck inside the room to spy. Apparently they're not impressed by what they see. Emily breaks off from the routine and rushes across to them. '*We've* got the room today.'

Renata snorts. 'Looks like you need it.'

'You're really going to dance to that noise?' adds Steph.

'Sorry we can't all aspire to be the backing group for a YouTube cover band with twelve subscribers,' Emily bites back.

Lorenzo and Saeed burst out laughing at that, while Duncan heads across to stand there awkwardly in case there's a fight. Before he can interject, the door flies open, hitting one of the girls in the back. Matt storms inside. It's immediately clear he isn't here for rehearsal and everybody freezes, animals caught in the headlights. He shoves past the girls and grabs Lorenzo around the throat. Pushes him to the floor and squeezes his neck with both hands.

'What the fuck?' squeaks Saeed. He's closest and grabs Matt's shoulders, but doesn't have the strength to prise him away.

'You're a prick!' Matt shouts, flecks of spit hitting Lorenzo's face.

I guess he found out what's been happening behind his back.

It takes all of us working together to pull Matt away.

He's practically vibrating with rage, his whole weight straining against us. When we tip him sideways he scrambles immediately upright. We stand in the way while Lorenzo rises coughing to his feet.

'What the hell's going on?' says Duncan.

Matt's face is beetroot red, sweat streaming from his forehead. 'She told me.'

Lorenzo rubs his throat, using the potential for damage as an excuse to delay his response. 'Mate . . .'

'*Fuck* you! You couldn't let me have *one* thing.'

'It's not like that—'

Matt lunges for him again. We act as a human shield. He's almost heavy enough to flatten us anyway. Lorenzo might have the muscle, but right now I think Matt might actually kill him if he gets the chance.

'Should I get somebody?' Emily asks from the door. Beside her, Steph and Renata are filming the action on their phones.

'Tell them,' says Matt.

Lorenzo opens his arms, like he's begging for mercy.

'*Tell* them.'

'Me and Becky,' says Lorenzo, fixing his eyes firmly on his feet. 'We've been, uh, seeing each other a bit for a few weeks.'

Duncan

A whole suitcase full of pieces slide into place at once. The sexy selfie Becky accidentally sent me was never meant for Matt. It was for Lorenzo. The alleged leg in her Instagram photo was Lorenzo's leg. Owen told me to ask him about the girl he's seeing.

Owen *knew*. I turn to him but he's too busy watching my friendship group implode in real time.

'It wasn't supposed to happen,' says Lorenzo.

'*Fuck* your excuses!'

Lorenzo puts his hands on his hips, lets out a sharp breath through his nose, and then looks up at him. 'You know what, it *was* supposed to happen. It should always have been me.'

Matt pushes against us. It's like trying to hold back a bull from a red cloak. 'So you had to take her for yourself?'

'It wasn't just me. She wanted it too.'

Laughing bitterly, Matt wheels away, trying to pace off his murderous energy. It gives me the space to turn to Lorenzo. The look he shoots back at me is fragile defiance. He knows what he's done is wrong. He *must*. But now it's been discovered there's no way he can let himself admit that to us.

'Come on, man, seriously,' he says. 'Can you blame her?'

It's almost like he *wants* Matt to pummel him. I brace myself for another charge.

Instead, Matt deflates, like his bones have turned to rubber. He swipes a hand angrily across his eyes, wiping tears across his cheek. The last time I saw him cry was . . . primary school? We found an injured pigeon on the playground and sat with it until it died.

I should say something, but I can't think of any words that could possibly fix the damage that has been done.

Amazingly, Saeed speaks up in my place. 'I can't believe you did that.'

Nobody responds. Saeed has *never* criticised Lorenzo. It seems to stun him into silence.

Saeed isn't even finished. 'It was me who told your gym friends you're still a kid. I messaged them on Instagram.'

Lorenzo practically reels, like he's been hit by a right hook. 'Don't lie.'

'You think you're too good for any of us. I got sick of it.' Saeed takes Matt by the elbow and leads him to the door. 'He's not worth it.'

Sensing the odds of a fight to the death are waning, Steph and Renata take the opportunity to slip out of the room after them, flashing a look of triumph at my sister before they go. That leaves me standing with Lorenzo and Owen.

'What . . .' I say, because apparently I've forgotten how to speak. 'You can't . . .'

Lorenzo stands over me, astonishingly huge, but I'm not frightened of him any more. All at once he seems diminished.

'Maybe you don't know me as well as you thought,' he says.

'Maybe I don't.'

I force myself to hold his gaze, long enough that it becomes uncomfortable. It's Lorenzo who looks away first, turning to face Owen.

'Did you tell him?'

'It wasn't for me to tell.'

'How else did he find out?'

Owen stands his ground. 'Ask your girlfriend.'

They hold each other's gaze for a long moment before

Lorenzo shoves past, bumping him with his shoulder. 'Forget this.'

Narrator: And then there were three.

The music is still playing, long since having moved on to another track. Angry guitars fill up the space, excusing any of us from having to speak right away.

Final rehearsal has proved a bit of a disaster.

Emily comes back to join us. 'They're not going to do the show.'

I drop my head. 'It seems unlikely.'

'But they *have* to.' There are tears in her eyes. 'I can't just *not* do it.'

'We'll do it,' I tell her, taking her hand. 'Even if it's just the two of us. I'll try not to look too stupid.'

I am legitimately *flabbergasted*. My eyes drift unfocused while I try to process what just happened. Tectonic divisions that had formed over years within our friendship group, easing gently apart or grating together, have finally fractured us apart.

It's over. There's no possible way we can come back from this.

'You knew?' I say to Owen.

At least he looks embarrassed. 'I saw them together last week. I'm sorry I didn't tell you. It just didn't seem like my place.'

I sort of wave a hand, like a charlatan offering a useless blessing, to show him I'm not angry.

'They have to make up,' says Emily. 'You have to *make* them make up.'

I try (and almost certainly fail) to keep the terrified scepticism off my face. 'You saw what happened.'

'Give them all a chance to calm down,' says Owen. 'Maybe it's not as bad as it seemed.'

I direct the full glare of my unfiltered terrified scepticism at him. He smiles sheepishly as he ties his hair back into a ponytail.

'Just talk to them. It's worth a try,' he says.

'They don't care what I have to say.'

'I don't think that's true.' Owen looks encouragingly at Emily. 'For ages you've thought that you were holding them back. Maybe you were actually the one thing holding them together.'

I think of Saeed telling me he was worried about Lorenzo's new mates. Matt showing me the picture of the tell-tale leg. When they needed it, they came to me for help.

As for Lorenzo . . .

'All right,' I say. 'I'll try.'

Chapter Twenty-two

Duncan

The last thing you should do when your friendship is hanging by a thread is play *Super Smash Bros.* together, so it's encouraging to find Matt and Saeed doing exactly that when I knock awkwardly on the bedroom door. Both of them sit on the floor, backs against the bed in classic gaming pose, hammering their controllers.

'You can join next game,' says Saeed without looking away from the screen.

I perch on the edge of the bed. 'Your mum let me up.'

'Cool.'

No *your mum* joke. That can't be a good sign.

Over the years, Saeed has perfected the most infuriating, dispiriting and outright tedious way to emerge victorious from any game we play together. It's frustratingly nostalgic to watch his Pikachu whittle away at Matt's King Dedede, tickling him with electricity before zipping away and calling down a vicious lightning bolt whenever he tries to follow. Dedede goes flailing off the stage, another life ticking off his total.

'I'm sorry about, um . . .' I say.

Matt doesn't so much as grunt in response.

'Have you talked to Becky?'

'She's turned her phone off,' says Saeed. 'We're taking our frustrations out on Nintendo characters' faces instead.'

It's better than what he usually does to relieve frustration. I've made very sure that not even a millimetre of my bare skin is touching his sheets. A black light would probably light the room up like a splattered disco ball.

'Did you really tell Lorenzo's gym friends he's still at school?'

'Yep. At the time I thought I was acting crazy because I was jealous, you know.' He misses a jump and whacks the pad in frustration as his character tumbles off the stage. 'Now I'm glad I did it. Bring him down a peg. He was always a dick about them.'

There were so many times I thought Saeed was eating up Lorenzo's tales of gym shenanigans, asking for more details, massaging his steroidal ego. Maybe it was real, for a while. A way of staying involved with something that wasn't his. Until it became play-acting, a way to determine what he was up against in the eternal struggle for Lorenzo's diminishing approval. No wonder he got sick of the competition and decided to nuke it from orbit.

King Dedede loses another life. Matt doesn't even flinch.

'I thought you were going to kill him,' I say.

'I should have done,' Matt mutters darkly.

'Do you know, like, how it happened?'

He shrugs, eyes fixed on the screen. 'She told me they started messaging and it went from there. Said it was jokey flirting at first but it turned real. She couldn't resist.'

The addition of an actual flesh-and-blood girlfriend to our group – and the subtraction of a virginity that *wasn't* Lorenzo's – introduced tension we could never have prepared ourselves for when sex was just a vaguely distressing concept on websites we deleted from our browser histories after viewing. None of us would have guessed it could lead to this. Back then, the worst we ever did to each other was throw the blue shell in *Mario Kart*.

'Are you going to talk to him?'

'Dude.' Saeed tears his eyes away from the game to flash me a warning look.

'Obviously I'm not excusing what he did,' I say. 'But is it worth losing all these years of friendship over?'

The match ends when Pikachu headbutts Dedede over the horizon of the level. Despite the dour mood in the room, Saeed celebrates his victory with a fist pump. Matt sets the pad aside and rests his head back against the corner of the bed.

'Honestly?' he says. 'Even before this I was thinking it might not be that much of a loss.'

A tug at my heart, like an important wire being jerked loose. 'Yeah?'

Saeed nods agreement. 'It's not been the same for a while.'

It takes me a long moment to respond, because if I speak straight away I'll only be able to scream *BUT*

DO YOU STILL LIKE ME THOUGH?! For so long I've thought the group was leaving me behind, when each of them was feeling the exact same way.

'I'm sorry,' I say.

Matt snorts. 'What for?'

'I don't even know.'

After a moment, Matt quietly says, 'I just liked being with her.'

'Well *obviously*,' says Saeed.

'I don't mean it like that. Just . . . I liked her. She made me feel good about myself, I guess. But I don't think I was a very good boyfriend.'

I always thought Matt was quiet because he was so sure of himself. Either that changed, or it was never the truth.

'Why do you think that?'

'I didn't know *how*.' He chuckles. I think it's the first time I've ever heard Matt actually chuckle. 'It was new and scary and I'm not . . .' He flaps his hands in the air, trying to find the right words.

I clap him on the shoulder. 'A social butterfly?'

'Yeah, or whatever. I was selfish too. I liked what her being my girlfriend *meant* more than I actually liked *her*. Can't blame her for getting fed up. It's just . . .'

'We know, mate.' I squeeze his shoulder a little more firmly.

Saeed throws his pad into Matt's lap, and then chucks me a spare. 'Let's just shut up and smash.'

'I don't really feel that way about you but okay.'

We play a handful of matches. Saeed grinds his way to soul-destroying victory in every single one of them. Gradually, as he repeatedly crushes us to dust onscreen,

Matt comes to life. He rushes for the best items and rumbles with laughter when he hammers me off the stage for the third time in a row.

It isn't quite like old times. But it's close.

'Are you guys still going to do the show?' I ask when another match ends in humiliating defeat.

They glance at each other, and it's pretty much the only answer I need.

'I'm not sure we should . . .' mumbles Saeed.

Matt is considerably more certain. 'There's no way I'm doing it after all this.'

I should try and convince them. There are a few arguments I could make: we've worked so hard; it means so much to my sister; drown your sorrows with the magic of dance! It was the first thing we'd really done as a group in a long time. Maybe we were forcing it, like we have been for a long time, even if none of us realised it. I can't try and force them now.

'That's a shame,' I say, standing up to leave. 'I was looking forward to pulling it off together.'

I wait for Saeed to make a dirty joke. When he doesn't, I leave without another word.

When Lorenzo doesn't answer his phone, I check his Snapchat. Sure enough, he's at the gym. At this point he probably spends more time there than at home. The last place I want to visit is his gym – I'm fairly sure an alarm would sound at the door if I tried to walk inside – so I'll have to try and speak to him later.

I send him a message – *We need to talk* – like I'm going to break up with him.

Narrator: As if that ship hadn't already sailed.

Another message arrives almost immediately. It's from Owen. *How's it going?*

I think the band has broken up for good, I reply.

Shit. You didn't even make it to your first album. And then, *You home?*

Ten minutes.

I'll bring over the last bit of Emily's costume. The show must go on.

Owen

By the time we're finished painting Emily's face, she looks like a forgotten villain from the fake clip show episode of *Doctor Backwash*. Face completely white, thick black rings around her eyes, inky trails running from the corners of her lips like she bit down too hard on a Biro.

She looks perfect.

Michaela holds up a hand mirror so she can consider her new appearance. Emily nods approvingly, and then looks to her brother for his opinion.

Duncan has spent most of the evening hiding in the corner, as far away from Michaela as it's possible to get without taking a leaf from my book and jumping out of the window. Apparently, Emily invited her over to help with the finishing touches for tomorrow's performance. Also apparently, Emily did not tell Duncan this was happening.

Now he nods enthusiastically and blinks sweat out of his eyes.

'It's definitely an *interesting* look,' says Michaela.

'Now let's see if this works!' Emily grabs the button I gave her to trigger my contraption.

The bulk of it hooks on to the back of her wheelchair, a wire running along the frame to the button in her hand. One press at the perfect moment of the routine and . . . well, if it works, it'll either be spectacular or ridiculous. Possibly both.

'You really made this yourself?' asks Mrs Cyman.

'Don't be impressed yet.' Cuthbert the cat winds around my ankles. I run a hand down his back. 'It's just two toy-gun firing mechanisms wired together and a lot of cardboard.'

We all stand back to leave enough room. Michaela ends up beside Duncan. He goes rigid, like her vision is based on movement.

Emily grips the button in both hands. 'Three . . . two . . . one and a half.'

'Please just press the button, dear.'

A mechanical click. A small puff of black paper feathers from the back of her chair. Cuthbert jumps a foot into the air and tears out of the kitchen. Nothing else does remotely what it should.

'I can probably fix it,' I say quickly, seeing how downcast Emily looks. 'It'll work.'

'It'll be amazing,' adds Michaela.

'Yeah!' chimes Duncan. 'You're going to look incredible. Like a big crow, or a, uh . . .'

'Grief angel,' I say. I'm not sure where the words come from, but they sound right. Duncan gives me a questioning look that I answer with a shrug.

I spend a few minutes fiddling with the contraption. The glue is making it stick where it shouldn't, I think. Or the paper is making it jam? I rip a few paper feathers away to clear the joins, try to ignore the tickle of the real thing against my back.

'I'd better get home,' says Michaela.

'Yeah, me too,' I add.

Mr and Mrs Cyman wish our respective mothers their best. Emily thanks us for our help. An unnervingly sweaty Duncan walks us both to the door. I take longer than necessary over my shoes to give them a moment.

'Thanks for coming,' says Duncan. His voice is actually *shaking*. 'I think she really appreciated it.'

Michaela smiles warmly. 'Of course. Look, about the last time we saw each other—'

Duncan waves her away. 'No, you were right. I'm sorry.'

She slips on her coat and opens the front door. Cold air drifts inside. Before she steps out, she nods towards me. 'At least it looks like you've started making better choices.'

When she's gone, Duncan slouches against the wall and lets out a heavy sigh.

'You are so smooth,' I say.

'I thought I might actually be having a panic attack. It's not even that I fancy her – I just didn't want her to hate me after what happened before.'

'Are you honestly telling me you don't fancy her even a little bit?'

'No comment,' he says, straightening up. 'And no *Battlestar* tonight. I need to at least *try* and sleep.'

I slip my shoes on. 'Maybe I have other plans.'

'Yeah, right. See you tomorrow before the show?'

Once the door is open, I turn back and hand him the

face paints. 'You keep hold of these. You saw how we did it?'

'Yeah, but it's probably better if we leave it to you.'

'Just in case,' I say.

He frowns. 'You *are* going to be there, right?'

I glance out at the street, then up at the sky, before turning back to him. 'Yeah. Of course.' I shove my hands deep into my pockets and stride away along the road.

Chapter Twenty-three

Duncan

The gym is supposed to smell like sweat rash and dried semen and other vaguely homoerotic odours I can freely insult to feel better about my incongruous presence here. Annoyingly, the air is pleasantly cool and faintly lemon-scented. I'll sulk about that later.

A turnstile blocks me from actually going right into the gym. I wave down one of the personal trainers, a young woman in skin-hugging gym-branded workout gear who looks like she could lift me above her head without breaking a sweat.

'Do you have a membership?' she asks.

Narrator: lol.

'I'm just looking for my friend quickly. I don't really do all *this*.' I wave my arms broadly to encompass the terrifying array of machinery ahead of me.

The trainer eyes me for a moment, which is clearly

long enough to decide that I'm hardly likely to sneak a free workout.

'Be quick,' she says as she lets me through the turnstile.

The gym is Saturday-morning busy, feet drumming against whirring treadmills, metal weight plates clattering, men grunting needlessly loudly. Obnoxious music pounds from wall-mounted speakers. This is pretty much my idea of hell. If Lorenzo wasn't somewhere here, I'd run away and never come back.

I practically tiptoe through the weights area, slipping past a woman thrusting a barbell towards the ceiling with her crotch and narrowly avoiding a saliva shower from a burly guy swinging a kettle bell and puffing like he's on the brink of a catastrophic prolapse.

Finally, I spot Lorenzo lounging on an inclined bench press like it's a reclining armchair, looking intently at his phone, nodding his head to the music plugged into his ears. He doesn't look up when I linger uncertainly beside him.

'I've got two more sets,' he says absently.

'Need a spotter?'

Now he looks, and it's a couple of seconds before he plucks out his earphones, like he simply cannot comprehend the absurdity of my presence here.

'I don't actually know what a spotter does,' I say.

'If you tried to spot me I don't think either of us would come out alive.' Lorenzo pockets his phone. 'What are you doing here?'

'Your dad told me where you were. Plus you're literally always here.'

He gets up from the bench, leaving a slick of shining

sweat behind. His vest clings to his skin as he glances around, checking to see who might be watching. When he's satisfied the coast is clear, he leads me to a door at the back of the gym. Beyond it is a studio, empty, blue mats spaced evenly across the floor like an oversized card game.

'I've been trying to get hold of you,' I say.

'I don't need anybody else telling me what a piece of shit I am.'

'I wasn't going to put it quite like that . . .'

He puts his hands on his hips, like he's ready to stand his ground, but he keeps his face turned away from me. 'Go on, then.'

'I don't really know what to say, to be honest. You know it was wrong.' I should have spent more time working out *what* I would actually say when I finally tracked him down. 'I just want to know why. You could have literally *any* girl.'

'I knew you wouldn't get it.'

'I get that you were jealous.'

Lorenzo plants both feet on a mat, the spongy material sinking under his bulk. He bounces on his toes slightly, like he's weighing up the integrity of his argument. Beads of sweat tremble on his forehead, threatening to make a run down his face.

'I just couldn't take that he had her,' he says. 'It should have been me.'

'That's not . . . that's not *anything*!'

'I know that!' he shoots back.

He still won't look at me. Somehow, I thought he might have a good excuse. A legitimate explanation that might smooth everything over, at least for a little while longer.

'Honestly, I didn't mean it to happen. We talked a little bit and got on really well. That had never happened before. Usually I get scared.'

'Scared?' I scoff.

'Yeah! People expect me to be confident, but it's not that easy. It was different with Becky.'

The more he says, the more I struggle to look at him. I hold my gaze anyway to see if he's brave enough to meet it.

'So you actually like her?'

'Yeah, of course!' He digs a heel into the mat. 'She told me she wasn't happy with Matt, that he wasn't being a good boyfriend.'

'He was scared too.'

Lorenzo sighs. 'I know that. But it was a chance to do better than him. It would make things the way they were always supposed to be. If Matt hadn't . . . honestly, I had enough on my plate without worrying about girls. People think it all comes natural, like I was *supposed* to get top grades, like I'm *built* to smash my workout goals, like I'll never have a problem with girls. Like it's effortless or something. It's tiring me out.'

'Who exactly is expecting all this of you?'

Lorenzo finally looks at me, eyebrows screwed down. 'Me!' He holds my gaze for a long moment, and then looks down at his hands. 'I've always been . . . I don't know. When I was a kid, I was so afraid my mum would be disappointed in me if she was here. And after so long forcing it, it was like there was always a certain way people expected me to be. I set the bar for myself too high. I have to live up to it no matter what. And it's impossible.'

I take a moment to think about it. It always seemed like everything he did was just how it was supposed to be. He was always the leader of our friend group. He was always the smartest of all of us. When he started hitting the gym it just made sense. We all thought he'd be the first of us to lose his virginity, which was why it was such a surprise when Matt got there first. I had never even considered the pressure we put on him. That he was walking around in shoes too big to fill. My mind reels trying to shift our entire history into a new context.

'You know I don't actually care about any of that, right?' I say. 'I just always wanted to be your friend.'

I reach for his hand. It's the wrong move. Lorenzo pulls away.

'It doesn't matter, man,' he says.

'So . . .' It's ridiculous to ask now, but after all this time I can't *not*. 'You've lost it, then?'

Lorenzo at least looks guilty about it. 'Yeah.'

'How'd it go?'

He shrugs. 'Yeah, all right.'

We spent years in desperate idolisation of sex. Having it was supposed to be a serious event. I almost feel sorry that he couldn't tell any of us about it. Or maybe I'm just sorry that *this* is the way it all ended up happening. We've been robbed of the moment it felt like our entire teenage lives were leading to.

'Becky shouldn't be with either of us,' he says sadly.

I choose my next words carefully. 'I'm sorry you've been struggling. It still doesn't excuse what you did.'

'I know that!' He wheels away from me. 'And I'm not *struggling*.'

'You don't have to keep pretending—'

'Just shut up,' he says, spinning back to face me. 'I know it was your new best friend *Owen* who told Matt everything. He saw us together the other night. You haven't been the same since he came around.'

I laugh. I can't help it. 'So it's my fault?'

'I didn't say that!'

'Maybe you didn't notice, but I haven't been the same for a long time.'

Lorenzo steps away from me. 'What are you on about?'

'I have depression.' I say it without deciding I'm going to. The statement only makes him look more confused.

'What, for real?' he says.

'I got diagnosed over a year ago. I've been taking medication for it.'

He narrows his eyes, like he thinks I might be joking. Then his expression softens. 'Are you okay?'

I smile. 'Yeah, I'm doing all right. The tablets help a lot.'

'I wish you'd told me,' he says.

'Maybe I should have,' I say. 'I was scared. I didn't know how you'd react.'

'What, did you think I'd break up with you or something?'

I don't return his smile. 'We've both changed a lot and . . . I didn't know. I thought – I *think* you might be better off without me.'

Lorenzo frowns. 'Is this because of Owen?'

'I'm not going to feel bad for making a new friend. He's exactly the kind of friend I needed.'

He stands there for a moment, clenching and opening his fists, like he's quietly pummelling the right words into shape. 'Have you told him?'

I nod. Lorenzo pushes past me to the studio door.

'Wait.'

He stops, leans on the doorframe, the music from the gym floor pulsing beyond him.

'What about the show tonight?'

He shakes his head. 'It was always a stupid idea. Anyway . . .' He drops his head. 'Do you think Matt will ever forgive me?'

'I honestly don't know.'

Lorenzo nods, like maybe he does, and then heads back out into the gym.

Chapter Twenty-four

Owen

I leave the house a couple of hours before the talent show is due to begin. That'll leave enough time for a dress rehearsal with whoever shows up. Or with me, if necessary. We can head off any last-minute costume disasters and we'll find out where we are in the running order.

Against all odds, it won't be the worst performance the world has ever seen. They – or maybe *I* – won't make complete fools of themselves.

I think I'm ready. Looking up, I see the Angels circling low in the failing light. When the show is over, I will let them take me one last time. I will finish my business in that other place. I will pull the two sides of myself back into a whole. Here, now. We're so close to where we need to go. It's time to see it through.

For a moment, I close my eyes. Salt stings my face. Waves lap around me. Motion sways through my body.

My spirit is crossing that distant ocean, searching the horizon for a long-awaited shore.

It won't be long.

I turn a corner and find Lorenzo lounging against a garden wall. He straightens up when he sees me. It's only when I'm a few paces away that I see the anger scribbled on his face.

'Did Duncan find you?' I ask. 'Are you doing the show?'

'You told him,' he says, blocking my path.

It takes me a moment to realise what he means. I focus on my other self, distant and detached.

'No, I didn't.'

'Who do you think you are, man?' he says. 'I've known him almost our entire lives. You've been here a few *weeks*.'

'I'm sorry,' I reply. 'I didn't mean to cause trouble.'

Lorenzo shakes his head. 'But you did.'

When he grabs me, there's no way I'm strong enough to even consider fighting back.

Duncan

My black studded waistcoat is too small, clinging to my belly like I've rolled across a freshly tarmacked road. Mr Spencer has confiscated our bandoliers ('They're not real bullets!' pleaded Emily, hurrying after him), and it's so hot backstage that my corpse paint is already melting off my face. I guess real corpses don't sweat.

Oh, plus nobody else has shown up yet. Not even Owen.

It's going really well.

'Don't freak out,' I tell Emily when she comes back proudly brandishing the bandoliers.

'I'm not freaking out. Are you freaking out?'

I straighten up and wipe sweaty paint from my face. 'No.'

She is in almost complete costume. The fancy-dress armour plating has been augmented with thick shoulder pads covered in spikes. A black and red tulle skirt billows over legs clad in shiny black leggings and heavy boots.

'You look badass,' I say.

Emily glances over to where Steph and Renata are going over their moves in the corner. 'I know. Do you think any of the others are coming?'

'Owen will, at least. He must be running late. But he'll be here.'

Owen

The darkness is almost absolute. A sliver of light breaks through a crack in the door, enough to show up stained tiles and litter across the floor. The air is tangy and sharp with ammonia. I throw my weight against the door again but it doesn't budge.

Lorenzo threw me into the old toilet block like I weighed nothing. Being so powerless reminded me of when the Angels come. Except this time I tried to fight. Wedged my feet into the ground. Clung to the doorframe. No use. He snatched my phone out of my pocket, shoved me through the door, and slammed it behind him.

'Please don't!' I bellowed. 'I need to go and finish this!'

There was the noise of something metal banging against the door. A padlock. Then he was gone. I don't think he even stayed to gloat.

I press my face to the crack in the door and try to glimpse outside. I need to know that I am still in the world. The darkness makes it too easy to believe that I have slipped away somewhere else. Somewhere in between. What if the Angels can't find me here? My chest begins to squeeze tight. The pain in my stomach writhes, making the feathers on my back tingle. Every ragged breath of the ammoniac air stings my throat.

You're still here.

The voice is born of the darkness. I recognise it immediately.

'No,' I say, and push hopelessly against the door again.

It's okay, says the boy. You're okay.

I can't see his smile, but I know it's there, like the Cheshire Cat carving itself out of thin air. 'I need to get out of here,' I say.

Where?

The space around me lurches. My stomach wobbles like the air pressure has shifted. Immediately the darkness is punctuated by flickering lights, a bay of them stretching across one wall. Panic spirals in my chest as I recognise them. I turn away to try and escape. My feet lift off the floor, gravity cancelled, and my momentum spins me around in the air. The circular window greets me, gaping down on the distant Earth below.

'Not here!' I shout. 'Anywhere but here!'

There is no oxygen. I sense it. My lungs begin to ache.

The boy steps out of the shadows. Although the satellite is rotating, the floor shifting from wall to ceiling, his feet stick to it the entire way until he is upside down.

This was your place once, he says.

I shut my eyes tight. 'I thought it was a dream.' I don't know if I speak the words or merely think them. Either way, the boy hears me.

Did you think my Forest was a dream too? he asks, amused.

'I don't know,' I say. But I do. 'No.'

When I open my eyes the boy is floating in front of me. Inert in the air while momentum continues to spin me around.

I can take you anywhere you want to go, he says. Smiling. Pleased with himself.

'Take me back.'

Home?

I shake my head. 'To Luana. I want to see it through.'

The boy cocks his head. Are you sure you're ready to face the truth?

'Yes,' I say. 'Yes.'

The boy nods. Lightning fast, he slams a palm hard into my chest. Somehow he stays fixed in place while my body is sent careening backwards towards the window. There is no way to prevent a collision. My back strikes the glass and I hear it crack.

The void inhales, silent, and the glass blows out.

I am expelled. Rushing soundlessly into empty space. Shards of glass pirouette past me, glimmering with the Earth's light as they spin and tumble. I am racing towards the planet. A meteor ready to crash to Earth or burn up trying.

Softness against my face. The blackness about me resolves into wings, feathers, wrapping my body in their embrace. Taking me—

The sound of waves breaking on shore.

Chapter Twenty-five

Duncan

The first performance is cut mercifully short when a wardrobe malfunction forces the audience to see a lot more of Marvin Pullman than anybody would consider decent. After that, another dance group spends three and a half minutes jiggling their arses to a bad cover version of 'Uptown Funk'. At least we're probably not going to be the worst performance of the night.

Probably.

We're sixth in the running order. Maybe fifteen minutes to go, and still nobody else is here.

The third act – an over-confident year-seven boy juggling kiwi fruit – takes the stage. There's still no sign of Owen. He hasn't responded to any of the half a million messages I've sent, and whenever I call it goes straight to voicemail. I *know* he wouldn't miss this. The whole thing was his idea! He's been here every step of the way.

Something must be wrong, but I can't leave now to go and find out what.

'How are you feeling? I ask Emily, deciding to make myself feel better by shamelessly projecting my anxiety on to her.

She's pressing her elbows hard into the arms of her chair. 'Like there are tiny narwhals duelling in my stomach.'

I squeeze her arm. 'We both know narwhals aren't real.'

She drops her hands into her lap and gapes at me in disbelief.

'I was joking,' I say. 'It stopped you being nervous for a second, didn't it?'

'There really is nothing your stupidity can't achieve.'

The year seven finishes his juggling act to a lukewarm smattering of applause. When he comes off the stage he eyes our costumes sceptically, waiting until he's out of reach before he offers any comment.

'Halloween's in October!' he shouts.

Emily whirls around to face him and brandishes a fist. 'How about I knock you there early?'

The boy throws a mushy kiwi at us and scurries away.

Steph, Renata and my sister's understudy are up next. They're dressed in matching sequinned tops that sparkle and flare like fireworks as they whirl around to a dance track, their moves perfectly synchronised, fast-paced and fun. It's easily the best of the dance routines so far.

When they come off stage to a loud round of applause, Emily claps for them too. They file past, breathing hard and smiling sheepishly.

'I think it might just be us,' I say.

Emily grins. 'I'd say it's not too late to back out, but I would disown you for ever if you did.'

Mr Spencer announces the next act, a boy and a girl comedy duo. Most of their jokes come at his expense, leaving him the only member of the audience not laughing warmly.

We are officially next. My heart feels like it's using my rib cage as a half pipe.

A voice at my shoulder makes me jump. 'I hope they don't laugh at *us* like that.'

I twist around to find Matt and Saeed dressed almost in full costume. Matt is already sweating heavily under the hood of his robe, and Saeed's bandoliers are too wide for his shoulders. They look perfect. The only thing they're missing is the corpse paint.

'I can't believe you came!'

Saeed grins. 'That's what your mum said.'

Emily thumps him, then pulls him into a hug, then pushes him away again, brandishing the yin-yang pallet of black and white paint and an already grubby sponge. 'There isn't time! We have to do your faces!'

They find a seat, and Matt begins painting hasty black circles around Saeed's eyes. I check my phone again. No calls or messages.

'Anybody heard from Owen? Or, uh, Lorenzo?'

'We can do it without them,' says Matt, swishing white paint haphazardly across Saeed's jaw. 'We know all the moves.'

That's true. Still, it's hard to believe Owen wouldn't show up to the final performance unless something bad had happened.

Emily grabs my hand and squeezes it reassuringly. 'Try not to worry.'

There isn't any more *time* to worry. No sooner have Matt and Saeed switched places than the comedy duo are taking a bow and making their way off stage.

I check the music is properly cued up. Check Owen's contraption is securely attached to the back of Emily's chair, the button stashed safely inside one of her wristbands. I really hope it works this time.

As we take our positions on the side of the stage, Mr Spencer offers us all a dubious look, before he smiles sweetly at Emily as if we've corrupted her.

'What are you called?' he asks.

Everybody looks at everybody else, expecting them to have the answer.

'What were you called before?' I ask Emily.

'I wanted to call us Kitten Cannon.'

I consider it. 'I guess it's *kind of* metal?'

'What about The Walking Dead?' suggests Saeed.

'Or The Farts?' offers Matt.

I'm not a metal head, but even I know those names are terrible. Owen would be able to come up with a brilliant name off the top of his head. I try to think what the bands he played to me before were called, but it was all just wilfully disagreeable nonsense.

Then I remember what he said to Emily last night.

'The Grief Angels,' I say.

Mr Spencer nods and hurries out to introduce us. The others throw me questioning looks, but I ignore them to check my phone one last time. There's only one message: Mum wishing us luck. Maybe Owen is sitting in the audience with my parents, ready to watch us go, keeping it as a surprise.

'Now for something completely different,' says Mr Spencer, the microphone whining with feedback. 'I give you, The Beef Angels!'

'Oh, for fuck's sake.'

The intro to the song begins: wind blowing across icy tundra, the rigging of an old ship creaking ominously. The lights go out and we hurry on to the stage to take our marks. It was supposed to be two of us on either side of Emily at the centre. Instead I'm left by myself, Matt and Saeed together on the other side. The faces of the audience are nothing but dim shapes in front of us. It's impossible to pick anybody out. I lower my eyes as the sound of wind is replaced by chanting voices, rising steadily in intensity until . . .

Movement beside me. The lights spring up as a snarling guitar breaks like a peal of thunder, crackling inside the school hall's rubbish speakers like it might explode the whole sound system. A couple of people in the audience gasp as they get their first proper look at us, students turning to whisper to each other as they recognise us through the costumes.

Lorenzo is next to me, exactly on his mark. Leather jacket, face painted neatly black and white. He glances at me and smiles.

The steady, marching drum beat kicks in, and we launch into the first move. I bring my arms up over my head and whip my body side to side, like I'm lashed to a ship's mast and being battered by a ferocious gale. The bandolier clatters against my chest. Beside me, the others perform the same action in perfect unison, Emily holding her hands out in front of her like she's wrestling with a ship's wheel in a storm.

The music shifts slightly, a second guitar picking a melancholic melody through the tumult. As we all freeze for a moment with our fists crossed above our heads, I have enough time to look into the crowd. My parents are sitting in the front row, grinning from ear to ear, but there's no sign of Owen anywhere.

A snare drum snaps four times, and on every beat one of us turns and fires an imaginary rifle into the sky. Emily mimes something falling into her lap, before the guitars spiral and we all run towards her, turning her in circles like she's caught in a whirlpool. Together, we lurch to one side of the stage, then back, thrashing our heads in time to the music. I catch Emily's eye and she grins at me.

Breathing hard, sweat beginning to pour down my face in the heat of the lights, the rest of the routine goes . . . smoothly isn't quite the right word. It's deliberately chaotic. We bang our heads and whip our limbs, fall down and drag each other like corpses. At one point Saeed is supposed to jump on to the back of the wheelchair, but his foot slips and he topples head first over Emily and on to the front of the stage. He recovers so quickly that it almost looks deliberate.

A screeching guitar solo marks the song approaching its end. We surge around Emily and take our positions, each of us gripping the base of the wheelchair tightly in both hands.

'Ready?' I say in Emily's ear.

She nods. The guitar solo ends on a squealing, sustained note. We heave Emily off the ground and lift her above our heads. At the same moment she presses the hidden button for Owen's contraption.

This time it works. Black wings spring open from the back of the wheelchair, unfurling wide, feathers shimmering in the lights. The crowd gasps. We turn her slowly on the spot as she lifts her arms high, like she's reaching for heaven. The music stops and the lights go out again, plunging the hall into darkness.

Muscles aching, we lower her gently back to the stage. The lights come up again. We stand there in a ragged bunch like startled rabbits, breathing hard. I glance at my friends. Most of the corpse paint has sweated away. If it managed to hide our identities before, it won't keep up the charade now.

There's a long moment of silence before anybody reacts at all. My parents go first, rising abruptly from their seats and clapping wildly. I wait for everybody else to join in, finally startled from their dazzled reverie to cheer us and throw their underwear on to the stage.

Narrator: Yeah, right.

Polite applause would be the polite way to describe it. Just enough that our self-esteem won't crumble to dust on the spot, but not so enthusiastic that we might feel prouder of ourselves than we deserve.

I turn to Emily, hoping she won't be disappointed. Instead she's beaming, first at my parents and then at me. I hug her, and before I know what's going on Matt and Saeed have joined in, bundling around us like a poorly organised rugby scrum. Only Lorenzo stands apart.

'Enough of that,' says Mr Spencer, striding across the stage and ushering us away through the curtains.

275

We all burst out laughing as soon as we're backstage, slapping hands and hugging again, smearing the last of our face paint on each other. Only Lorenzo lags behind.

'That was amazing!' says Saeed.

Matt looks him over. 'You fell pretty hard, mate.'

'Yeah, but I've got too much adrenaline to be in terrible pain yet!'

Emily extricates herself and turns to face us all. 'Thank you all *so much*. That was way better than Kitten Cannon ever would have been.'

She takes my hand and squeezes it.

'I'm really proud of you,' I say.

Lorenzo walks past us without stopping. I throw him a smile but I don't know if he sees it. Steph and Renata push past him to reach my sister.

'Well done!'

'That was really cool.'

Emily beams at them. 'No it wasn't, but thank you.'

I check my phone again. Still no call or message. 'I wish Owen had seen it.'

From across the room, Lorenzo beckons me over. The face paint makes him look like a panda, but he looks so serious that I don't smile.

'I'm sorry about earlier,' he says when I reach him.

'It doesn't matter,' I reply. 'Well, it *does* matter. A lot of it needed to be said.'

Lorenzo nods. 'Maybe we have changed more than I realised. But I still want us to be friends. It felt like Owen was getting in the way of that.'

'I had kind of figured,' I say, smiling to let him know it's okay.

He doesn't smile back. Instead, he glances away, the muscles in his jaw working. There's more he needs to say. A sick feeling spreads through my gut.

'What did you do?'

Lorenzo takes a phone from his pocket. It isn't his own. It belongs to Owen. 'Something really stupid.'

In a breathless confession he tells me what he did to Owen. Tells me he's probably still there now.

'It's been hours! He's terrified of dark places like that!' I shout, shrugging him off as he tries to apologise. The others throw me questioning looks as I rush past them and out of the door.

The Fisher of Souls

The beach is solid stone instead of sand. Bright sunshine beats hot on their shoulders, lighting up the island in its solitude at the heart of the ocean. Here, free of the Forest, the eternal night is radiantly repealed.

Owen vaults the side of the boat and drags it up the gentle slope until it is free of the water. The rough, sand-coloured stone scrapes against the wooden hull. The slope is slick with green algae, before desiccated seaweed crackles underfoot above the tideline. Luana steps out of the boat and shrugs off her furs.

'We made it,' she says, as if she can't quite believe it.

She peers up at the structure ahead of them. A kind of temple dominates the island, built from the same stone that is under their feet. Square walls rise into a thick spire at its centre, smaller pinnacles rising symmetrically either side. It is riven with carvings, too beaten and burnished by millennia of weather for the shapes to be legible. What might once have been faces and limbs and lavish ornamentation have been reduced to shallow veins and dimpled bulbs in the rock.

'This is where the Fisher of Souls lives?' asks Owen.

Then he laughs at how it sounds, as if they are going to knock on a neighbour's front door to ask for the return of an errant ball. Turning, he finds the endless ocean at their backs, no sign of the lighthouse or the Forest they left behind.

'We must have come a long way,' he says.

'We did.'

They approach the temple. Narrow channels are cut into the ground, water flowing from the ocean towards the walls from every direction. It streams into the temple, gurgling through inlets girded with salt.

Following the wall, Owen grazes his hand along its surface, tracing the lines etched into the stone like a tattoo. Dust crumbles away and clings to his fingertips.

Finally they reach a tall entrance, crossbeam cracked and sagging like a tired spine. Nothing but darkness beyond. The flagstones here have been polished by the passing of countless feet. More streams of water trickle inside.

'Any idea what we can expect?' Owen asks.

'None. You'll be the first person living to ever see it,' she replies. 'Are you ready?'

Owen nods. They step inside.

It takes a moment for his eyes to adjust to the dim light. The air is cooler here. As his vision settles, he sees water running down either side of a long, low passage, splashing up on to the path ahead. The passage walls are carved too, indecipherable words and figures, hollows choked with long-melted candle wax. Owen and Luana stay close at each other's sides as they follow the path to another archway at its far end.

'Spirits must be ensnared through these channels,' says Luana, pointing to the rushing water. 'The temple is like a fisherman's net.'

'How does it take them from the water?' asks Owen. 'Is it some kind of witch? Like you?'

Luana shakes her head. 'No, not like me.'

Beyond the next archway, the passage opens on to a much larger chamber. The channels of ocean water flood into exposed pools ranged around the wide space, glittering in the crooked beams of sunlight that cut down from gaps in the spire high above their heads. It's like entering a cave, the air heavy and moist, leaving dew on their bare skin. The sound of every cautious step is masked.

In the corner of his eye, somebody stands against the distant wall. Owen turns quickly to look, but there is nobody there. Another figure crouches at the edge of the nearest pool. This time Owen pivots slowly, still finding it gone by the time his eyes can focus in the gloom.

'Do you see them?' he whispers.

Luana turns carefully on the spot. 'Yes.'

People seem to crowd around them now, always

lingering just out of sight, lurking at the fringes of their vision. The chamber is rife with them.

'Spirits,' says Luana. 'Trapped in this place.'

'Can we free them?'

'Let's worry about ourselves first.'

The largest pool at the end of the chamber begins to bubble and swirl, pale mist pouring off and sweeping quickly across the stone floor. It gathers in the centre of the space, lifting up to take physical form. A hulking shape looms over them, mist resolving into long, scrawny limbs sheathed in loose, pale flesh. A ragged cloak of shadows and mist obscures its body and head. Slowly, a kind of proboscis extends from where its head must be, a thin, elongated straw of muscle with a heavy bulb bulging at its end.

Owen is frozen by fear. Awe. Excitement at having finally found it. He has pictured this moment so many times since he was brought to the Forest, but never considered what he would actually *do* when it arrived. Indecision itches through him and roots his feet to the ground.

The Fisher of Souls takes a laborious step closer and lowers its bulb in front of Owen's face. It lights up from inside, images playing behind its fleshy surface. Faces and places he's sure he recognises, doused with the hazy quality of dreams.

Memories.

'Get away!'

Luana pushes past him, slashing a knife at the bulb. Its light stutters as the Fisher rears away. She swings again, wildly, and the Fisher swipes a long limb at her, knocking her tumbling across the floor to collide with the wall.

Owen turns back to face the Fisher of Souls.

Alone.

Chapter Twenty-six

Duncan

The park is empty, the path lit up in orange blotches of light. I'm out of breath, legs aching, but I keep hurrying towards the old toilet block. The nearest lamppost is broken, leaving me to stumble through the weeds and litter that line the path to the door. I shove it as hard as I can but it doesn't budge.

'Owen?' I shout.

No response.

Footsteps and heavy breathing behind me. Lorenzo pushes past. I was so busy focusing on not collapsing with a stitch that I didn't notice him following me.

'It's locked,' he says, fumbling in his pocket. He brings out a key, opens the padlock and throws it away. Another shove opens the door wide. It's pitch black inside.

'Hello?'

Still no answer. I take out my phone and switch on the torch. Pale white light washes over the graffitied tiles and rusty pipes. I shine it quickly through the broken stall doors and across the filthy sinks. There's nobody here.

'Where is he?' I say, whirling to face Lorenzo.

He shines his own phone around the space, eyes wide and sharp in the glow, the shadow of his face paint making him look ghoulish. He shakes his head. 'I left him here.'

Before I can even think about what I'm doing I push him hard in the chest. It's like striking a post box, the impact jarring through my arms. It's enough to send him staggering back against the wall. 'What did you really do to him?'

'Nothing, I swear!' He slips out of my reach. It's strange to see *him* frightened of *me*. 'I locked him in here. Somebody else must have let him out.'

'Did you give a key to anybody else?'

He shakes his head, looking so helpless I know he isn't lying.

I check my messages again before remembering that Lorenzo took Owen's phone. None of this makes any sense.

'I'm sorry, okay?' says Lorenzo.

'It's not me you need to apologise to! You have no idea what Owen's been going through. I've been trying to help him deal with it. He needed a friend.'

Lorenzo watches me carefully. 'And that's it?'

'No. I needed him too,' I say. 'I needed a new friend for the new person I was becoming.'

Lorenzo sniffs, nods. 'I'm sorry I couldn't be that friend for you.'

I take a breath. 'Well, my terrible secret is out of the bag now, so maybe we just see how we go. Right now we need to find Owen.'

'He might have just gone home.'

'I don't think so.' But I don't know *why* I don't think so . . .

We leave the toilet block and return to the main path like we might magically catch sight of him sitting on a bench and waiting for us.

'When I shut him in there, he said he had to go and finish something,' says Lorenzo. 'You don't think he meant . . .?'

I shake my head. 'No way. I think—' The truth hits me all at once. There's only one other place he's likely to be going. The same place he's gone every single time before. 'The train station. Maybe we can catch him if we hurry.'

So despite the pain in my lungs and the creeping ache in my legs, we start to run again.

The End of the Ocean

Crumpled against the wall, Luana looks diminished, as if some vital part of her has been snuffed out. Owen runs to her, grabs at her shoulders and shakes her, shocked at how light she feels. When he puts an ear to her mouth, he feels no breath against his skin. So he does the only thing he can think to do – he shakes her harder, murmuring a wordless prayer, as if he can bring her back by sheer strength of will alone.

'Come *on*,' he says.

And her eyes open. Luana lifts her head, blinks. Still she doesn't take a breath. She is awake – *alive* – but not breathing.

'There was nowhere else to go,' she says, brow crinkling, as if trying to recall the order of a dream. 'Not yet.'

Behind them, the Fisher of Souls waits patiently, shadows whirling. The streams of water and diluted spirits continue to flow into its hideout.

'You're dead,' says Owen. 'You always were, right from the start.'

Luana smiles wryly. 'Not quite. I told you I'm trapped in this place, as you would have been. I thought I couldn't cross the Water until I could take my family with me. But now I'm here, I realise they are not. They made the journey a long time ago and I simply could not accept it.'

When she tries to stand, her legs buckle underneath her. This place, halfway across the Sunday Water, is sapping her strength.

'It's time to face it,' says Luana.

Owen takes a breath, to prove to himself that he still can, and turns back to the Fisher. The shadows and mist flicker around it, camouflaging its true form. It is so much bigger than him, bigger than anything he should ever be expected to fight.

Discovering the truth about Luana gives him the strength he needs. This whole world is a place of death. The Forest, the shoreline, the limitless expanse of the Sunday Water. Owen has been sent here time and again not only because he lost his way. Trapped in between life before and life after, he has teetered on the brink of losing himself. If he had allowed the Forest to claim him, the person he has found the freedom and support to become would have died.

He fought. And every time he won.

The Fisher towers higher. The bulb extending from its head lights up again and sways hypnotically in front of

Owen's eyes. Under its surface, faces and familiar shapes flicker. Owen sidesteps it, tries to get away, but the Fisher moves quickly. Its long limbs creak like tree branches. Wherever Owen moves, the bulb hovers ahead of him, until there is no choice but to peer directly into it.

The faces become clear. There is his mother and father. They hold each other tight in their old living room, rocking side-to-side to the rhythm of unheard music. There they are in the park, Owen bouncing on his father's shoulders and giggling. There is a childhood cat curled in his father's lap.

'None of that is true,' says Owen, trying to dodge away.

Except they *are* true. Those memories are real, or real enough, pieced together from the debris of what he remembers and what he has been told since. Yet they still lie. They tell one side of the story, the only side that has been told since his father died.

The bulb lingers, selective memories thrumming across its surface. Owen covers his eyes but somehow the images burn through his fingers. He swings a fist at the bulb, but the Fisher flicks it deftly out of reach. It is trying to lure him – to where? To trap him inside a past, a life, that was never real.

'No!' Owen screams. He won't accept it. 'I hated him!'

His voice echoes around the temple. The Fisher stops, shadows and mist pulling tight to its body, the light in the bulb sputtering.

Tears run hot down Owen's cheeks. 'I loved him too. I did. And I never wanted him to die,' he says, the words spilling out of him like struck oil. 'But I never liked him. I always wished for a way to get him out of my life.'

A strip of shadow tears loose from the Fisher, breaking apart in the beams of sunlight that pierce the temple, dissipating into the air. The bulb grows dimmer.

'When he died, it let everybody rewrite history. And that rewrote mine too. Everything I remember – the way he treated us, the way he made me feel – was turned into a lie.'

Another ribbon of shadow peels away. The bulb grows dimmer still, the faces inside it flickering out.

Owen takes a shaky breath. 'He never let me be who I wanted to be. Never gave me the chance to work it out for myself. I don't know if there was a person I was always meant to be, if I *am* that person anyway, but now I have the chance to find out.'

He looks up at what remains of the Fisher.

'I'm glad he's gone.'

The remaining shadow unfurls from the Fisher, swirls around it like a cyclone, stripping the creature of its limbs. The bulb empties, splits open and falls away, cracking against the ground like a plastic bauble. When the last of the cloak is gone, a boy – *the* boy – stands at the centre of the chamber, a smile playing on his lips.

'You,' says Owen.

Finally, the truth.

'I knew it before, I just couldn't . . .'

The boy's smile grows wider. I gave you the space you needed to find it.

Not only this place. Having Luana at his side, and Duncan too, to help him navigate through it.

Luana staggers to Owen's side, clutching her ribs, still empty of breath. 'My family was never here,' she says. 'The Fisher never took them.'

They passed through, and found their way across the water.

'You should have told me.'

The boy cocks his head. I tried. Many times. You wouldn't accept it.

'I trapped myself here.'

'And I could have done the same,' says Owen.

Now you must move on.

'Can I join them?' Luana asks. 'Finally?'

There is no other choice.

The far wall of the temple rumbles as it sinks into the ground, bright sunlight flooding the chamber. Beyond it, the ocean shimmers.

The boy watches on. It was not your fault.

Luana nods, and turns to leave the temple. Supporting her on his shoulder, Owen helps her walk out and down a gentle slope to the water's edge. She pulls off her tattered boots and lets them fall to the stone beach.

'We made it here together,' she says. 'Now we must take different paths.'

Owen wants to hug her, but she seems too fragile now, like the hardships of the Forest have sloughed the flesh from her bones.

'I have somebody,' he says.

'I faced my grief alone. I thought that was how it had to be,' Luana says, resting a hand on his shoulder as she steps into the tide. 'You proved me wrong.'

She lets him go and wades out into the water. It draws up around her knees, her waist, deeper with every step.

Without glancing back, she ducks under the sparkling surface. All at once she becomes a passenger on the ocean, physical form dissolving into a phosphorescent shimmer that rides the current to another life.

Owen watches until there is nothing but the purling waves.

When he is sure she is gone, he turns back to the temple. The boy stands expectantly in a wide shaft of sunlight.

'I'm ready,' says Owen.

The boy smiles. Nods. Owen pulls off his T-shirt and feels his feathers drink in the heat of the sun. He flexes a muscle he didn't know he had, the muscle that has hurt inside him for months as it grew, and black, shining wings unfurl from his back. He twitches them experimentally, once, twice, and then beats them hard against the air. They bear him up, feet leaving the ground. He wobbles, swings his arms to find his balance, but the wings hold him steady. Beating them harder, he rises away from the temple, the ocean opening up below him all the way to the horizon.

The Angels swoop down to join him, wheeling and looping around him playfully as he soars. This is the last time Owen will see this place. He is almost free.

After one last look across the Water, he cocoons his wings around himself and thinks of home.

Chapter Twenty-seven

Duncan

When all of this is over, I will either dedicate myself to a life of fitness and wellbeing so I need never feel such terrible pain again, or retire from exercise for ever. My lungs are liquefying and the stabbing pain in my side is like being run through with a rapier. Now I've been forced to slow down, Lorenzo trots comfortably alongside me. I'd demand he carry me if I wasn't so furious with him.

'I know I can't make it right,' he puffs.

Between heaving breaths I manage to say, 'The adultery or the kidnap?'

'Shit.' Lorenzo spits a glob of phlegm into the road. 'I'll . . . I'll stay away for a while. After this.'

Maybe he expects me to protest. Even if I had the breath to do it, I wouldn't argue otherwise. The fact that he's willing to step back shows there's still some of the friend I knew left inside him. But we can't just forgive him for everything he's done.

'And I'm sorry you couldn't tell me about your . . . you know. Depression.'

'It's okay,' I breathe.

'No, it's not. You should have been able to tell me stuff like that.'

I throw him a look intended to wordlessly convey that it *is* okay and we can talk about it later when I'm not dying of some kind of explosive hernia.

When we reach the high street we have to push past Saturday-night drinkers and haphazardly technicolour hen parties. Music spills from bars and restaurants. Smokers linger outside the train station, making me choke on their combined smog as I gasp for breath. Lorenzo buys tickets while I try not to vomit up my pancreas. Then we hurry down the stairs to find a train already in the platform, doors open. They begin to beep as they prepare to close.

Lorenzo shoves me hard enough that I am propelled staggering down the last few steps. The momentum sends me flailing towards the nearest door. I've got one leg inside the carriage when the doors slide shut, clamping my thigh like toothless jaws. Lorenzo reaches between them and wrenches the doors open again before bundling us both inside. Now the doors slam closed. The train hesitates, as if checking for damage, before it begins to move.

'That was close,' says Lorenzo. 'You should really come to the gym with me for some cardio.'

'I'd rather have lost the leg.'

A solid minute passes before I can successfully stand upright. Then I start moving along the first carriage, holding on to the seats to keep my balance as the train picks up speed. It's mostly empty, just a few single travellers listening to music or watching catch-up TV on their phones. We cross into the next carriage.

'How do you know he's here?' asks Lorenzo.

'I don't.'

He could have got an earlier train. He might not have come this way at all. Only a nagging feeling in my gut tells me I'm right.

Still, uncertainty rises in my throat as I glance into every seat of the second and third carriages and don't find him. Sweat drips down my face. We reach the fourth and final carriage. If I was wrong, it'll be a long time before we can get back home and look elsewhere.

Somebody sits facing away from us at the end of the carriage. I approach slowly, terrified of finding a stranger there.

Owen is slumped across two seats, fast asleep. Clutched in his lap is the white cardboard box that holds his father's ashes.

Chapter Twenty-eight

Owen

We will shortly be stopping at . . . Maywood.

The announcement wakes me up from a sleep that feels absolute. I might have been asleep for days, months, years. I rub my eyes groggily and wonder if this is a dream. If the boy has taken me somewhere else outside of the world. Finding Duncan and Lorenzo sitting opposite me doesn't make it any less surreal.

'Good morning,' says Duncan.

I look out of the window at the passing darkness and rub my eyes again.

'It's not actually morning. I thought a joke would make it less creepy that we were watching you sleep.'

They're both sweaty and dishevelled. Traces of black and white paint cling to the edges of their faces, eyebrows, lips.

'The show,' I say, remembering. 'How did it go?'

'I believe the correct terminology is that we rocked.

295

Actually, we ran away before they announced the winner.' Duncan takes out his phone and checks his messages. 'Apparently we came third from last.'

'Oh. That's disappointing.'

'I *was* kind of hoping for the unlikely underdog victory. Emily still seems happy though.' He pockets the phone. 'Are you okay?'

Lorenzo leans forward. 'I'm sorry, for . . . what I did. I don't . . . well, I know *exactly* what came over me. But it was stupid.'

The darkness. The satellite. And then the bright sunshine of the temple washing it all away. I reach a hand behind me to check my back. There are no wings. The feathers have gone.

'How did you get out of the toilet block?' asks Lorenzo.

The train decelerating saves me from having to answer the question. It doesn't matter. *He* doesn't matter. We stand up together and wait by the doors. I hold the white cardboard box securely in both hands. I don't know when I picked it up, but I know it's right to have the ashes here.

We pile out on to the platform. It's well lit but eerily quiet at this time of night. A couple of station staff in high-vis jackets hang around near the exit. They might not take too kindly to what I'm planning to do next.

Lorenzo seems to have the same thought.

'I'll keep them busy,' he says, and heads off quickly towards them.

'People usually say that before they run off and get shot by guards,' I say.

While Lorenzo lures the staff into a non-lethal

296

distraction, I lead the way to the end of the platform. It grows darker as we leave the shelter of the electric lights. A sign for the Samaritans is attached to the end guard rail, asking people to seek help if they're struggling. I stop at the edge of the platform. Open up the cardboard box.

'Do you want me to go away?' asks Duncan from behind me.

'No, it's okay.'

I take out the hard cardboard tube and twist off the top. The ashes are nothing more than grey and black powder. I push my fingers into it and dig out a handful. It's strangely soft, like icing sugar. A small cloud of it wisps away on the breeze.

'You were a bully,' I say, and throw the handful of ashes on to the tracks.

It drifts away, sinking slowly, disappearing into the gloom. I claw out another handful.

'You made me feel small,' I say, and throw again, before taking another handful. 'You stopped me being whoever I wanted to be.'

A sharper breeze blows some of the ash back to leave a pale shadow on my clothes. I grip the tube in both hands and hold it in front of me.

'That's who you were sometimes. And I loved you anyway. You will always be a part of me.'

I thrust the tube forward. The remaining ashes fly out in a grey cloud that quickly breaks apart on the air, disappears into the darkness beyond the platform.

'But now I have to see who I can be without you. Goodbye.'

I dust off my hands. Turn my eyes to the night sky, where I know the Angels will no longer be circling.

I find Mum waiting for me in front of the mantelpiece where the ashes used to sit. It's strangely bare without the white cardboard box. Only the framed family photograph remains, stripped of its last piece of context.

'You finally scattered them?' she asks.

I cross the room and pull her into a hug. 'I'm sorry.'

She squeaks in surprise, reaches up to stroke my hair.

'It's okay,' she says. 'I'm glad you could finally do it. Did it help?'

'Yes.'

'Then that's all that matters.'

We stay locked together for a while, breathing into each other's shoulders. She smells like home, whether that's here or there.

When we eventually break apart, Mum reaches for a photograph laid flat on the mantelpiece. Unframed, I had missed it before.

'I was unpacking some of your dad's things earlier and found some photos he had never shown me,' she says. 'I think he must have been about your age when this was taken.'

She hands me the photograph. It's creased around the edges, colours faded like it's been left in the sun. A snapshot of history. A boy is grinning past the camera. Dark hair cut into a too-straight fringe above bright and mischievous eyes. Lopsided dimples pushed into his cheeks.

My heart wrings like a wet washcloth when I recognise him.

The boy.

The devil on the water. The Prince's escort to the next life. The true nature of the Fisher of Souls.

My father when he was still a child.

'I thought you'd want to see it,' says Mum.

I nod, the gesture sending a tear streaming down my cheek. It splashes on to the photograph. Mum rests a hand on mine and searches my face. 'What is it?'

'It's . . .' I wipe away another tear. Turn the photo towards her. 'He still could have been anything.'

And so can I.

Chapter Twenty-nine

Six Months Later

Duncan

Is it possible to die from eating spicy noodles? Because I'm pretty sure I'm about to die from eating spicy noodles.

Narrator: Goodbye, old friend. It's been real.

I chew the tiny mouthful and swallow it as quickly as I can. When I gasp for air I expect smoke to pour from my mouth. The heat is melting my tongue, burning holes in my cheeks, stoking my teeth to red hot coals.

'Hubris,' I pant, fanning my mouth with both hands. 'Tell the people I died a hero.'

Owen winces. 'I've got more bad news for you.'

'Steam is billowing from my ears?'

'No, you just licked your lips.'

The tingling, clawing, cauterising heat, once quarantined inside my mouth, spreads across my lips like a spell he has summoned. I wail in agony and grab the emergency bottle of milk from my desk, gulping it so enthusiastically that it floods over my chin. It's cool enough to douse the worst of the pain.

I shake my fist at the bowl of noodles, bright red and steaming on my desk, so hot that in their native China they can only be ordered online by masochists and idiots and masochistic idiots. 'I will have my revenge!'

Everybody else our age is out celebrating (or commiserating) their exam results by trying to sneak into pubs or burning their set texts in a bonfire of academic emancipation. We're scorching our taste buds off so we won't be able to taste the family meal we're all going out for later.

Saeed and Matt messaged the group chat earlier to share their grades. Unsurprisingly, they both did okay. I haven't seen much of them this summer. Apart from a couple of *Smash Bros.* sessions, we've mostly stayed in touch by sharing memes I've already seen ages ago but have to pretend are still funny. It'll probably stay that way, now they're going to different colleges, apprenticeships.

Lorenzo sent a quick *Congratulations*. He's still in the group because kicking him out seems so final, but he never replies. After the show, whenever we saw him at school we just sort of pretended we had never been friends. Which was weird. And sad. It probably couldn't be any other way. I messaged him privately to ask about his exam results. He aced everything, of course.

My results were fine. Owen's a little less than fine. We'll both be staying on for sixth form. It's going to be strange without the others. They will always be my friends, a big part of who I am, even if they move into the past and stay there.

We'll always have the Asda road gate.

'Your turn,' I say.

Owen glares at the noodles, as if he can intimidate them into mildness. 'I made a lot of promises my mouth probably can't keep.'

'There's no backing out now,' I say, thrusting the fork at him. 'This was your idea and you must suffer the consequences for my amusement.'

Grudgingly, he winds some noodles around the fork. I still can't work out if he's really changed over the last six months, or if I've just got to know him better. Those flashes I used to see of what I thought was the 'real' Owen come more frequently now, and he does less to smother them each time. He can still be quiet, like his mind is drifting in another world. I figure *that's* the real Owen too – the quiet and the loud and everything in between.

He shoves the noodles into his mouth and chews rapidly as if he can out-run the sting.

'It's not so –' his eyes go wide – 'oh no.'

What follows is two solid minutes of lamentable baying, gulping of milk until it's all gone, followed by even louder baying.

My bedroom door is thrown open and Emily rushes inside, brandishing her fists. 'Who's hurting you?'

We both point to the bowl of noodles.

My sister rolls her eyes, picks up the fork, and slurps up a wriggling mouthful. She chews thoughtfully for a moment before giving an appreciative nod. 'Not bad. A little bland. Now come through to the kitchen, we've got something to show you.'

Owen throws me a questioning look, but I just nod for him to follow her.

Our parents are gathered around the kitchen table, each gripping a mug of tea. Positioned behind them is an oddly shaped present wrapped in mismatched paper.

'I got you a gift for getting through this year,' says Mrs Marlow. 'We all think you deserve it.'

Owen turns to me. 'Did you know about this?'

I nod. 'The noodles were a distraction. I hope you appreciate my martyrdom.'

He stands there dumbfounded until Emily pushes something into his hand. The button that triggered her wings at the end of the talent show performance.

'You never got to see them in action,' she says. 'Press it.'

Owen smiles uncertainly, but does as he's told. The wrapping paper bursts open, the black wings ripping through it from inside, revealing the present underneath: a brand new electric guitar, complete with amp.

'No way!' he exclaims.

Mrs Marlow smiles. 'I know how much you missed your old one.'

He pulls her into a smothering hug. I resist the temptation to remind everybody it was my idea.

When he picks up the guitar, he runs a hand lightly along the strings before slinging the strap over his head. It's already plugged in. The amp buzzes when he switches it on. He plays a simple chord, grinning as the rich sound reverberates around the kitchen.

'Any requests?' Owen asks, looking to me.

'How about "Bowel Liquefying Acquiescence" by Egregious Flatulence?'

He narrows his eyes. 'Is that a real song?'

'No, but the fact that it could be says a lot about your taste in music.'

Owen sticks his tongue out at me and shakes his ponytail loose. He adjusts his fingers on the fret board and plays a power chord, a blunt chugging sound that he repeats until it becomes a pounding march. Emily joins in by drumming erratically on the arms of her chair. I begin nodding my head, and our parents follow, each of us awkwardly picking out different rhythms, all of us together in the same tune.

Acknowledgements

Much of this book was written during one of the hardest periods of my life, and the list of people who helped me through it would be longer than is acceptable for even the most indulgent of acknowledgements pages. Instead, I'll offer thanks to those who directly helped bring this book into the world.

To Ella, as ever, for indulging my strange ideas as well as gently shooting them down when required, and for her constant support.

To Olivia, for her belief in this book and the excellent work she did helping me to whip it into shape.

To Sarah, for her enthusiasm for this book when it was only a few sample chapters.

To Leo Nickolls, who created a cover that made my jaw drop.

To Non, Darran, Simon and Ashley, for their boundless support for my writing and general existence.

To Will, Peat and Sam for an education in 'your mum' jokes and the rigorously upheld scoring system that briefly consumed our working lives.

To Piggy and Barb, my angels, my muffins, who make life infinitely better and writing significantly more difficult.

I must also acknowledge the books that quite explicitly influenced this one: *A Monster Calls* by Patrick Ness, *Skellig* by David Almond, and *Eren* by Simon P. Clark. Thank you for making my imagination sing.